The Whistleblower

Anonymous

First Published 2008
by Impress Books Ltd
Innovation Centre, Rennes Drive,
University of Exeter Campus, Exeter EX4 4RN

© the author 2008

The right of the author to be identified as the originator of this
work has been asserted in accordance with the
Copyright, Designs and Patents Act 1988.

Typeset in 10/12 Sabon by Swales & Willis Ltd, Exeter, Devon

Printed and bound in England by imprint-academic.com

British Library Cataloguing in Publication Data
A catalogue record for this book is available from the British Library

ISBN: 978 0 9556239 3 6

For Richard

Author's Note

Neither the City nor the Cathedral, nor the University of St Sebastian's has any existence in reality. Both Arrowsmith College and the Priory Residential Home are similar fictions. All the characters in the novel are also entirely imaginary; they have no counterparts in the real world.

PROLOGUE

SECRET LIFE OF KINKY CLERIC

The Provost of St Sebastian's Cathedral has been
EXPOSED by a STUDENT he GRADUATED . . .

Saucy Susie reveals that he is a regular client . . .

[Accompanying this article were three photographs. The first
was of a pretty young woman in gown and mortar-board receiving her degree certificate from a distinguished-looking clergyman in academic dress. The second showed the same young
person, but this time she was dressed in a tight black satin costume with nipped-in waist, high leather boots and a fearsome
whip. The third was more fuzzy. It seemed to be of a middle-aged
gentleman with very few clothes on. He was cavorting with the
girl and, on close inspection, appeared to be the same clergyman
as in the first photograph.]

There is a sense of outrage in the normally quiet precincts of St
Sebastian's Cathedral this morning. The Very Reverend Doctor
Cyril Woodcock, the Provost of one of the most beautiful cathedrals in the south of England, has been exposed as a liar and a
hypocrite.

Woodcock is well-known in ecclesiastical circles as an able
administrator and one of the best preachers in the Church of

England. Only last year he was a finalist in a competition run by our rival newspaper, its annual '*Times* Preacher of the Year Competition.' According to our Religious Affairs Correspondent, 'Woodcock was the favourite, but he was pipped at the post by a rather inspiring nun!'

Today he is not thinking about sermons. Last week, your *Sunday Enquirer* was approached by the luscious Miss Susie Strict. The severe and beautiful Miss Strict regularly offers her attractions through a well-known escort agency in London. 'We only advertise in the best places and our services do not come cheap,' she insisted. 'I wouldn't like you to think that the Provost would use any old girl. My agency charges at least two hundred pounds for an hour for my time . . .'

This did not protect the unfortunate cleric. He did not know that only six months ago, Miss Strict, under her real name of Julia Patterson, graduated with an Upper Second degree in Dance and Drama from the local University of St Sebastian's. The Provost, as the Visitor of the University, conducted the Degree Ceremony and gave her her diploma at a public ritual in front of hundreds.

'My mum and dad and little brother came down from Wolverhampton to see me graduate in my academic costume. They were really, really proud that I'd done so well. I shook the Provost's hand. There's a photo of me. He gave me my certificate and afterwards we all had lunch. My family were thrilled to see the Provost close to. My mum said that he looked a very holy man and he gave an ever so funny speech at the ceremony,' Miss Strict told the *Enquirer*.

'It wasn't easy to get a regular job after I graduated and of course I had a lot of student debts. So I thought I'd just help out a bit at the agency and they introduced me to some very nice men. Some of them were very generous and I soon had my own personal client list. One of the other girls got ill and she asked me to take over one of her regulars. She said he turned up about once a month and was no trouble at all. I just had to spend forty minutes or so spanking his bottom.'

'Well of course I recognised the Provost straight away. I could hardly keep a straight face and I almost told him the truth once I got his trousers off. But I didn't want to spoil the old fellow's fun so I kept quiet. But then I thought that it really wasn't right. There he was pretending to be ever so holy, saying prayers and giving sermons and all that and all the time he was cheating on his wife and visiting escort agencies. So I took a few photos of him with my mobile phone. He was so excited he never noticed and the next day I contacted the *Sunday Enquirer*.'

This is yet another blow for the Church of England. Cyril Woodcock was tipped for the very highest office in the Church. He is not the first clergyman in his family. His father was for many years Archdeacon of Wellington while his grandfather was Bishop of Basutuland in the 1920s. There was never a breath of scandal about either of them. Cyril Woodcock himself was until today a respected member of the British establishment. He was said to be heading for great things. There was even talk that he might some day become Archbishop of Cannonbury. Yet like so many of his fellow vicars, he just could not resist temptation . . .

After a tip-off early yesterday, Woodcock and his wife were seen driving their car out of the St Sebastian's cathedral precincts, heading for an unknown destination. Mrs Woodcock looked stony-faced. Through its press secretary, the cathedral has announced that the Provost has tendered his resignation. The official communiqué declares, 'He wishes to spend more time concentrating on his family and his academic work. He has an important book on the Holy Spirit to write.' When your Editor confronted the cathedral spokesman on the telephone with the true facts, the Press Secretary stuttered that it was all most regrettable. 'It could happen to any of us . . .' he said and put the receiver down. Since then the telephone has been permanently on the answering machine . . .

For an in-depth interview and further pictures of the saucy Miss Strict, please turn to our double-page feature on pages 6 and 7.

CHAPTER ONE

Miss Strict Strikes Back

It was a beautiful day in mid-October. The leaves had turned and were gently drifting off the trees as we drove through rural Shropshire. Ahead of us were the misty Welsh hills and the air felt fresh and clean. My wife and I were on our way to visit my father-in-law, Sir William Dormouse. Although nearly ninety, the old man continued to live in the castle of his ancestors on the Welsh border. Victoria was excited. She was devoted to her father and this was the countryside in which she had grown up. In a real sense she was returning to her roots.

I had just retired. For many years, I had taught Christian ethics at St Sebastian's University, but three years ago I had been offered a retirement job at a small liberal arts college in the United States. I, Professor Harry Gilbert, had held the Thomas Jefferson Porpoise Distinguished Chair of Theology at Sweetpea College, Virginia. It had been a successful and happy experience, but we had increasingly missed our friends and relations in England. In particular, Victoria was worried about her father. By any standard he was not young and the family felt that the time had come for him to hand over the castle to his eldest son Billy and to move into some sort of sheltered accommodation. Even Sir William was becoming adjusted to the idea. It was time for us to come home.

Billy and his wife Selina had invited us to stay at the castle for several weeks. The idea was that Victoria would help her sister-in-law find a suitable place for the old man and, at the same time, we would identify a nice retirement cottage for ourselves. We still owned our old house near St Sebastian's. It had been locked up while we were in America, but someone had come in weekly to clean and mow the lawn. Most of our furniture was still there and it would have been possible to move straight back. But Victoria was Sir William's only daughter and she wanted to be nearer her father. We felt that our life in St Sebastian's belonged to the past. We wanted something new. So we planned to stay on the Welsh border while we went house-hunting.

We passed through lush green valleys dotted with sheep and stark black and white Shropshire buildings. Eventually, we came upon a huge pair of stone gates surmounted by two Welsh dragons. We drove through them down a long gravelled drive. I could remember a time, not so long ago, when the drive was almost impassable with puddles and potholes, but now it was smooth and well-maintained with a fresh layer of gravel. We also passed a series of cottages. They all looked prosperous and in good repair. Then, in the distance, we had our first glimpse of the vast grey castle with its Regency turrets and romantic battlements which was my wife's ancestral home. A Welsh flag was flying from the roof and crows and ravens were circulating round the towers, outlined against the cool October sky.

Sir William was waiting for us, standing on the porch wearing a disreputable greenish tweed jacket; he was leaning on his cane with the silver dormouse handle and he looked frail. Bess, his elderly black and white sheep dog, was lying at his feet. Victoria was out of the car and hugging her father almost before I had stopped. I moved more slowly, checking that the handbrake was on properly. Leaving the luggage in the boot, I followed the pair of them, Victoria clinging to her father's arm, through the stone passages to the Great Hall.

I was astonished to discover that we were actually going to sit there rather than in Sir William's usual lair of the old housekeeper's room. In the past, despite the magnificent fireplace and the enormous portraits of distinguished Dormouse forebears, the hall had been uninhabitable. An icy blast straight from the North Pole had blown continuously through the ill-fitting lead of the stone mullion windows. It seemed as if every draught in Shropshire would gather round the feet of unfortunate visitors and even the faithful Bess would sneak away from her master for the comfort of the housekeeper's old wood-burning stove.

All this had changed while we were in Virginia. Sir William had always been a highly competitive games-player. In his later years he had become interested in blackjack and after studying a scientific treatise on the game which I had bought him as a Christmas present, he had become an expert. Admittedly his first foray in casino gambling had been a fiasco. He had arrived in Las Vegas prepared to enjoy himself and break the bank. Unfortunately his skills were quickly spotted. He had been hauled into the manager's office and informed in unmistakeable terms that he was no longer welcome in any of the Nevada casinos.

He had been more circumspect on his next attempt. Wearing a large stetson hat and a Hawaiian shirt, he and Victoria had presented themselves in one of the smaller Atlantic City casinos. Sir William made a point of losing a little money, before he settled down to what he described as 'an amazingly lucky run . . . Eh? What!' He repeated this performance in a different establishment every night for a fortnight with highly gratifying results. He was substantially richer when he came home than when he arrived and the money had been spent on an extensive programme of repair. The roof no longer leaked; the walls had been repointed; the furniture had been mended and the final glory was a magnificent new central heating system . . . a master-piece of thermo-technology. For the first time in its history, it was possible to be warm in every room in the castle.

We both chorused our approval of the new arrangements. Victoria practised sitting on every chair in the room and was astonished to find that not a single one collapsed under her. Then, while she was taken on a tour to admire the mysteries of the new boiler-room, I went back to the car to gather together our things. Lugging two heavy suitcases, I followed Victoria and Sir William down a long corridor where blood-stained Welsh and English flags were suspended high over our heads. We then went up a flight of stairs and down another long passage until we found ourselves at the other end of the building. We mounted a further stone circular staircase up to a landing at the top. This was the guest room that looked across open fields. The bathroom was down the hall. We had stayed there many times before, but we could not believe how comfortable it had become. There was a new carpet and the curtains actually covered the windows. The bed was soft, the water was hot and there was a cashmere blanket draped over an armchair. It might have been a boutique hotel.

Our long day had included a transatlantic flight. Bleary-eyed, Victoria and I unpacked and made our way back. We found Sir William in his usual cosy study, the old housekeeper's room. Billy and Selina were already occupying the main part of the castle, but they had gone off to Selina's brother's cottage in Tuscany for a short autumn holiday. Sir William's room looked much as usual. The furniture was old and battered. There was a mahogany long case clock with a brass face and one wall was lined with books. In front of the stove was my father-in-law's special leather armchair and an old brown velvet sofa. Both looked as if they had been clawed continuously by the family cat since the time of the first baronet back in the early 1800s.

Sir William himself had taken off his tattered tweed coat and had put on a musty maroon smoking jacket. To our amazement he was sitting on a new seat. It was a strange contraption covered with an unfortunate knobbly brown tweed. 'Saw this in *The Field*,' he announced. 'Damned clever! Just what I need now I'm getting a bit stiff!' He pushed down on a lever and the chair thrust him upright. 'That's the ticket!' he muttered. 'D'you want a go?'

'Really, Daddy,' Victoria sniggered. 'It's hideous.'

'Just the thing to get me up,' he said. 'I'm not as young as I once was, you know.'

Victoria poured sherry from an old crystal decanter with a tarnished silver label as Sir William complained about his various physical ailments. 'Memory's bad too,' he sighed. 'Can't remember the proper method for blackjack any more. I keep forgetting to count the cards. Damn and blast – whole system's shot to pieces! Maybe I ought to go into a home. I don't want to be a nuisance to Billy and Selina.'

'I'm sure you're not,' Victoria said.

As usual, Bess was stretched out by Sir William's feet. He stroked her ears as he announced, 'if I do go somewhere, they've got to take us both. I'm not leaving my dog behind. We're a package deal,'

'We'll find you a nice place,' Victoria said. 'That's one of the reasons we've come down to Shropshire. Harry and I want to buy a new house anyway and we want you to be somewhere near. We'll see if we can find you somewhere warm and comfortable with nice nubile young nurses to look after you. . . and of course Bess will go with you.'

'You're a good girl!' conceded Sir William. He pressed the lever for the umpteenth time and enjoyed the sensation of being evicted from his armchair.

Over the next fortnight we looked at several cottages, but none was exactly right. Then, when Selina and Billy returned home, we took a break ourselves and drove down to the Cotswolds for the weekend. One of Victoria's school friends, Vanessa Mandril-Fortescue and her husband James lived just outside Upper Buttercup in a charming Georgian double-fronted house and Victoria was eager to see them again.

Several years ago James had retired from his job in the City and was doing some part-time consultancy. When we arrived on the Saturday afternoon, he was sitting under a large magnolia tree wearing old flannel trousers, a rumpled tweed jacket and a panama hat. He was speaking loudly into a mobile telephone about the drop in the stock market. Vanessa greeted us carrying a tray with a pretty tea pot, cups and a large chocolate cake. Sitting outside in the afternoon sun, Victoria looked longingly at the mellow stone cottage behind us. 'Really Harry,' she said, 'we should have done this long ago.'

'There's a very pretty converted chapel for sale just outside the village,' Vanessa said. 'Just Harry's kind of thing. There's a picture of it in this week's *Country Life*. Shall I get it?'

Vanessa and Victoria started talking about houses and James turned his attention to me. 'So old boy,' he said, putting his mobile in his top pocket, 'you've finally retired. About time. I understand you made a packet at that college of yours in the States. Though you've never seemed to have much to worry about on that score. I wish I were in the same boat. This part-time consultancy job hasn't been going so well this past year . . .'

James began a long ramble about the difficulties of the monetary world, the dangers of recession and the catastrophic fall in the market. I had always found financial affairs paralysingly boring and, after our drive down and the excellent chocolate cake, was having difficulty staying awake. Happily, my host did not seem to notice. Then, in the middle of James's lament about the unpredictable behaviour of the Nikkei index, my mobile telephone rang. I woke with a start, reached into my inner pocket and mumbled 'Hullo . . .'

To my astonishment, it was a call from the Archbishop of Cannonbury's chaplain. He apologised for disturbing me and said he had been given my number by Sir William. 'Professor Gilbert,' he said, 'the Archbishop has something he would like to ask you about rather urgently. He wonders if you might be free to come to his club, the Acropolis, on Monday at about four for tea.'

'For tea?'

'He's due to go there after giving a speech about homosexuality in the House of Lords.'

'We've just arrived in the Cotswolds,' I said. 'But yes, that would be all right. Can you give me some idea what it's about?'

'I don't think I can go into detail,' he said. 'But there seems to be a problem at St Sebastian's. And the Archbishop wants to talk to you about it.'

'Right,' I said, 'I'll be there.'

Not surprisingly, I was curious about this call. I had known the Archbishop since we had been students together at Cambridge. We still exchanged Christmas cards, but we seldom met. Although we were both ordained clergymen, I had chosen an academic career while he had risen to dizzy heights in the established Church. I wondered what he could possibly want to consult me about. Still St Sebastian's was my old stomping ground. Perhaps there was some problem with the university.

We had a delightful couple of days in the Cotswolds with our old friends. Then on the Monday, when Victoria returned to Shropshire, I took the train from Upper Buttercup station to London. It was lunch-time and I ate some very nice smoked salmon sandwiches which Vanessa had packed up for me. I was surrounded by tweedy ladies going up to town to do some early Christmas shopping and a few serious businessmen talking urgently into their mobile telephones. Opposite me was a smartly-dressed young woman with dyed blonde hair. Her fingernails were painted a shocking pink and she was reading a copy of the *Daily Recorder*. I could not help but notice that on the front cover was a picture of a scantily dressed young woman brandishing a very large whip. Underneath was the headline: 'MISS STRICT STRIKES BACK'.

When the woman left the train at Reading, she disposed of the newspaper in the luggage rack. No one seemed to be looking so I took it down and prepared to enjoy whatever scandal was being reported. I have to admit that even I was a little disconcerted. It turned out that young Miss Strict was a graduate of St Sebastian's University. When she left, she had amassed considerable debts which she decided to clear by taking a part-time job as a dominatrix at a high-class escort agency. (This was the newspaper's description of her place of work, not mine.) I thought it was unfortunate that any new graduate was so burdened by debts that she would even contemplate taking up this sort of career. When I was at Cambridge, students had grants to finance their education.

But there was worse to come. Apparently, during the course of her duties, Miss Strict had recognised one of her clients as someone who held a high position in St Sebastian's Cathedral. Seizing the chance to make even more money, she had reported the whole story to the *Sunday Enquirer*. As a result the unfortunate cleric had to resign. This was not the end of the story. It turned out that her family were furious that she had given the *Enquirer* her real name. They felt humiliated by the whole affair and there was a sad interview with Miss Strict's mother who was a clerical officer at a hospital in Wolverhampton. She was mortified and was ready to disown her daughter and her activities altogether. Miss Strict herself was defiant. She told the

Daily Recorder that she had earned forty thousand pounds from her escapade. As a result, she was now debt-free; she had given in her notice to the agency and she intended to put down a deposit on a small flat in London.

I have to say that I was appalled that a young woman would think of paying for her education in such a way. That, of course, did not excuse the clergyman, who, in its mealy-mouthed way, the *Recorder* had refused to name. The editor of the paper was obviously furious that the *Enquirer* had scooped the story first and its leading article was sanctimonious in its condemnation of Miss Strict's avarice and lack of charity. It was full of sympathy for the unfortunate clergyman who had been led astray by this bold young bluestocking.

As a supposed expert in Christian ethics, I spent the rest of the journey pondering the rights and wrongs of the situation. Was the *Recorder* right to condemn young Miss Strict? Could Miss Strict's activities be justified on the grounds of the greatest happiness of the greatest number? Should the *Sunday Enquirer* be condemned for pandering to people's prurient interests or was it to the public good that hypocrisy and vice be revealed? And what was the moral status of the *Recorder* in prolonging the story? These were hard questions even for the emeritus holder of the Thomas Jefferson Porpoise Distinguished Chair of Theology and I was still thinking about them when I passed through the noble portals of the Acropolis Club.

I went straight up to the drawing room where the Archbishop was hiding behind a copy of the *Church Times* in a dark corner. In front of him was a plate of half-eaten tea cakes. When I greeted him, he jumped to his feet and shook my hand. 'Good to see you Harry,' he said. 'It's been too long. I know you and Victoria have just got back from Virginia and I feel bad calling on you so soon, but I really am at the end of my tether.' He signalled to a waiter to bring over another pot of tea and some more tea cakes and we sat down.

'You'd better see this,' he said, as he pulled a newspaper cutting out of his pocket. It came from the *Sunday Enquirer* and it was the whole sad story of Miss Strict and her client. It turned out that the unfortunate St Sebastian's cleric was no less a person than the cathedral Provost himself.

11

'Oh dear!' I said.

'Oh dear is right! There's no choice. I've got to discipline him. He's got to go and I've got to find someone to take his place.' He drew his leather chair nearer mine and lowered his voice. 'Look, Harry,' he continued, 'I know you've just arrived back in this country and I'm sure you're looking forward to retirement. But, you see, now St Sebastian's Cathedral doesn't have a Provost and the university doesn't have a Visitor. And it's rather a critical time. The university is facing a quality inspection and the gossip is that there may be trouble. The whole cathedral Chapter is very upset what with one thing and another. They didn't exactly get on with each other even before this crisis. What we need is a steady hand on the tiller. I wondered if you might consider a little proposition . . .'

'You surely don't want me to be the Provost, do you?'

The Archbishop hesitated. 'Well actually Harry, yes I do. At least for a short time, just as a temporary measure. To tide us over the difficulty. Until we can can fill the post in the long term. We really are in a bit of a fix . . .'

I was flabbergasted. I had never had any ambition to rise in the Church. I was looking forward to retirement. It was time to bow out and cultivate a garden, not to embark on some new exhausting post, fraught with conflict and difficulty. But the Archbishop was shrewd. He knew just how to play me.

'It'd only be for a year or so. Just to sort things out. And, as you know, the Provost's House is really rather splendid. Pevsner describes it as one of the most beautiful houses in England. Victoria would love it and she is the perfect person to make it as beautiful inside as it is outside, Anyway we need you. You'd be doing me, and more importantly, the dear old Church of England a real favour.' The Archbishop picked up a tea cake and bit into it. Butter escaped and dripped down his cassock. He looked me straight in the eye. 'Think about it, Harry,' he said. 'I could almost say it's your duty. Look at it as an act of solid Christian charity.'

The Archbishop could not stay long. He had to go back to the House of Lords to collect a group of visiting bishops. We parted with expressions of mutual esteem and I promised I would consider his proposal. 'Please . . . Please . . . We need you . . .,' he said as he climbed into his chauffeur-driven car.

Somewhat dazed, I rang Victoria. Mobile telephones were banned in the club rooms, so I had to use a grubby little cubicle by the entrance desk. Despite the smoking ban, there was still a ghostly smell of stale tobacco. Inevitably, Victoria had not yet arrived back at the castle, so I left a message on her voicemail. But I needed to talk to somebody so I telephoned my old friend Magnus Hamilton.

Several years ago, Magnus and I had been colleagues at St Sebastian's University where he taught Hebrew and Old Testament. Although he had come to the university with superlative references from Oxford, his research had dried up and over the space of nearly thirty years he had published little except acerbic reviews of other scholars' work. At the same time, he was a very brilliant teacher; he was adored by his students who imitated his mannerisms and adopted his catch-phrases. It was hard to believe, but under his tuition, Hebrew was the most popular undergraduate course in the whole Theology department. Sadly his abilities were not recognised by the university authorities. As far as they were concerned, research was the only thing that counted and Magnus had remained a junior lecturer for his entire career.

Then, to everyone's amazement, he won an indecently large sum of money on the premium bonds. He promptly decided to retire from full-time work. He booked himself on a round-the-world cruise and Victoria had taught him ballroom dancing before he left. He had found his vocation. He was a huge hit with the elderly ladies on board and was in constant demand as an escort and dancing partner. Unlike the University of St Sebastian's, the Trans-World Shipping Company recognised talent when it saw it. As soon as the voyage was finished, he was offered a regular job as a gentleman host.

Since then, he had been employed on several different cruise ships. He complained constantly about being pursued by the octogenarians, but when another summons from the Company came, he could not resist. After packing his dinner jacket in his leather suitcase, and checking that his shoes were still comfortable, he would set off. Invariably, he returned laden with a

13

selection of elegant little souvenirs from his admirers – gold cigarette cases, thin platinum watches, a rainbow of thick silk ties and elaborate sets of silver hairbrushes in pigskin cases.

I knew that he had been away. When we arrived at the castle, there was a postcard waiting for us from Turkey. It was a mounted photograph and it showed Magnus in the loud orange and green shirt he had bought in the West Indies. He was standing in front of a ruined temple, surrounded by a troupe of grey-haired ladies. Everyone was smiling at the camera except Magnus who looked exhausted.

I worked out that he must be back by now and I rang him at his flat in St Sebastian's. He picked up the receiver on the second ring and I could hear mournful Mediterranean music playing behind him. 'Welcome back, Magnus,' I said.

'Ah, it's you Harry. God it's been a nightmare! Worse even than usual! Never again! Just a minute. I've got to turn the music down. I can't hear myself think.'

'What on earth is that ghastly noise?' I asked.

'Terrific stuff. Purchased it in Athens. It's a group of Greek Orthodox monks chanting. Do you know they go up in baskets to their monasteries and never come down again? After dealing with all my old ladies, I knew just how they felt. In fact, I thought I'd try it out for myself when we went to Mount Athos.'

'You weren't really going to enrol as a monk?'

'Believe me, by that stage on the cruise I'd have done anything to escape. Somewhere where no women were allowed under any circumstances sounded very attractive. But when it came to the point they wouldn't have me. There was some stupid business of not being properly baptised. Apparently a nice C of E christening in the parish church when you're a baby doesn't count, Anyway, how are you? Back for good now I hope. Is Victoria well?'

'She's fine. But, look Magnus, I need to talk to you. The Archbishop of Cannonbury summoned me to the club out of the blue. And he made me a job offer. You won't believe what he wants me to do!'

'He wants you to be Bishop of BongoBongoLand to drive some sense into his fellow-bishops in preparation for the next Lambeth Conference.' Magnus had always had an inventive imagination.

I laughed. 'Well . . . not quite as daunting as that! No. He's invited me to become the next Provost of St Sebastian's Cathedral.'

'No! . . .' said Magnus. And there was a long pause while he thought about it.

'Well, Well!' He came back. 'Does he indeed! It's because the present Provost is in hot water, isn't it? I would have thought he'd been caned enough for his misdemeanours! Doesn't the Archbishop believe in Christian forgiveness?'

'Magnus! Really! How do you know about it anyway?'

My friend chuckled. 'I saw the *Sunday Enquirer* when I caught the train back from Southampton. It's not my normal choice of Sunday reading, but I was so exhausted after my labours on the ship, that I thought I should read something completely untaxing. In fact I got a winner. There are few more pleasant spectacles than a member of the established Church on the hop.'

'Was he a nice man? He was appointed after I left St Sebastian's. His predecessor was ghastly as I remember.'

'A real creep!' agreed Magnus. 'He became Suffragan Bishop of Puddlethorp you know. I only ever met this one a couple of times. He seemed all right. The usual Church of England ineffective ass if you know what I mean.'

I tried to sound offended. 'Magnus, I am an ordained clergyman of the Anglican Church. Am I the usual ineffective ass?'

'Only sometimes,' pronounced Magnus. 'Even after all these years you still believe the best of people instead of really taking on board the eminently sensible doctrine of original sin. In my experience, the vast majority of the human race is uniformly ghastly as you'll very quickly discover if you're foolish enough to take on the provostship. You're not really going to say yes are you?'

'I don't know what to do. The Archbishop put on a lot of pressure. I'll have to talk about it with Victoria, but perhaps it really is my duty . . .'

'Victoria's the last person you should consult. You know she's a complete sucker for beautiful architecture and even I accept that the Provost's House in the Cathedral Close is one of the most pleasing buildings in England. No . . . you need someone objective to talk some sense into you. Why don't you invite me to dinner at the club? I've got nothing decent to eat in the flat and I could be with you in an hour if I catch the six o'clock train.'

I realised that that was exactly what was going to happen. After we had said goodbye, I booked a table for two in the club dining room and left another message for Victoria telling her that I would not be home until well after midnight. Then I went back up to the drawing room and immersed myself in the Archbishop's discarded *Church Times*.

Just before seven, Magnus arrived clutching a gigantic package. Deeply tanned, he was wearing a khaki suit with a floppy red and white bow tie. The porter looked suspicious as he ushered him into the lobby. He was only partially reassured when Magnus insisted that his parcel was not a bomb, but an important Greek antiquity.

He then shoved the parcel into my arms. It weighed a ton. 'Here, Harry,' he said. 'Found this on Crete and couldn't resist.'

'Do you want me to unwrap it now?'

'Why not? It's just the thing for the Acropolis.'

Inside I discovered a very battered two-foot-high female stone figure. She had enormous breasts and a very round stomach. I was a little taken aback. 'What is it?' I asked.

'It's a female pre-Minoan fertility goddess. I found her in a little shop on a back street in Knossos and couldn't resist her. I thought she would make a nice pair with my African god that I keep in my room at the university.'

I remembered the African statue. Indeed it was notorious throughout St Sebastian's. It stood at least three feet high. Magnus put it on a table and used its enormous phallus as a peg for his coat.

'Didn't they go?'

Magnus shook his head. 'They're really rather incompatible. Too much of a good thing, if you know what I mean. And then I realised that she was just the present for my friends the Gilberts. It will challenge Victoria's interior decorating skills to the utmost. Particularly in the Provost's House. I would recommend putting her in the dining room. It'll put the entire cathedral chapter off its pudding! And anyway I must pay you back for the nice dinner I am about to eat.'

I rewrapped the statue, tied it up with string, and asked the porter if he could keep it in his office until I left. Then we went straight into the dining room. The first person we saw was the Archbishop who was seated at a large table with a group of African bishops, all of whom seemed to be talking at once. They appeared to be united in their disapproval of the activities of their American counterparts. The Archbishop looked agonised, but smiled wanly at me as we passed.

We were shown to a table in the corner of the great room. After we had chosen what we were going to eat and had ordered some wine, Magnus leaned back in his chair. 'So,' he said, 'you've been bamboozled. The Archbishop looks a bit under stress which is, after all, what he's paid for, and you immediately feel that it's your duty to help him out of a hole and sort out St Sebastian's Cathedral.'

'Well I can't make any decision at all until I've talked it over with Victoria.'

'Oh come on, Harry,' Magnus was impatient. 'You know jolly well she won't be able to resist the chance to live in the Provost's House. It's the perfect background for her. Well, it'll be splendid for me to have you both back. You know I'm still doing a bit of Hebrew teaching for the university?'

'Really? . . .' I was amused. 'You always said it was such a corrupt crappy place and you couldn't wait to leave. What happened?'

'Well . . .' Magnus looked embarrassed. 'They caught me at a weak moment and they asked me very nicely. When I came back from my first cruise, I found that I sort of missed the students . . . though they get more ignorant every year. I can't imagine what they teach them in all those schools.'

'The thing is I promised Victoria we'd move to Shropshire to be near her father. Sir William's become more feeble recently and he needs some sort of residential care . . .'

'You know,' Magnus said, looking at me penetratingly, 'the Provost's House is quite magnificent.'

'I know, I know . . . and the Archbishop really is anxious for me to do it. But, when all's said and done, it's rather embarrassing. After all I did leave St Sebastian's under a cloud.'

'So did I . . . well sort of. But that doesn't matter now. We've got a new Vice-Chancellor. And after all you'll be mainly looking after the cathedral. The Visitor is only called into the university when there's a crisis.'

'I know. But honestly, Magnus, I'm still rather cross about the way I was treated. I was bullied into leaving. So I don't really see why I should bail them all out just because the Provost can't keep his trousers on.'

'I always thought Christianity taught that you should forgive people, seventy-times-seven if I remember rightly. That's what the school padre used to say . . . Never let the sun go down on your anger and all that,' he added sanctimoniously.

'Oh shut up, Magnus,' I responded. He was an old friend, but at times he was infuriating. 'Anyway, what's going on at the university now? Remember I've been away for three years.'

'They certainly need you, Harry. The place is a mess. A crazy Irish Australian called Flanagan is now in charge. They appointed him not because he had any claims to erudition or indeed any intellectual interests that I've been able to discover. But he is a financial genius.'

'Well that's all right then,' I said. 'At least there's some money in the kitty. When I was there, cash was always a problem. Remember when the university was threatened with amalgamation with Arrowsmith Teacher Training College?'

'Well that threat has receded. But this Flanagan chap is mad. It's true that the place is now solvent, but he's done it by introducing the most appalling new curriculum. Most of the students are studying such subjects as Professional Golf, Exotic Dance and Brewing Technology.'

I laughed. 'I don't accept that. They'd never get it past the Higher Education Quality inspectors.'

'That's just the point,' said Magnus. 'Honestly I'm not exaggerating. The most popular undergraduate discipline this year, the one that attracted the most students, was Celebrity Studies.'

'Don't be absurd.' I did not believe him.

'Honestly it's true. They seriously study the love life of film starlets. Next weekend there's to be an international conference, an international conference mark you, on the Plight of the Female Celebrity focussing on the cases of Geri Halliwell and

18

Amy Winehouse. Apparently, hundreds have enrolled for it and the Vice-Chancellor is dancing all the way to the bank.'

'But why aren't the Quality Control people doing something about all this?'

'I told you, that's just the point. The Vice-Chancellor has managed to fob them off for the last eighteen months or so, but we've just heard that St Sebastian's is going to have a full-scale inspection early next year. It'll be a disaster. Everyone knows that, but apparently Flanagan is completely unabashed. He insists that everything will be fine and he won't even talk about it.'

'Perhaps everything is all right.' I was determined to try to look on the bright side. 'All these inspections only come down to having all the right paperwork in place. No one cares about the reality.'

'But the paperwork's non-existent. You know what the Registrar is like.'

Unfortunately, I remembered all too well the deficiencies of Registrar Sloth. 'And,' Magnus continued, 'he's recruited his wife – no interview or advertisement or anything like that – to be the new Quality Control Officer. She is paid an enormous salary. She sits surrounded by paper which she systematically loses and the whole thing is a complete shambles from first to last.'

'That doesn't sound good.' It was true that Mrs Sloth was even more incompetent than her husband. I could see the situation was serious. 'So you think the university needs a Visitor who will crack the whip a bit.'

Magnus giggled. 'That's an unfortunate expression given the present Provost's troubles,' he said as he tucked into a large plate of moules marinière.

When I finally crept into the castle at half past one in the morning, Victoria was reading in bed with both our Siamese cats curled up on her lap. They had travelled back with us from America in the hold of our aeroplane, but the authorities had insisted that they go to a cattery for a month for a thorough veterinary inspection. In fact the total cost of their travel and medical arrangements had been more than double ours. They had finally arrived at the castle roughly at the same time as Victoria that afternoon and she had been delighted to see them.

After I had kissed everyone, Victoria got straight down to business, 'I got your message,' she said, 'but your telephone was turned off.'

'We're not supposed to use mobiles in the club. Now listen, Victoria, I've got some important news.'

'The Archbishop wants you to do something for him.'

'Yes he does. You're not going to believe it, but he wants me to be the Provost of St Sebastian's. Just temporarily.'

'But they have a Provost . . .'

'They had a Provost,' I corrected her. 'He's just been sacked for cavorting with prostitutes. Well, actually, just one prostitute. One of the girls who graduated from the university this year was paying off her student loans by working in an escort agency. She recognised the Provost as the man who gave her her degree and she went straight to the *Sunday Enquirer* with the story. They wrote her a huge cheque.'

Victoria put her book down. She grinned. 'That was very bad luck for the poor old provost. I can't remember any of my contemporaries at Girton going in for the oldest profession when they left. It's not exactly what you expect of a sweet girl graduate.'

'Your friends all got government grants to support their education.'

Victoria became grave. 'You're right, of course. That is dreadful. A student shouldn't be so desperate for money that she would decide to be a hooker.'

'Well I think as far as selling the story to the newspaper, she recognised a commercial opportunity when she saw it. But the fact is, it won't do as far as the Provost is concerned and he and his wife have left St Sebastian's, bag and baggage, already.'

'Poor wretched woman . . .' Victoria shook her head, 'It's not fair. She hasn't done anything wrong.'

I continued. 'As you know, the Provost's House is quite spectacular. The Archbishop emphasised that, if we take it on, you'd get the chance to decorate it. And it would only be for a year or so. We can buy our own house now, just as we planned, and it will give us a chance to fix it up while I try to sort things out at St Sebastian's. And they'd pay me something too.'

'But they were beastly to you at the university Harry and, as Provost, you'd have to be their Visitor.'

'I know. I've thought about it. Magnus invited himself up to the club for dinner. He told me about the university. Things aren't good at all. I have a nasty feeling that it may be my duty to do it.'

'You mean it would result in the greatest good for the greatest number.' Victoria always mocked my attempts at systematic ethics.

I was serious. 'Perhaps . . .' I said. 'Anyway, unless you really hate the idea, we ought to go for a look at the very least.'

'I'm not likely to hate the idea of living in that wonderful house,' murmured Victoria as she turned over to go to sleep.

The next day, we told Sir William about our possible plans. He was very amused. Then we set off for St Sebastian's on the train. The city looked very familiar and it was a glorious autumn day. The sun was shining as we walked through the Monks' Gate into the cathedral precincts. Visitors were wandering around the Green Court. At one end was the Provost's House, a glorious symmetrical Queen Anne building of old red brick with white small-paned sash windows. Across from it loomed the grey stone mass of the cathedral. 'It is beautiful,' I said.

Victoria sighed. 'All right, Harry. I agree, but one or two things must be made clear. You promise that it's only for a year, or at the very most two.'

'No more,' I said.

'And I must find a room for Daddy and Bess in one of the St Sebastian's nursing homes.'

'Of course,' I promised.

'And you won't get flustered and upset by university politics.'

'I'll only be the Visitor. I won't get involved.'

'Huh!' My wife was not convinced. 'And you won't become entangled in cathedral politics either.'

'They won't take any notice of me. I'm just an ignorant academic,' I said.

'And you'll let me decorate the house the way I want to. You won't interfere.'

'You can have it exactly as you want. The Church will pay so you may have to talk it over with someone in the diocese.'

Victoria nodded. 'All right, Harry. We'll go. But please, please, please, pretty please, try not to get mixed up with things you don't understand . . .'

CHAPTER TWO

Our Lot is Cast in a Goodly Heritage

So, the decision was made. I wrote my letter to the Archbishop and received a very grateful effusion by return of post. There was to be no delay. It was a case of crisis management and it was thought important that the new Provost should be put in place as soon as possible. Victoria and I were permitted to stay in the castle for just one more week and then we had to move.

Victoria felt wretched leaving her father. He had suddenly become an old man and she thought she should be looking after him, rather than gadding about redecorating the most beautiful house in England. Sir William was philosophical about the situation. He had accepted that he needed more help. When we finally departed and Victoria kissed him goodbye, she insisted that she would be returning very soon with a list of first-class residential homes near St Sebastian's. 'I promise the carers will be pretty,' she said.

The old Provost had sent in a remover's van and all his possessions had already disappeared from the house. Happily he owned a holiday cottage in Northumberland so he and his wife were not homeless. Meanwhile Victoria was busy looking at pattern books from various grand interior designers while I made arrangments for some of our furniture to be transported from our old house to the Provost's residence. In fact, the house was already exquisitely equipped. One of its previous occupants had been a bachelor. He had loved pretty things and, when he died at the immense age of ninety-seven (there had been no retirement age for clergy in those days) he had left his collection to the cathedral. Nonetheless, we felt we wanted to have a few of our own treasures around us so I made a list of the things that needed to be collected from our old house.

On the day of the move, Victoria and I drove to St Sebastian's. There was a new system of one-way streets past Arrowsmith College, but at last we found ourselves in the cathedral precincts. A group of noisy French students were screaming at each other and dropping litter on the steps of the cathedral. Lugging a heavy cat basket – it is surprising how much two well-fed Siamese weigh – I staggered across the Green Court in the direction of the Provost's House. As I walked through the front gate, I almost tripped over a vast ginger-and-white creature who was sitting next to the doorstep. He was dismembering and noisily consuming an unfortunate squirrel. As I passed by he stared at me with luminous green eyes. Then, quite deliberately, he spat. Our two cats peered out of the cat basket and immediately became shivering, tremulous wrecks. Victoria followed behind carrying a small bag and a jewel case. The ginger beast pointedly turned his back on her and proceeded with his luncheon.

Our cats became more and more agitated. We rang the bell and a grey-haired lady carrying a feather duster appeared. I recognised her as the wife of one of the university porters. She used to 'do' for me in my study when I taught at St Sebastian's. 'Good afternoon, Mrs Thomas,' I said.

Mrs Thomas beamed, 'Recognised me you did!' she said. 'I told Evan that Professor Gilbert wouldn't forget a face. And how are you, Sir? And Mrs Gilbert too?'

Victoria rose to the occasion. She was proud of being Welsh and had learned to speak the language from her nanny when she was a small child. '*Da iawn, diolch. Hyfryd gwrdd a chi eto! Ydych chi wedi dod 'n helpu ni heddiw?*' (Very well, thank you! Lovely to meet you again! Have you come to help us today?)

24

Mrs Thomas was enchanted, '*Ydw! Ydw! 'W i wedi gweithio yn y Ty Provost am sbel.*' (Yes I have. I've been working at the Provost's House for quite a while.) 'But a long time it is since I've spoken the old language, Madam. To tell you the truth, Evan grew up in Pembrokeshire and English always came easier to him. And then when we moved to St Sebastian's and the children were in school, they didn't like me to speak Welsh to them. It marked them out, you see. So what with one thing and another, I only ever spoke it to Mam when she came to live with us, her arthritis being so bad, and she's been gone these ten years.'

By this time we were all inside the hall and the front door was shut. 'Who does that large ginger beast belong to, Mrs Thomas?' I asked.

'He's Canon Blenkensop's cat. He's called Marmaduke. Terrible he is, but the Canon won't hear a word against him. He's always catching birds and squirrels. Then he fights with all the other animals in the precincts. I should look out for your two if I were you. Precentor Samuel's dog had to go to the vet after being bitten and I heard that the bill was more than sixty pound.'

'I don't think we'll have to keep them in. It looks like they'll be too scared to go out. Can't Canon Blenkensop keep him under control?' asked Victoria.

'It's not just his cat, Madam. No one can keep Canon Blenkensop under control either if you'll pardon my saying so. He didn't like the last Provost at all. He walked all over him at Chapter meeting so everyone said and the Provost was right scared of him.'

I felt the conversation was becoming rather too gossipy. 'Would you mind taking my wife's bags upstairs, Mrs Thomas?' I said.

The hall had a wonderful cornice and was beautifully proportioned, but the paintwork was stained and shabby. I saw what the Archbishop had meant when he said that the house needed Victoria. She would have a wonderful time putting it all to rights. The walls were decorated with imposing gold-framed portraits of my predecessors. It was a daunting thought that my image might be hung here in future years.

Beyond the hall was a sizeable study where I supposed I was to write my sermons. There was a magnificent old Isfahan carpet on the floor and the furniture looked to be of museum quality, but again, although everything was clean, there was an undefined air of shabbiness and neglect. We shut the doors and opened the cat basket. Slowly and reluctantly Brutus and Cleo emerged from the depths. They crept out, looked about them and promptly retreated under a handsome walnut tallboy.

Mrs Thomas then showed us the rest of the house. Balancing the study was a magnificent dining room with a long mahogany regency table and twelve William IV dining chairs, all with fine needlepoint seats. Hanging over the table was a huge Venetian chandelier. It was superb, and sparkled in the autumn sunshine.

'That can't be easy to keep clean . . .,' I remarked to Mrs Thomas.

'No,' she said, pleased that I had noticed. 'I have to get the men to take it down and then I wash each piece by hand. Two whole days it takes me.'

'It looks beautiful,' I said.

The drawing room was situated on the first floor and ran the full length of the house. It was the shape of two symmetrical cubes placed together and with the right paint colours and curtains, it would be the most perfect room for a grand party. Then on the next floor there were six bedrooms and two old-fashioned bathrooms, all overlooking the cathedral. Much needed to be done to make them as pleasant as they could be.

The inspection took us some time and the cathedral clock was chiming the hour as we descended a small winding staircase, which led to the old servants' rooms and, finally, to the somewhat primitive kitchen. Victoria made a face when she saw it. 'What sort of budget will the diocese allow me?' she asked.

'I have no idea. The Archbishop didn't mention it. I don't think you should spend too much, Victoria. The Church of England has more important things to do with its money than lavish it on housing for a couple of already very privileged people.'

'Nonsense!' said Victoria. 'You're doing the Archbishop an enormous favour, putting off your retirement to take on this job. And, in any case, the Church is a steward of this wonderful property and it's its duty to exercise that stewardship in the best way possible. It shouldn't just let things rot.'

I did not want to argue. Having spent the whole of my professional life pondering ethical dilemmas, it was all too easy to see both sides of any problem.

Finally, at the back of the house was a lovely walled garden. It had been a mild autumn and the traditional English roses still bloomed as they clambered over the mellow brick walls. There was a spacious lawn and old mulberry and quince trees heavy with fruit. The air was sweet with the fragrance of its ripeness.

'"Our lot has been cast in a goodly heritage,"' I quoted.

Victoria snorted. 'Try not to be pompous, darling,' she said.

Mrs Thomas brought us coffee in the study while Victoria tried unsuccessfully to entice the cats from under the tallboy. They were completely traumatised by the move and the encounter with Marmaduke had been the last straw. Just as Victoria gave up and started to pour out, there was a huge rat-tat-tat on the front door. I hastened to open it and, to my amazement, there was a rotund figure hidden behind a large bunch of golden chrysanthemums. Although I had never met him, I knew instinctively who it must be . . . the Vice-Chancellor of St Sebastian's University.

'G'day, mate,' he said as he shook my hand. 'Alf Flanagan, here.' He could not have been much more than five-foot-two inches high, but he made up for his lack of inches in girth and personality. Wearing a grey flannel suit that barely met around his middle, he sported a St Sebastian's tie while a large maroon handkerchief flowed out of his breast pocket. Before I could get out a word of greeting or welcome, he bounced over the front doorstep and into the hall.

'Good to have you back in St Sebastian's. I've heard all about you from your old friend Magnus Hamilton. Just what we need! A breath of fresh air! Incidentally is that your cat? He's dispatched that wretched squirrel in a most unchristian fashion.'

'Our cleaner told us it belongs to one of the canons.'

'Rough little bugger! He hissed at me when I went past.'

I introduced the Vice-Chancellor to Victoria and she asked him if he would like to join us for coffee. Mrs Thomas brought in a tray with a cup and saucer and some home-made shortbread fingers. He was on his feet in an instant.

'Well hullo, Mrs Thomas, and how are you? I was saying to Evan just the other morning that it's been too long since we saw each other. And how are young Bronwen and Huw getting along?'

Clearly Flanagan was superbly good at people-management. Mrs Thomas was thrilled by the encounter with her husband's boss and disappeared down to the kitchen smiling. The Vice-Chancellor then turned to Victoria and asked all about her father. He had met him previously more than a year earlier. He had even stayed overnight at the castle to discuss some university business while Victoria and I had been in Virginia.

'A real top bloke! A bonzo sportsman and a gentleman if ever I met one. Eighty-eight is he now? It's a great age!' I could see Victoria melting. Anyone who liked her father could do no wrong in her eyes. I made a little promise to myself that I would not allow myself to be manipulated by his bluff Australian charm.

Alf Flanagan spread himself on the sofa and dunked his biscuits into his coffee.

'When d'you plan to start at the cathedral?' he asked.

'Actually,' I said, 'I'm supposed to begin straightaway. The last Provost has already moved out all his things and our furniture is due to arrive tomorrow.'

'Poor sod!' he said. 'Cyril Woodcock was an idiot in many ways, but he was an improvement on his predecessor and it could've happened to any of us.'

'How is his wife?' Victoria asked. 'It can't have been much fun for her.'

'Well she was half the trouble. Double gussetted if you know what I mean! Anyway she gave him hell about it all. And to make her feelings clear, when they left she drove the car straight across the Green Court. The gardeners were not pleased. You can see the tyre tracks by the Monks' Gate.' Turning to me, he smiled. 'Let's talk of more pleasant things. I want you both to come to Flanagan's for lunch on Monday.'

'Flanagan's?' Victoria looked puzzled.

'The new university restaurant. A fair-dinkum place even if I say so myself. You'll remember it as Brewster's Brewery just behind the university.'

I did remember it. Brewster's Brewery was an old St Sebastian's business. In my years at the university it had been very run down and the managing director, the last scion of the original family, was said to have a serious drink problem. The Vice-Chancellor continued his explanation, 'We've taken over the building. I got a nice lump of European money to keep the operation going. I'd just closed the Chemistry department, which was a waste of space if ever there was one. I'd managed to get rid of the professor, but I was stuck with some of his underlings. So I set them to organise a department of Brewing Technology. It's been a top enterprise. We make all our own beer: Flanagan's Finest, it's called. Place is booming! We've got outlets all over the country and we're planning to export to Europe this year. That's organised by the Business Studies department. It gives them something useful to do . . .'

'But what about the restaurant?' asked Victoria.

'Well it's all part of the enterprise. The Travel and Tourism department train the waiters and waitresses as part of their hospitality course and we use the old brewery offices as a small catering department to produce the food. It's a thoroughly professional enterprise.'

'It must cost a fortune,' my wife observed. 'Presumably you have to pay all the cooks and waitresses the government minimum wage even if the beer comes very cheaply.'

Alf Flanagan roared with amusement. 'Pay them? . . . I've never heard such nonsense! They pay us! They're students! This is all part of their course! St Sebastian's University is famous throughout the United Kingdom for providing the very best work experience for its undergraduates. You should just see their curriculum vitaes when they leave us!'

'So Brewing Technology and Travel and Tourism and Catering are all academic disciplines now? Is that right, Vice-Chancellor?' I always like to get things clear in my own mind.

'You bettcha! They're some of the most successful departments in the university. Now you must call me Alf,' he said. 'We're going to see a lot of each other in the future.' He glanced at his watch and heaved himself off the sofa. Then he turned to Victoria and smiled. I could sense another blast of Australian charm coming through.

'You're obviously your father's daughter,' he said, 'and I want to make you a sporting proposition. I've got a cracker of an idea . . . I know you're quite an expert on art and antiques and suchlike. I've seen your pieces in *Country Life*. As part of our programme of continuing education, we're planning to run a series of talks for the local community. I thought a set called "Make a Fortune from Your Old Junk" would go down a treat. Perhaps you'd even consider holding it in the drawing room here, that'd pull in all the old pussies of the precincts. And then you could have an Antique Roadshow evening with some celebrity or other. I'm sure Harry here would let you use the Chapter House and you could invite a panel of experts. We'd give them all a free dinner at Flanagan's and of course pay all their travel expenses. People could bring their rubbish for you to value. They'd love that. Perhaps we could even have an auction. The Business Studies department would organise it for you. Twenty per cent of the proceeds to the university, that sort of thing. I'm sure you'd enjoy it!'

Victoria took a deep breath, but before she could utter a word, the Vice-Chancellor was looking at his watch again.' Well that's settled then! My secretary will be in touch. I've got to go to a Council meeting. Let them all have their say and then do exactly what I was going to do anyway, that's the ticket . . .,' he said as he headed for the front door. He bounced off in the direction of the Trinity Gate. As he passed, he directed a sly kick in the direction of Marmaduke who was occupied in tossing a disembodied squirrel leg into the air.

For the rest of the week, Victoria was busy organising the house and ordering new curtains and carpets. I met with the Canons of the cathedral and was preoccupied with ecclesiastical problems. I realised from my first meeting with the Chapter that the Precentor, Percival Samuel was terrified of the Senior Canon, Reg Blenkensop. Blenkensop in his turn bullied the Precentor mercilessly. Officially the Precentor was responsible for the cathedral music. He was a willowy young man who seemed much attached to the works of Hindemith and Messiaen. In contrast, Canon Blenkensop insisted that the only composers worth having were Handel and Elgar, although he was prepared to make a concession occasionally for the works of Bach. They quarrelled about it ceaselessly and it was clearly a delicate situation.

On my first Sunday, I preached a sermon at Matins and was delighted to see a number of old friends at the service. I did notice, however, that despite the Precentor, the anthem was by Handel. Cleo and Brutus were becoming used to their new home, but did not dare venture outside. Marmaduke spent much of his time sitting on a bench in our front garden, glaring at our cats whenever they had the temerity to look out of the window. Occasionally, a passing tourist would take his photograph. He would stop whatever he was doing, present his best profile to the camera and give a self-satisfied smirk.

On the Monday, the day of our lunch with the Vice-Chancellor, the sun was shining. Magnus had telephoned us to say that he was to be of the party and we arranged to meet him outside the restaurant. When we arrived at the university, we parked our car by the old Victorian red brick brewery. Over the front door was a large sign with 'Flanagan's' in big letters and a logo of an academic wearing a mortar board. If Alf Flanagan had been its model, it was certainly a flattering portrait. Magnus was waiting for us by the main entrance.

We found Flanagan in the entrance lobby and he led the way up a flight of stairs to the dining room at the top of the building. A youthful waiter wearing jeans and a sweatshirt with the same logo led us to our table which had a splendid view of Old College with the cathedral spire in the distance. The seats were comfortable, the room was busy, and the young staff seemed attentive. 'Well, what d'you think?' asked our host.

Victoria and I looked at each other. 'It's delightful, Alf,' I said. 'It's just hard to think of it as an academic part of the university.'

'Gotta move with the times.' Alf Flanagan was in a jovial mood. 'If you stand still nowadays you go under. I'm sure it's just the same in your cathedral. Can't keep doing the same old thing!'

As a follower of a religion which had lasted two thousand years, I was not sure about this. Still, I was now Visitor of St

31

Sebastian's University by virtue of my position as Provost of the cathedral and it was my duty to support the Vice-Chancellor.

Alf Flanagan was enjoying himself. 'Actually the Brewery has been a godsend. Not only does it provide premises for Brewing Technology, Catering and the restaurant, we use the European grant to finance all the university's sporting activities. I've developed our golfing and swimming facilities to a near-Olympic standard and we now offer Sports Studies as an undergraduate degree and various diplomas in Professional Golf, Pool Management, Life Saving and Sports Coaching. You see one thing leads to another . . . We now attract students from all over the world, all paying full foreign students' fees. And of course the Dance department has gone from strength to strength since we added Artistic Dance to our other programmes . . .'

'What on earth is Artistic Dance?' asked Victoria. 'I thought all dance was meant to be artistic.'

Magnus giggled while Flanagan became a little evasive. 'Oh it's an American speciality,' he said. 'But,' he got back into his stride, 'the biggest area of growth is Celebrity Studies. That's another part of the Entertainment Faculty located in the Old College.'

'Place is full of students. We'll be like Arrowsmith Teacher Training College soon,' Magnus complained.

'Of course it's full of students,' the Vice-Chancellor beamed. 'That's what a university is for! To attract students! To spread culture and learning! Here at St Sebastian's applications have quadrupled in the last three years.'

'The noise!' Magnus moaned. 'And the people! It's unbearable.' Looking over the menu he ordered a deluxe hamburger with cheese and mushrooms and a double-portion of chips.

'Now you must try Flanagan's Finest. That's the main point of the place, after all,' said the Vice-Chancellor as he signalled to a waitress. She brought over a large pitcher and four glasses. After he had poured out, he picked up his glass and made a toast. 'To my new Visitor and his charming wife,' he said. 'Let this be the beginning of a prosperous alliance!' I looked at Magnus who sniggered.

The following week I was invited out to lunch again. This time it was to the university Senior Common Room and Magnus was to be my host. He had also asked an old friend, Felix Glass. Felix had been a senior lecturer in philosophy when I was a member of the staff. He was an expert on the work of the great German Immanuel Kant and, as my views on ethical theory were not exactly the same as his, we had enjoyed many stimulating discussions over the years.

Things had changed while Victoria and I had been in the United States. As a result of Alf Flanagan's cost-cutting strategies, the Philosophy department had been closed and it looked for a time as if Felix would lose his job. However, to everyone's astonishment, he had turned his attention to fiction and had published two successful campus novels both loosely based on St Sebastian's. The first, *A Campus Conspiracy*, was actually inspired by my original difficulties at the university – though if Magnus had not let me in on the secret I am not sure I would have recognised myself. The second, *Degrees 'R' Us*, was a sequel and focussed on Felix's own problems at the time of the closure of his department. Magnus was a prominent character in both volumes and held out hopes that they would be taken up by Hollywood and that he would be invited to play himself. He had already practised his Oscar acceptance speech. In any event, both books had done surprisingly well and had had glowing reviews in national newspapers.

The Senior Common Room, panelled in dark oak, was located at the far end of the Old College. Magnus and Felix were standing in the queue when I arrived, and they both ordered cheese sandwiches, crisps, and packets of biscuits. Magnus bought a bottle of Muscadet for us all. This was another change. There was certainly no alcohol for sale in the days when I was the Professor of Christian Ethics, but Felix told me that the sale of wine was another commercial enterprise of the Vice-Chancellor. Indeed I saw several of my old colleagues enjoying bottles of Flanagan's Finest with their lunches. As always, I was concerned about my expanding waistline. I selected a tuna sandwich and an apple. They looked rather austere on the university plain white plates, but I tried not to look wistfully at my friends' crisps and biscuits.

We chose places in the corner where we could talk uninterrupted. At the next table were a couple of law lecturers whom I dimly remembered, but they were absorbed in their newspapers and did not notice me. I turned my attention to my companions. 'So how are you Felix?' I asked.

'He's just been promoted,' said Magnus coyly. 'He's now Professor Glass.'

'Really?' I said. 'How splendid! When did that happen?'

Felix looked embarrassed as he explained that he was not exactly a professor of philosophy.

'What then? Philosophy's your subject. Don't tell me you've been seduced into Brewing Technology or something . . .'

'Well, as you know, I was rescued from redundancy by agreeing to head the Vice-Chancellor's Entertainment Faculty. The academic programme is divided into three faculties now. Humanities, Social Science and Entertainment. Entertainment is by far the biggest.'

I shook my head. I tried to imagine what my old tutor at Cambridge would have said to this programme. He had been appalled when I switched from Classics to Theology at the end of my second year on the grounds that Theology was not really an academic subject, at any rate not as compared with Classics and Mathematics.

'But I managed to persuade Alf Flanagan to let me continue to teach philosophy to small groups of interested students.' Felix went on. 'I didn't just want to be an administrator. And I must say, I've had some very good undergraduates . . .'

'So why can't you be the Professor of Philosophy if the subject is still taught?' I asked.

'Well . . . it's all rather embarrassing . . .'

'Ask him what he's now called,' Magnus grinned

'I'd rather you didn't.' Felix squirmed in his seat.

'Tell us, Felix. I'm sure there's nothing to be ashamed of. After all, a Chair's a Chair . . .'

'It's all a big mistake.'

'A mistake?'

'Well, it really doesn't make sense.'

'Go ahead, Felix,' Magnus prompted.

'All right, all right! I'm the Immanuel Kant Professor of Entertainment!' Magnus dissolved into giggles.

'You can't be!' I said.

'Well,' Felix said, 'Flanagan insisted. What he really wanted was for me to be the Walt Disney or the MGM Professor of Entertainment and he wrote around trying to get a massive endowment from the studios. As it happens, Hollywood isn't finding things too easy at the moment so that came to nothing. So the compromise was he allowed me to be the Immanuel Kant Professor provided it was made clear that it was for entertainment rather than philosophy. And it's understood that if he does find some sucker to give the money, then poor old Kant will have to be dropped.'

'It could be a lot worse,' consoled Magnus. 'Think if you were the Frodo Baggins or the Harry Potter Professor of Entertainment. Flanagan is quite capable of that sort of whimsy.'

'I know,' said Felix grimly. 'I live in dread . . .'

Magnus looked through his post as Felix told me about the growth of his faculty and the changes that had taken place in the university since I had left. All the new departments belonged to Entertainment. There was now Dance, Drama, Fashion, Film, Sports Studies, Travel and Tourism, Catering, Celebrity Studies and, of course, the notorious Brewing Technology. In effect the whole institution had been reorganised and there was no doubt that it was financially booming.

'But I don't understand,' I protested. 'All this reorganisation takes time. It's complicated. All the new degrees have to be approved by the central higher education Quality Control Agency. You have to have armies of qualifed external examiners to make sure that your standards are the same as that of degrees in the more conventional subjects. How have you got all this organised so quickly?'

Felix squirmed again. 'I worry about that every day. To be honest nothing is properly in place. Flanagan insisted that we started and took in students as soon as ever we could and preferably before that. At present we rely on a very cursory system of moderation because we simply do not have enough external examiners and Flanagan won't give us enough money to pay for them.'

'But what are you going to do?' I persisted. 'I understand there's to be a quality inspection later this academic year. You've got to get it organised before then.'

'I know, I know!' Felix wiped his mouth with his handkerchief. 'I go on about this to the Vice-Chancellor whenever I meet him. But he's incredibly good at ignoring problems and he refuses to discuss anything. He keeps referring me to Mrs Sloth who's the new Quality Control Officer in the university.'

'Jenny Sloth, the wife of the Registrar?' I asked.

'The very same . . .' Felix sighed.

Christian charity temporarily failed me. 'But she couldn't run a booze-up in a brewery,' I said.

'And she can't see the necessity for an external examiner for Brewing Technology and, in any case, she has already lost the documentation three times!' remarked Magnus brightly.

'Only twice actually.' Felix was deeply gloomy.

I thought the time had come to change the subject. After all this was meant to be a pleasant lunch amongst old colleagues.

'How is everyone else? How is my old arch-enemy John Pilkington?'

John Pilkington was the Head of the Department of Theology and had been determined to get rid of me. Magnus was amused. 'Oh he's risen to great heights. He's become Dean!'

'Dean! No!' I said. 'But what happened to the old one? That nice lesbian you liked? What was her name? Patricia Parham?'

'She's gone off to Miami Beach to be the Head of Women's Studies on an enormous salary.' Magnus informed me. 'There was much wailing and gnashing of teeth when she went, partly because she was so nice, but mainly because her partner was the best car mechanic in the town and everyone's cars have fallen into little pieces since she left.'

'But how did Pilkington get it?' I asked.

'He was the only candidate,' said Felix, who was also clearly not happy with the situation. 'I've also had my battles with Pilkington as you may know. The only consolation about his elevation is that he is as worried as I am about the coming quality inspection. And when all's said and done, he is conscientious.'

'Never mind!' I consoled him. 'At least you've written a couple of novels and you must have got some royalties on them.'

'And movie rights,' Magnus added pointedly. 'I'm still waiting for my call from a Hollywood casting director.'

'You may wait a long time,' Felix said. 'I helped with the screenplay, but there were problems and the whole thing seems to be snarled up in some financial wrangle . . .' He smiled. 'Still the books did quite well . . .'

When we had finished our lunch, Magnus insisted that we paid a visit to the Great Hall. The university had been given a picture of its patron saint, St Sebastian, and Magnus was eager for me to see it. I happened to know the artist who lived in Virginia, but I was unprepared for what I found. The picture was at least twelve feet tall and was hung at the far end of the room next to an antique longcase clock. It was larger than life in every sense of the word. Every vein and every muscle was outlined in sharp relief. The flesh was intensely flesh-coloured and, at intervals, golden arrows skewered bank notes to the body as streams of scarlet blood flowed from the wounds. Over the saint's head was a golden halo and his face was lifted upwards toward heaven. It looked bizarre against the Victorian oak panelling.

'Good God!' I said. I regret to say that sometimes I forget that I am a clergyman.

'Absolutely!' Magnus smirked. 'It's quite memorable, isn't it?'

'It's incredible! What's it doing in the Great Hall?'

'It's to drum up custom for weddings,' Felix said.

'Weddings? What weddings?'

'Actually gay weddings,' Felix explained. 'Of course the university doesn't discriminate; it does offer a straight wedding package, but that picture rather pulls in the gay market.'

'How does it work?' I had understood that universities were in the business of teaching and research. Flamboyant life-cycle ceremonies were the preserve of cathedrals. Now it seemed the Church had a serious rival.

Magnus started laughing again. 'It's one of the Vice-Chancellor's money-making schemes. He set up a company called Mixed Blessings. He employs an administrator who mainly uses student labour and every Saturday and often on week-days the college building is taken over by one wedding after another.'

'Does the Mixed Blessings administrator teach as well?' I asked. 'Are you now offering a degree in Matrimonial Management?'

Felix shuddered. 'Don't suggest it! Don't even think about it! Flanagan would be onto it like a dog after a rabbit!'

'Now that you're Provost, Harry, perhaps you could officiate,' Magnus suggested. 'It would be a nice little earner for you!'

As we were chuckling about this, we heard the voice of the Vice-Chancellor in the distance. As he came round the corner, we saw he was showing a delegation of Japanese visitors around the university. They were heading in the direction of the Great Hall; Flanagan was wanting to show off the portrait.

He was delighted to see us and seized the opportunity to make elaborate introductions. There was a great deal of bowing and quantities of Japanese business cards were thrust into our hands. I felt inadequate that I had nothing to give in return. Magnus, however, rose to the occasion. Leading the delegation to the foot of the portrait, he rattled off several very fluent-sounding Japanese phrases. His audience giggled uncertainly and then relaxed when Magnus said something else. When he had finished there were more smiles and bows and Flanagan led them all out.

I knew Magnus was a suberb linguist, but this time he had surpassed himself. 'That's very impressive,' I said. 'Where did you learn how to say that?'

'Stopped off in Tokyo on one of the cruises,' he said. 'Bought a phrase book for tourists. Thought it might come in handy as a gentleman host. I hoped there might be some meek Japanese ladies who would be content to sit quietly rather than dance exhaustingly all the time.'

'Did it work?' I asked.

Magnus shook his head. 'No. The cruises are only marketed in America. The only Japanese person I ever met on board was one of the cooks. Still I did practise a bit with him.'

'They seemed pleased. What did you say?'

'Well I took them to the picture and asked them if they'd ever seen anything so camp in their lives. I'm not sure if I got the right word for camp which is why the reaction was a little uncertain. They may have thought I was saying something improper. Then I told them to make sure that the Vice Chancellor gave them something to eat. Business visiting is very exhausting and one must always keep one's strength up. They liked that!'

Felix and I looked at each other and shook our heads. For all his faults, Magnus was incredibly talented.

Later in the week, Sir William and Bess came to stay with us at the Provost's House. Our cats were not pleased. In their view, Marmaduke was a terror and Bess an affront. But some things have to be endured and they decamped to a high chest of drawers and spat at the poor dog whenever she went past. My father-in-law was in good form. He had always liked St Sebastian's and we got the impression he was looking forward to his new life.

True to her promise, Victoria had found a very nice residential home within walking distance of the precincts. It was located in an old regency mansion known as the Priory and there were extensive grounds. There was plenty of room for both Sir William and for Bess to walk about and there was no objection to dogs. Indeed, on our visit, we were introduced to a small white poodle in a jewelled collar who belonged to one of the old ladies.

There was one room vacant. It was not very large, but it was on the ground floor and it overlooked the garden. We stayed to lunch and the meal was just what my father-in-law liked; basic well-cooked school food. Then we were shown the programme of entertainment and were pleased to see that the other old people looked well-cared for and comfortable. I was a little perturbed that there seemed to be almost no men amongst the inhabitants, but Victoria was not troubled. 'Daddy's always liked ladies,' she said.

We took him round the following Saturday. Sir William was enthusiastic about the grounds, but felt that the gardeners were not sufficiently supervised. 'Damned untidy herbacious border,' he remarked. 'It should have been thoroughly cleared for the winter by now. And the lawn edges are a disgrace!' I feared that the Priory staff would have a hard time under his aegis.

He also liked the room. I thought he would find it too small after the castle, but he was unbothered. 'I'm used to army quarters, remember. This is very cosy. As long as I've got my new arm chair and we can fit in Bess's basket, I'm happy.' He ogled all the young carers who were very amused by him. The other old ladies were put in quite a flutter at the idea that a real-life baronet was going to join them and he was remarkably gallant to them all. He even got on with the matron. He addressed her as if she were his sergeant. 'I say, you're doing a fine job here, Matron,' he said. 'Carry on the good work, carry on the good work!'

So it was decided. Victoria drove him back to the castle to help him select which of his possessions he wanted to bring. Since for many years he had lived mainly in the old housekeeper's room which was not much bigger than his new residence, the choice was not difficult. It was all packed up by Victoria's brother Billy and sent off in a van. Victoria followed to set up the new room, leaving her father behind for one last week. During this time, his tenants on the estate organised a surprise farewell party for the old man which touched him very much.

Meanwhile, Victoria was busy. She persuaded the matron to have the room repainted in cream and a dark brown carpet was fitted. This was the scheme Sir William was used to in the castle. She hung a couple of pairs of old gold velvet curtains at the windows and somehow managed to fit in an incredible quantity of furniture. There was his old leather armchair, the new self-lifting contraption, a Regency mahogany gentleman's wardrobe and a couple of sidetables as well as his bed and a flat-screen television. On the walls, she hung several engravings of Shropshire as well as three or four small ancestral portraits from the castle and an array of family photographs. There was a replica of the arms of his old regiment and pictures of his old school and college. Just before he arrived Victoria set out an enormous bouquet of red-hot pokers in one of the castle vases.

Billy and Selina drove him and Bess down. 'Feels like my first day at prep school,' Sir William remarked, as we all arrived together in front of the Priory. The sun was shining, the matron was cordial to us all, though she was surprised at Bess's size. She had been expecting a small dog. Bess walked to heel impeccably at Sir William's side and all was well. Sir William liked his room. He demonstrated the raising action of his chair to any member of staff who was willing to be an audience and he admired all Victoria's arrangements. It all seemed too good to be true.

Then suddenly there was a disturbance. We heard the sound of an old lady screaming hysterically down the corridor and there were accompanying yaps of terror. Victoria rushed down the passage to investigate the problem. It was not good. Bess had made a category mistake. She had taken the small white poodle to be an errant lamb and had hemmed it up into a corner. The poodle's owner was weeping and wringing her hands. She was sure that her darling Pookie was about to be eaten.

Victoria called off Bess who responded instantly. Sir William limped over to apologise; he reproved the poor sheepdog (who was, after all, only being obedient to her training) and promised that henceforth Bess would be kept on a lead in the house. He was so remarkably charming that old Mrs Mackenzie – that was the name of Pookie's owner – surrendered completely. The two old people sat down together and Victoria went out and asked one of the carers to bring everyone coffee.

'Do you play cards, madam?' asked Sir William.

'Oh yes,' fluttered Mrs Mackenzie. 'We're always looking for someone for our canasta group and my friend Mrs Germaney is a bridge fiend.'

'Yes, yes! Very good! But what about blackjack? Do you play blackjack?'

Mrs Mackenzie looked nervous. 'Isn't that a gambling game? I'm not sure my dear father would have approved of that!'

'No, no!' said Sir William. 'You can always play with matchsticks. It makes it more interesting if there's something to play for. I'll demonstrate.' He dug into his pocket and produced a pack of playing cards. 'Now madam,' he said, as he happily started dealing out the cards, 'Let me show you. You'll soon get the hang of it!'

CHAPTER THREE

You Wouldn't Want
Everybody to be Unhappy

We settled down to our life in the precincts. Victoria was very preoccupied with her father, but things seemed to be going well at the Priory. Sir William had established a good rapport with the matron. Bess had become a general favourite and now understood that, despite all appearances, Pookie was a dog like herself. The rules of blackjack had been taught to several old ladies and was widely established as the game of the moment. Sir William, to his great satisfaction, had also demonstrated that he was the best Scrabble-player in the home.

On our third Sunday, Victoria invited Magnus to lunch following the cathedral service. It was a damp day and there was a slight mist over the Green Court as I made my way to the West Front. Despite the inclement weather, there were still a great many tourists in the precincts. The doorway into the cathedral was blocked by a large group of Japanese visitors all taking photographs. I wondered if it was the same delegation that I had met at the university. Perhaps unsurprisingly, they showed no sign of wanting to join us for prayer.

When I finally arrived in the vestry, I found the rest of the

Chapter waiting for me. Hurriedly, I put on the Provost's Cope. This was one of the treasures of the cathedral. It was extremely heavy and it was covered with magnificent hand embroidery in gold, red and white. When I was a professor at the university, I had always admired it. I did not realise how hot and uncomfortable it was to wear. Just before we were due to begin, choir and clergy came together and I recited a brief prayer. Then, as the organ struck up the first hymn, led by the choir, we all filed into the nave. I brought up the end of the procession.

The service followed its usual course. I was somewhat disconcerted to discover that the choir was to sing yet another anthem by Handel. I made a mental note to myself that I must defend the Precentor's choice of music against the assaults of Canon Blenkensop. Nothing else untoward happened until we were on the third hymn. I was due to be led by the Verger into the pulpit for my sermon, when I saw Marmaduke sauntering up the cathedral aisle. He turned this way and that as he walked, much as a royal personage graciously greets his subjects who have been standing all night in the rain to catch a glimpse of him. Then, to my horror, he sprang up onto the altar which stood at the top of the nave. Waving his tail, he sharpened his claws on the white linen cloth. Then he walked across it leaving a line of muddy footprints. They would have delighted the forensic department of Scotland Yard. Turning himself round several times, he stretched himself out and settled for sleep in the warmth of the candle flames.

I was horrified and thought about sending the Verger to turn him off. But, having confronted him several times in my own garden, I knew he would spit and struggle. In all likelihood there would be an unseemly scene and probably the Verger would end up wounded and in need of immediate first aid. Therefore, coward that I am, I pretended not to notice and started to deliver my sermon. Marmaduke did not seem to feel any obligation to listen. He slept soundly, snoring slightly until I finished. Then he leapt down, waited until I had been led back into my seat and proceeded back down the aisle with exactly the same aplomb as before.

'Is this normal?' I whispered to the Precenter under cover of the final hymn.

'That damn cat does it whenever it rains. He sits, terrorising everyone in the precincts on fine days and then he comes into the cathedral to throw his weight about whenever it's wet,' he said.

'But that's outrageous. We can't have a cat disrupt the service like that. Look at the state of the altar cloth.'

The Precentor shrugged his shoulders and started singing the last verse of 'Praise to the Holiest in the Height' very loudly in his fine deep baritone.

Back in the vestry, we all disrobed. Before he could leave, I tapped Canon Blenkensop on the shoulder. 'Can I have a word?' I said.

The Canon looked at his watch. 'I've only got a minute,' he said. 'I've an important luncheon engagement.'

I took a deep breath. 'It's about your cat,' I began.

Canon Blenkensop frowned. 'Marmaduke? What about him?'

I realised that this was not going to be an easy conversation. 'As you know, Reg, I'm a cat-lover myself, but we really can't have Marmaduke wandering all over the cathedral during the services. It's distracting for the congregation and really, it's not very suitable in the house of God.'

'Why not? As our Lord said 'Suffer the little children to come unto me.' Surely that includes all God's creatures.'

'I think there is a difference between children and animals,' I said mildly. 'And anyway I wouldn't allow a child to march all over the altar and leave his footprints everywhere. It's not reverent.'

'I think you're making a fuss about nothing. He doesn't do any harm.'

'I'm sorry Reg,' I tried to sound firm. 'Marmaduke really cannot come into the cathedral in future. You must keep him under better control.'

The Canon looked at his watch again. 'I'm sorry Provost,' he said, 'I really must go to my lunch. All I can say is that no one has ever complained before . . . Splendid anthem wasn't it?' And with that he turned on his heel and strode out of the vestry.

Although Magnus had been at the service, we had agreed to meet back at the Provost's House. I found him sitting in my study drinking sherry while Victoria was on the telephone in the kitchen. I helped myself to a drink and sat down opposite. 'Well . . . what did you think?' I asked.

44

'Very jolly! I particularly liked the anthem,' he said. I sighed inwardly. The problem was that Canon Blenkensop's musical tastes, in contrast to those of the Precentor, probably did match those of the general public. 'And I loved that Cope of yours,' he continued. 'Very stylish! Almost worth being Provost for!'

'It's very uncomfortable to wear and I don't get to keep it,' I said. 'It's over a hundred years old and it belongs to the cathedral.'

'And that cat was quite an addition. He looks a tough customer!'

'He is. He terrorises Cleo and Brutus. They don't dare go outside and we've had to organise indoor sanitation for them. They haven't had that since they were kittens, but they're too frightened to face that ginger beast who dominates the whole precincts.'

Magnus laughed. He knew what it was to be bullied by a cat. His tabby was called Pushkin. He was known to insist on an indoor lavatory and the most expensive cat litter. 'I can't understand it,' I continued, 'Marmaduke seems to run the place.'

'I thought that was your job, Harry.'

'Well perhaps the Almighty has put that cat here to keep me humble . . .'

At that moment Victoria came into the room and poured herself a large glass of sherry. She looked flushed.

I felt a chill of foreboding. 'What's the matter?' I asked.

'That was the Matron of the Priory on the telephone. She's been trying to get hold of me since Friday. The gardeners have complained.'

'How has your father managed to upset the gardeners?' Magnus was amused. He always found it difficult to take domestic crises seriously.

'He ticked them off. He told them that the herbacious borders hadn't been properly weeded and that several of the perennial clumps should have been lifted and divided a couple of months ago. Then he rang Billy to send some cuttings from the castle grounds and he is demanding that the gardeners plant them.'

'What's wrong with that?'

'They say it's against union rules. They're only prepared to take their orders from Matron. And apparently Daddy walks

45

about the garden like a fieldmarshal, looking down his nose and pointing his stick at everything he disapproves of.'

'He's behaving like Marmaduke! And how do the gardeners show their displeasure?' I asked.

'Well they're scarcely gardeners. They're a couple of youths on some ex-delinquent employment programme and Matron says they don't react well to authority figures. They went to see her insisting on their rights. They told her that if she didn't keep the old bugger under control, they'd give in their notice.'

'It sounds as if the Priory would be better off without them if that's their attitude.'

'Well I made that point, but apparently labour is almost impossible to find in St Sebastian's. You have to take whatever you can get.'

'Perhaps Sir William could organise a volunteer corps of gardeners from among the old ladies. Probably several of them are veterans of the Second World War Land Army and he could be their commander-in-chief,' suggested Magnus helpfully.

We all giggled. Then Victoria became serious. 'I'll have to go and see him after lunch and talk to him. I'm sorry to send you off before tea, Magnus, but we must calm him down a bit before there's real trouble.'

There were further difficulties later in the afternoon. Victoria did manage to persuade her father that he was no longer the lord of the manor and that he could not go about giving orders to the gardeners, however inadequate. She had just arrived home and was looking forward to a quick glance at the Sunday newspaper when there was a knock on the front door. We really did not want to be disturbed, but I knew my duty. I rose from my chair and opened the door. Outside, looking as if he were about to burst into tears, was the Precentor. 'Provost,' he said, 'I feel dreadful disturbing your Sunday evening, but I just don't know what to do. Could I have a minute of your time?'

I gathered him up and led him into the study while Victoria tactfully melted away into the kitchen. 'Sit here,' I said pointing at an armchair beside the fire. 'Let me pour you a drink. You look a bit as if you need one. What would you like? How about a little whisky?'

The Precentor huddled into himself, but cheered up a little when I suggested a large gin and tonic instead.

With trembling hands he told me that he had just had another argument with Reg Blenkensop. Apparently, earlier in the afternoon, the Canon had marched over to the Precentor's house uninvited and had insisted that the matter of cathedral music be sorted out once and for all.

'He had heard that I was planning a special service for the Bishop of Tuckenham's visit in a fortnight's time,' the Precentor told me. 'I don't know how he found out. He always seems to know the coming anthems almost before I do. I think Mrs Blenkensop has struck up a friendship with the girlfriend of one of the lay-clerks and that's how he gets all his inside information.'

'Anyway, I know the Bishop is one of the more musical members of the bench so I was planning to have a treat for him, a special arrangement of extracts from the Schoenberg Mass in F.' I tried to look as if I were familiar with the work. The Precentor continued, 'Canon Blenkensop stormed around my study and said it was a totally unsuitable choice and no wonder people stayed away from church if they had to listen to that sort of rubbish. Rubbish . . . that's what he said!' The Precentor's voice became higher and higher in indignation. 'Schoenberg was one of the finest composers of the twentieth century. His work may not have the immediate appeal of Ralph Vaughan Williams or Arthur Sullivan which is the limit of Reg Blenkensop's taste, but it's infinitely more subtle . . .'

'I'm sure you're right,' I tried to soothe my agitated colleague. 'What did Reg want in place of the Schoenberg?'

'He suggested that if I wanted something special for the Bishop, we could have Bach's 'Jesu, Joy of Man's Desiring' cantata, but really one of Elgar's anthems would be more suitable. How dare the man interfere! He's a complete Philistine! He's almost tone deaf and he's had no musical education at all! The only thing he ever did when he was at Oxford, besides scraping a third in theology, was play rugby for the university . . .'

'Was he really a rugby blue when he was an undergraduate?' I was impressed.

'Oh yes . . . he boasts about it all the time. But that doesn't give him the right to lay down the law about cathedral music. I just can't bear it any longer . . .'

'Oh dear!' I said rather inadequately.

The Precentor was not to be halted. 'He just wants to control everything, every detail. I'm the Precentor and the responsibility for cathedral music is part of my job description. I tried to tell him so, but he wouldn't let me speak. He just cut across me. He accused me of being a modernist and having no respect for the traditions of the Church of England. And then he told me that he had told the printer after the morning service to change the proposed service sheet and put Bach's 'Jesu, Joy' as the anthem rather than the Schoenberg. The printer always prints it out before lunch on Sunday so it can't be changed now. It's too bad! When I tried to protest he told me to attend to my duties and he went out and slammed the door. His horrible cat was waiting for him, eating a pigeon in my garden, and the two of them went off together leaving a mangled corpse in my rose bed.'

'Oh dear!' I said again.

'And that's not all, Provost.' There was no way the Precentor's indignation could be assuaged. 'I think you ought to know that he wants to introduce a scheme so that visitors will have to pay to come into the cathedral in the future. It's an outrage! Our cathedral is a house of God. It belongs to all faithful people and its doors should be open to anyone whatever their financial circumstances.'

'Yes,' I said. 'I had heard something about that. It's supposed to come up at the next Chapter meeting. There's an item on the agenda about imposing an admission charge. But surely the other Canons won't approve of it?'

'You don't know what he's like, Provost. He marches about the place like a sergeant-major barking at us and giving his orders. The whole Chapter is terrified of him. Your predecessor, Provost Woodcock, wouldn't even be in the same room as him without his wife present.' The Precentor gave a little smile. 'Mrs Woodcock was the only person who could stand up to him and even then, when they did have a battle, it was sort of an honourable draw between them!'

'Perhaps I'd better set Victoria on him,' I suggested.

The Precentor looked doubtful. 'She looks far too charming ever to defeat Reg Blenkensop,' he said. I thought back on various occasions in our marriage when Victoria had completely humiliated several of her enemies in the neatest, most elegant way, but I felt this was not the right moment to reminisce.

'I did speak to Reg about Marmaduke,' I said.

'He's a monster. He dominates the Green Court. He slaughters the birds and squirrels, he spits at the tourists and he bit my dog.'

'I heard about that,' I said.

'The vet bill was seventy-five pounds and poor Otto really needs intensive psychiatric help to get over it. And as for that cat's behaviour during services . . . it's beyond belief.'

'I'll see what I can do,' I said.

'Please, Provost.' The Precentor downed his drink and stood up. 'I don't know how I can continue any longer if this goes on,' he said as I led him through the hall. 'We're counting on you to do something about this reign of terror.'

As I let my unfortunate colleague out of the front door, I noticed that Marmaduke was sitting outside on the study window-sill. It was almost as if he had been listening to every word. As soon as the Precentor turned the corner, he sauntered off.

When I went back to the study, Victoria was sitting on the sofa. She shook her head. 'Poor wretched man. Reg Blenkensop is a real bully. You're going to have to do something about him.'

'I know. It's going to be a problem . . .'

Victoria smiled slyly. 'I think you also have an ethical dilemma here, Harry.' Victoria often teased me about my views. She had always thought my job a bit of a joke. I saw myself as a Christian utilitarian which meant that, with many qualifications and reservations, I believe that the right thing to do is whatever leads to the greatest happiness for the greatest number of people.

'Why is there a difficulty in my situation?' I smiled back at her.

'Well I expect if you did a survey of cathedral congregations, the majority of them are made happier by the tunes of Handel than by the dischordance of Schoenberg. Therefore, according to your own principles, Blenkensop is right and the Precentor is wrong. The fact that the Precentor is a nice, sensitive man and Blenkensop is an oafish bully is irrelevant. According to your ethical theory you can only judge a situation by its results.'

'You're looking at the matter too simplistically,' I teased her back. 'Overall, as a general rule, it produces even unhappier results if bullies are allowed to win. Therefore, it's right to support the Precentor in this instance. We may have to endure some ghastly Schoenberg and miss out on some splendid Handel. But this leads to the ultimately happier result that aggressive behaviour is discouraged.'

Victoria laughed. 'You are sweet,' she said, 'I've never heard such a roundabout way of demonstrating what everyone knows anyway.'

'What does everyone know?' I asked.

'That people like Reg Blenkensop and his horrible cat should be clobbered on every possible occasion,' she said as she went off again to the kitchen.

On the day of my first Chapter Meeting, the three Canons, the Archdeacon and the Precentor assembled in a panelled room next door to the old Chapter House. The magnificent Chapter House with its carved stone seats for every canon, residential and non-residential, was only used occasionally on high days and holidays. The small Victorian annexe, known as the library was far more comfortable for everyday business.

One of my duties as Provost was to act as chairman of Chapter Meetings. I sat in a large Chippendale armchair at the head of a mahogany table with the Canons arranged in order of seniority. Canon Sinclair, who was within a year of retirement was on my right. He had just been diagnosed with the beginnings of Parkinson's disease and was a little shaky. The Archdeacon, a brisk sensible man, who was responsible for diocesan affairs sat on my left. The great bulk of Reg Blenkensop was on the other side of Sinclair and the red-haired Canon Trend who was said to be a promising young man destined for great things, was next to the Archdeacon. The Precentor was uncomfortably isolated by himself next to Blenkensop with no one opposite him; he looked pale and tired after his most recent confrontation. I made a mental note to have a leaf taken out of the table. Then the Precentor could sit fronting me at the end so we could all see one another at future meetings.

The minutes of the last meeting had been circulated. We

embarked on the agenda which was unexceptional. After an hour we had covered all the items except the last which was ominously headed 'Admission Fees'. This item had been suggested by Canon Blenkensop and he introduced the subject. 'Gentlemen,' he began. 'As you know a considerable number of cathedrals are now charging for admission. Some are even asking for fees to enter the precincts. This of course has many advantages. It preserves the quiet of the cathedral neighbourhood and deters undesirables from putting off genuine visitors.'

'I thought Christianity was founded for the benefit of undesirables. Publicans and sinners our Lord called them,' quavered Canon Sinclair . . . rather bravely, I thought. I realised that here was a potential ally. I would ask Victoria to invite him to lunch.

Reg Blenkensop magisterially ignored this interruption. 'I am not suggesting we take this step at this juncture despite its advantages. In the first instance I am merely recommending that we charge a nominal entrance fee to the cathedral itself . . .' He paused, clearly expecting general agreement and approbation.

'But why?' blurted out the Precentor. 'Our cathedral is a place of prayer and worship. It's not a tourist attraction. This is not Disneyland. God's grace is free. We shouldn't think of charging people.'

'It would make a considerable difference to the cathedral's finances . . .,' began the Archdeacon. He was of a practical turn of mind.

'Precisely,' continued Blenkensop smoothly. 'You've hit the nail on the head, Archdeacon. It would bring many great benefits. We would find it easier to keep the fabric of this great building in repair and we have to face facts. It is a major tourist attraction. Every year thousands of visitors come to see our historic buildings. They drop their wrappers on the Green Court; they stamp out their cigarettes on the pathways; they toss their empty beer cans in the cloisters; and, unsuitably dressed, they sun themselves on our benches. At present they do all this for free.'

'Surely then you're suggesting an entrance fee to the precincts?' I asked.

'Not at this stage. It's always more sensible to proceed slowly. To test the waters, we should charge visitors who wish to come into the cathedral. This will deter all those hoardes of French adolescents whose teachers dump them in the building as if we were a kind of baby-sitting service.'

I could not resist it. 'But you reminded me only yesterday that Jesus said "Suffer the little children to come unto me."'

Canon Blenkensop went purple. 'Provost, I have to say with all due respect for your great learning and your academic qualifications and so on, you have no experience whatsoever in cathedral administration. You are only here as a caretaker and your interference in this matter is not welcome. No indeed! I must insist on my right as a member of the Chapter that the motion be put to a vote.'

At this point Marmaduke sauntered into the Chapter House. He leapt on a radiator just inside the door and settled himself comfortably to enjoy its warmth. I felt his cold green eyes balefully staring at me. The whole Chapter looked at him and then looked back at me.

I made up my mind. 'I'm sorry Reg. It's a big decision. I want further investigation as to how it has worked out at other foundations. Would you look into it, Derek?' I turned to young Canon Trend.

'Yes Provost,' he mumbled, looking away from Reg Blenkensop.

'We will examine the matter again in six weeks' time when we have more solid information,' I declared. 'Now, if there is no other business, we can adjourn.'

The Canons rose slowly from their chairs. Blenkensop stood rigidly, put a pair of gold spectacles in a leather case, and picked up his papers. Without speaking, he marched to the door and passed out into the cloisters. His cat followed him.

'Oh dear,' said old Canon Sinclair, shaking his head. 'This kind of conflict is always so unpleasant. It is indeed!'

Despite all my worries about the cathedral, I still wanted to keep in touch with the university. After all, as Provost, I was the official Visitor. In particular I was anxious about the coming quality inspection later in the academic year. Felix Glass was clearly uneasy about it. Early in the week I made a telephone call to the Vice-Chancellor's secretary to ask if he could spare the time to have a little chat. Alf Flanagan was efficient. The very same afternoon he rang me back to invite me up to the university. Felix, as Head of the Faculty of Entertainment, would join us and he would explain to me what was happening.

On the appointed day I made my way to the Vice-Chancellor's office. Nothing had changed. It was still located in the Old Building on the top floor. When I arrived, I knocked on the door and heard a loud cuckoo coming from inside. Flanagan opened the door himself. He was wearing his dark suit, this time with a florid purple and gold tie. The silk handkerchief which flowed from his pocket was black. He shook my hand heartily and drew me inside. 'G'Day, mate,' he said.

The room was much as I remembered it under his predecessor. There was the same emerald green fitted carpet on the floor. The furniture was reproduction mahogany and the pictures were undistinguished but inoffensive. However, I could not fail to notice an enormous brown cuckoo clock hanging behind the Vice-Chancellor's large pedestal desk. The desk itself was covered with an untidy array of papers. Felix was already sitting on the sofa.

Despite his girth, Flanagan was clearly a man who found it difficult to stay still. I sat down in one of the armchairs, but the Vice-Chancellor continued to pace the room. 'As you know,' he began, 'we are to have a visitation from the Higher Education Quality Control people within the next few months. I've tried to put them off as long as I could, but like death and taxes, they catch up with you in the end. I can't imagine what they expect to find. The whole thing's damned silly in my opinion, but there it is.'

'How long will they be staying?' I asked. 'Should Victoria and I be doing something for them at the Provost's House?'

Alf Flanagan suddenly became enthusiastic. 'That'd be great mate! They'll certainly be impressed by the architecture and Victoria could keep anyone sweet. I understand the delegation will be in St Sebastian's for five days, Monday to Friday, so we must find plenty for them to do. We don't want to have them asking awkward questions, do we?' He roared with laughter. Felix looked agonised.

Flanagan was impervious to the effect he was having on his audience. 'I've already booked the best rooms at the White Hart Hotel. They'll have their breakfast there, but we'll give them a fair-dinkum lunch in Flanagan's and dinner in the Old Hall. I'm going to line up the lecturers in the Catering department to ply them with plenty of their best food and drink. Hopefully they'll go off to sleep after meals and won't be too much of a nuisance to us!'

He rummaged among the papers on his desk and handed over several menus and a wine list. 'Got to keep the buggers happy whatever it costs. That'll be the job of your department, Felix. You'll need to find some of your prettiest little sheilas to act as waitresses. Make sure they're careful. However tempting, it wouldn't be a good idea to drop soup all over them. And I've just ordered a couple of cases of Bordeaux and Burgundy from my wine club that we can put in the cellars . . .'

'But Alf,' Felix sounded desperate 'A visitation from the Higher Education Quality Control Committee requires more than just entertainment. They'll want to see documents to show we're doing our jobs properly. Things like grade criteria and external examiners' reports and teaching statistics and minutes of committee meetings and so on. Then all our partnership-institutions need similar paperwork to justify our giving them degrees. And I'm sorry to fuss, but we don't have anything like a comprehensive record. Everything was started up too quickly . . .'

Flanagan turned to Felix in the manner of a kindly uncle. 'Don't get so hot and bothered, mate. It'll all be fine. I've asked poor old Registrar Sloth to manufacture whatever paperwork we need.'

'How can he manufacture the paperwork?' I asked. 'Surely the documents should reflect what is actually going on and should already be in place.'

Felix shot me a grateful look, but Flanagan was unrepentant. 'Oh he'll just fix them up a bit. A touch here, a touch there. There's no need to worry Harry. I know what these bureaucrats are like. I went through all this at Fandonegal, my last university. They whinged a bit but as long as you gave them piles of pen-pushing stuff, they're quite happy. You've just got to produce a convincing paper-trail. It doesn't matter if it bears no relationship to reality.'

I felt that somehow I was losing the plot 'I'm not following this,' I said. 'Could you go over it again?'

The Vice-Chancellor put on a golfing cap which was lying on a side-table and he picked up a golf club from his umbrella stand. He started practising his putting. 'You know, I've just been elected onto the board of the St Sebastian's Golf Club,' he said. 'How many students are registered for the diploma in professional golf this year, Felix?' he asked.

'Nearly a hundred,' Felix mumbled.

'You see, Harry. Everything's booming. Golf, Celebrity Studies, Artistic Dance. The students are practically breaking down the doors to come to us . . .'

'Could we get back to the paper trail?' I insisted.

'I think you're too upset about it all. It'll be a piece of cake. If a paper-trail doesn't exist at the moment – and I'm sure that it probably does – then we'll just have to invent one. The quality inspectors won't know the difference.'

'The Registrar's doing this?' I asked. I could hardly believe what I was hearing. During my time at St Sebastian's the Registrar, Dr Robert Sloth, had lived in a complete haze. Nothing ever got done. A mild narcoleptic, he slept through most meetings. It was impossible to imagine him producing a credible set of documents, even if such a thing were tolerable.

'He's just appointed his wife as Quality Assurance Officer,' Flanagan pointed out. 'If he can't do it, she will.'

I was almost speechless. Reminding myself that I was a clergyman and, in theory at least, Alf Flanagan's boss, I pulled myself together. 'Vice-Chancellor,' I pronounced. 'This is most unwise. We cannot falsify documents. It would be dishonest and unethical and unworthy of the traditions of St Sebastian's. And even if we were prepared to engage in this sort of activity, the Registrar's wife is the last person in the world who should be asked to do it. She was absolutely hopeless when she worked in the university library. She was notoriously lazy and incompetent and I simply cannot imagine her creating a document which would deceive anyone . . .'

'Ah . . . you mustn't underestimate the lady . . .' Alf Flanagan reproved me as he tried to knock a golf ball into his wastebasket. It veered off in the wrong direction and nearly hit Felix's foot. 'Damn!' he said.

I was about to remonstrate further, but the Vice-Chancellor was distracted. He went to his desk again and rummaged among the papers. 'Ah . . . here it is! Now don't you worry about any-thing, Harry. Leave it all to me! I've got just the thing here to cheer you up.'

He sifted through the litter and pulled out a shiny photograph of a blonde young woman of about twenty-five. 'Before you go I wanted to talk to you about Olive O'Shea. I've just made a brilliant appointment.'

'Who is Olive O'Shea?' I asked.

'She's a watercolour artist. Had a small one-woman show in the fringe at Edinburgh a couple of years ago. She's married to old Lord Barridon. You'll remember him. He used to be a junior minister in the foreign office some time ago, but there was a bit of a scandal about kerb-crawling or something twenty years back and he was thrown out. But he still sits in the House of Lords.'

'But Lord Barridon must be nearly seventy by now. What's he doing with a young woman like that?'

Flanagan winked. 'Well . . . what can I say? Anyway I need someone to be a Director of Hospitality for the university. We need a front-woman to charm the pants off everyone and she's just the person to do it . . .'

He handed me a job description for the new post. I noticed that the salary was in the professorial range. 'It seems an awful lot of money to pay for a glorified hostess.' I said 'With a salary like that, you must have attracted some excellent candidates. What are Lady Barridon's qualifications and experience for this sort of post?'

Alf Flanagan shook his head. 'Oh she's a real cracker, mate. You'll love her. She's got loads of influential friends who know important people, if you know what I mean. Actually we haven't advertised the post yet and we'll have to go through the motions of interviewing, but she knows the job's hers. She's already put it on her curriculum vitae.'

'She's not the easiest person to work with Alf . . .' began Felix.

The Vice-Chancellor patted his colleague's shoulder and looked across at me. 'This bloke's always such a worrier,' he said. 'It'll all be all right on the night, just you see!'

At this point, Flanagan's secretary knocked on the door to inform him that his next appointment was waiting. It was time for us to go. We both stood up and thanked the Vice-Chancellor for his time.

'Now you mustn't be concerned about a thing, Harry,' he said, as I opened the door to leave. 'It's all under control . . .'

Felix wanted me to go to his room to talk things over. It turned out that he had been allocated the same study that had been mine during my eleven years at the university and I felt at home straightaway.

'You see,' said Felix, throwing himself down into an armchair. 'It's impossible to get any sense out of Alf. He won't concentrate on the matter at all . . .'

I tried to be encouraging. 'Well he's been through all this before. The Quality Control people did an inspection at Fandonegal University when he was Pro-Vice-Chancellor there. As at St Sebastian's, he'd introduced all sorts of educational partnerships with some very shady institutions . . .'

'Most of whom have since transferred here . . .' interrupted Felix.

'I seem to remember that the final report was pretty critical,' I continued, 'but Fandondegal got away with it in the end. The *Times Higher Education* magazine covered it pretty thoroughly at the time.'

'But he can't believe that Registrar Sloth or that idiotic wife of his could create a decent smoke-screen if they tried with both hands. And as for Lady Barridon, or Olive O'Shea as she insists on calling herself . . .'

'Yes . . . what was all that about?' I asked. 'Why's he doing this for her? Is she his mistress?'

Felix shook his head, 'I don't think so . . . she seems genuinely attached to Barridon. But she's completely unsuitable for the job. She has only two subjects of conversation – one is herself and the other is her activites. She has no interest whatsover in anyone else. I had to sit next to her at a formal dinner last month and she talked non-stop about her talents through the whole first course. She didn't ask a single thing about me. Then the conversation at the table became general. She tried to interrupt several times, but the other guests had things to say. So as soon as the second course was finished, she got up, pulled poor old Lord Barridon out of his seat, announced she was developing influenza and disappeared off home.'

I laughed. 'Oh dear! She sounds very much as if she's what

my old mother would have described as 'All mink coat and no knickers!''

Felix looked rueful. 'That's exactly it . . . But what is the Vice-Chancellor doing giving her the salary of a professor and ignoring the demands of the Quality Control Agency. Do you think he's gone mad?'

After dinner that evening Victoria and I were having coffee in the study. Brutus and Cleo were perched together looking anxiously out of the window. The Green Court was in darkness. In the distance we heard the unmistakeable sound of a cat fight. Marmaduke was on the prowl. I was telling Victoria about my conversation with the Vice-Chancellor. 'You know,' I said, 'I don't think the university has any of the required documentation for this Quality Control visitation. Flanagan kept talking about creating paper trails where none exist. As I was leaving, Felix said that they have never even recruited external examiners for most of the new degree programmes. The inspectors will be outraged if they find out.'

Victoria laughed. 'I expect someone will create some fictitious papers . . .'

'They can't produce non-existent external examiners. It would be disgraceful. And anyway, if they got caught, the whole degree course and possibly the whole university would have to close down.'

'But do you think anyone would check?'

'I don't know. Probably they wouldn't. But the whole thing's a scandal. And I can't see how, as Visitor, I can ever approve of such a policy.'

'I don't think they're going to ask for your permssion, Harry.'

'No, they won't. But if I know what's going on, then I can't stay silent.'

'What are you going to do?' asked Victoria. 'You certainly can't tell anyone.'

Indignantly, I said that I certainly would if necessary. 'There have to be proper standards. That's what the role of a Visitor is, to ensure fair play and all that . . .'

'But imagine the consequences . . .' Victoria smiled to herself. 'Think about the situation in utilitarian terms. If what really matters is the greatest good for the greatest number, then calling attention to the fact that the university is making up its reports would have appalling results. The standard of St Sebastian's degrees would be called into question. The staff and students would suffer. There would be a major investigation and they might even close the place down. All your erstwhile colleagues would lose their jobs. It would be a disaster. Surely a few little white lies and turning a blind eye would end in a much happier situation for everyone.' Victoria looked smug as she passed me a box of chocolates, one of the housewarming presents we had received from the residential Canons.

I sighed. I could see that here potentially was a very knotty situation. I did not feel strong enough to tackle it that night. 'I think I'll have to face the problem when it comes,' I said, and ate the last two chocolates in the box. One was an orange cream – a flavour I greatly dislike.

Exasperated, I went to answer the telephone which was ringing in the kitchen. It turned out to be Magnus who said he had run out of food for his cat and he wondered if we might be able to lend him some. About twenty minutes later he arrived at our front door. I led him into the study where he picked up the empty box of chocolates. 'What a pity!' he said. 'It looks like you've run out.'

He was displeased when he saw the brand of cat food we could offer him. 'You don't really make your two eat this cheap stuff, do you? Pushkin's digestion would be upset for a week if I gave him muck like this. Oh well, I'll just have to defrost some fish out of the freezer.'

Victoria went out to the kitchen to refill the coffee pot as I told him about my conversation with Flanagan.

'Inevitable,' he said. 'Flanagan's batty. Thank God I only do a little part-time teaching. If I were dependent on the university for my livelihood, I'd be seriously worried. He's turned the whole place upside down with his schemes. It's overflowing with students doing degrees in God-knows-what. None of it academic as far as I can see. Do you know they have a degree in Striptease?'

'Don't be ridiculous,' I said.

'It's true! It's part of the Dance and Drama department. Flanagan went into partnership with an organisation in Florida called the Pussy Galore College. They pay the university a fortune and send students on exchange. Now you see these little girls running about campus dressed in a few feathers and very little else.'

'But he can't put "Striptease" in the university prospectus.' Victoria had come back into the room.

Magnus sniggered. 'He doesn't! It's called Artistic Dance. Flanagan mentioned it to you when we all had lunch together, remember?'

'I thought he looked a bit shifty about it,' said Victoria.

Brutus jumped down from the window and hopped onto Magnus's lap as Victoria poured him out a cup of coffee. Magnus sprawled on the sofa as I complained about the Vice-Chancellor's plans to manufacture documents for the Quality Control Agency. 'Sloth and his wife are supposed to do it,' I said.

Magnus groaned. 'It'll be a disaster.'

'That's what I told Flanagan,' I sighed. 'Don't you think I ought to do something about it, Magnus? I am the Visitor, after all . . .'

'I wouldn't if I were you. You're only supposed to be filling in temporarily. Why make trouble?'

'But there's a principle involved,' I objected.

'Harry somehow believes that blowing the whistle will lead to the greatest happiness for the greatest number in the long run,' Victoria smirked. 'But I demonstrated to him that it could only lead to general misery.'

'That sounds most probable,' agreed Magnus. 'You wouldn't want everyone to be unhappy, would you Harry? Let them do whatever they want – Celebrity Studies, Fashion, Brewing Technology, Tourism, Striptease . . . as long as it keeps the place full and the money coming in.'

Victoria nodded her head. 'Please Harry. Stay out of this. You promised me that you wouldn't get mixed up with things you don't understand when you took this job.'

'But I do understand. I understand all too well. Alf Flanagan is planning to cheat.'

'Cheat? Of course they are!' Magnus said. 'They always have; they always will! What's new? Victoria's right! Just lie low and enjoy your fancy Cope, Harry.' Picking up the empty chocolate box, he looked at Victoria. 'You haven't got another one of these things, have you?' he asked.

CHAPTER FOUR

He's Created a Monster

For the next fortnight, Reg Blenkensop served as Canon-in-Residence. The practice at St Sebastian's Cathedral was that each residential Canon led the services for two weeks at a time. As Provost, I was not part of this rota, though of course I attended the cathedral whenever I could. Blenkensop's stall was next to mine in the choir. Every day I attempted to make pleasant conversation, but it was to no avail. Before the services, Blenkensop robed himself in sulky silence and would only speak to me if he was compelled to discuss details of the liturgy. When any other canon was present, he would have long animated chats with them. Generally, he reminisced about the good old days of the previous Provost or he talked of his time as a rugby blue when the Oxford University team was so exceptionally well-managed.

I have to confess that during this period I did become very tired of dischordant modern music. I had told the printer only to accept the order of cathedral services from me or from the Precentor. This meant that there was no possibility of Blenkensop sabotaging the Precentor's choices. As a result, we had a plethora of difficult anthems. However, I told myself that this was better in the long run than allowing a bully to prosper.

Unfortunately I was not so successful in improving Marmaduke's behaviour. He continued to stalk around the cathedral whenever he felt like it and he systematically decimated the unfortunate small fauna of the precincts. He also took to spitting at me whenever I was anywhere near him. This did not improve the atmosphere in the Green Court. However, the other Canons and the Precentor did their best to be friendly to both sides. Altogether it was all very awkward and embarrassing.

At the next meeting of the Chapter, young Derek Trend, keeping his eyes firmly on his papers, hesitantly reported that he had been in contact with a number of cathedrals. He gave a very diplomatic account of the advantages and disadvantages of introducing formal charges. By the end of his exposition, we were no nearer reaching a decision.

Blenkensop remained adamant in his championship of the cause and was supported more mildly by the Archdeacon. Old Canon Sinclair, trembling and with much lamentation over any possible unpleasantness, came out against the motion and was whole-heartedly supported by the Precentor. Trend refused to declare his colours. He was a young man who knew the unwisdom of offending any of his elders and, as a result, succeeded in pleasing none of them. So it all came down to me and I said that I wanted to discuss it with the Archbishop. Therefore, to Blenkensop's fury, it was agreed that no formal decision would be made until after Christmas.

We were worried about the cats. There was already a cat-flap cut into the scullery door which led out to the Green Court. Victoria tried very hard to persuade Brutus and Cleo to go outside and enjoy the fresh air. They would have none of it. They spent most of the time on my study window-sill peering out in terror in case Marmaduke was in the vicinity. On one appalling occasion, Marmaduke actually marched into the scullery and proceeded to consume two large saucers of food which we had just put down. Mercifully, our two were sitting with me in the study and Victoria managed to chase the ginger intruder out before there was an almighty cat fight. However, the two Siamese knew from the smell what had happened and for two days they were both off their food. After that we had to keep the cat-flap locked.

Even though the weather was becoming colder, Marmaduke did not moderate his activities. Every day I saw him out pacing about, hunting some wretched creature or preening himself for tourists' photographs. The peaceful ambiance of the cathedral was frequently disturbed by his appalling caterwaulings. It sounded as if someone were being murdered and probably someone was.

On my way to and from services, I often came across Mrs Blenkensop. She was a mousey, little woman. In contrast to her husband, she always smiled and said 'Good Morning!' She was invariably burdened with large numbers of shopping bags. On a couple of occasions I offered to carry them over to her house, but she refused. She said she was used to heavy shopping. I could not help but notice that the bags seemed equally divided between numerous tins of cat food and large quantities of expensive cuts of meat. Clearly both Reg Blenkensop and Marmaduke were fond of their food.

At the beginning of November, I was invited to preach at Cannonbury Cathedral. I thought it would be a pleasant interlude and I drove down to the beautiful mediaeval city thirty miles away. I was particularly anxious to learn about their Dean and Chapter's experience with admission charges.

I had been at theological seminary in Cambridge with the current Archdeacon, and he invited me to lunch after the service. Sitting in the splendid Archdeaconry overlooking the magnificent cloisters, we drank sherry as my old friend told me about the disagreements that existed within the Chapter. 'They forced the charges through, Harry,' he said. 'I have always been opposed to admission fees, but the Dean was determined. He had just been on a management course for clergy and he persuaded the entire Chapter.'

'Couldn't you stand against it?' I asked.

'There was nothing I could do. As you know, we've had problems with the roof. We've tried to raise enough money for repairs, but it's been quite hopeless. We've been running at a deficit for years and we can't let the cathedral actually fall down.

The projections of future income were very pessimistic and the Chapter was convinced that charging was the only answer.'

He took a deep breath, before he started again. 'To tell you the truth, I hate it. You saw the barriers just outside at the entrance to the cloisters. Nobody can come in without paying. We lock the doors of the precincts at night and God's glorious church is only open between the hours of nine and seven to those who can afford to pay. Even those who live in the town have to make a token yearly subscription for the priviledge of walking around. It's unchristian and dreadful, but there was really very little alternative.'

'And has it worked?' I asked.

The Archdeacon nodded ruefully. 'Amazingly well. Last year we had over fifty thousand tourists all paying ten pounds each. And of course the relative quiet in the precincts is blissful. All the social problems are left firmly in the town.'

'That sounds very much in accord with the teachings of the Gospel,' I said.

'It's dreadful, isn't it?' he agreed. 'What it all comes down to in the end is money. It governs everything. The Church seems to think of nothing else. Well . . . when they're not cowering at the thought that a woman might become a bishop or wondering how much of a witch-hunt they should have against gay priests . . . As if half the clergy aren't gay anyway! Honestly . . . You were sensible to choose the academic life, Harry.'

I sighed. 'But I'm a Provost now.'

'Indeed, so you are. And how is it going?'

I told him about my problems with Blenkensop and hinted about the difficulties at the university. 'The Archbishop just wanted me to fill in,' I explained. 'I knew there were one or two problems, but I thought it was basically a caretaking job in a beautiful house. But unfortunately it isn't.'

As the Archdeacon's wife went off to look after lunch, my mobile telephone rang. It was Victoria. Her father had been coaching the other Priory residents at croquet. He had not been looking where he was going and he had tripped over his mallet. An ambulance had been called and he had been taken to hospital. Victoria was sitting with him in the X-ray department.

I asked how Sir William was. Not surprisingly, he was very

shaken, but he could still walk and nothing appeared to be broken. They wanted to X-ray his ankle as it was possible that he might have a fracture in one of the small bones.

'He's as stubborn as always,' pronounced my wife. 'His foot has swollen up like a ballon, but he was furious that the ladies insisted on stopping the game and calling Matron. He wanted to carry on regardless. He was way ahead of everyone else and you know how he likes to win.'

'Will the hospital want to keep him in overnight?' I asked 'After all he is in his late eighties. He was lucky not to break a hip.'

'They don't seem too worried. I think he'll be sent back to the Priory, but I'll stay with him until he gets the final "all-clear",' she said. 'You know, Harry,' she went on, 'one of the old dears he was playing with was Canon Blenkensop's mother. Did you have any idea she was another resident of the Priory?'

'No. No one told me. What's she like?'

'Rather a nice old biddy. She's built on a large scale like her son and she can never have been pretty. Also she's not helped now by the fact that her false teeth don't fit very well. Daddy says he finds it difficult to hear what she says because she mumbles. But she's a game old bird. She's one of the group Daddy's teaching black-jack to and she says it's a nice change from canasta. Actually, it was she who insisted on summoning Matron and calling the ambulance.'

'Well we owe her a debt of gratitude then . . .'

'Yes I agree . . . I thought I'd take her some flowers when I next call in to see Daddy. It would be nice to get to know her. She might have a story or two to tell me about her loathsome son!'

'She probably thinks he's wonderful in every particular. Mothers are often unrealistic,' I pointed out.

'Yes . . .,' remarked Victoria dryly, 'if I remember rightly, your mother had some very peculiar illusions about you!'

As the nights drew in, it was the custom for the cathedral to turn on its floodlights. The great building was lit from six o'clock until midnight. I have always thought that floodlighting was the great twentieth-century contribution to architecture. High above the town, the towers of the cathedral looked magnificent floating in a golden glow against the blackness of the night. Close to, the play of light and shadows was overpowering and I loved to see the illuminated cathedral from the windows of the Provost's House. However, during the last week of November, for no reason that I could discover, the lights were turned off at ten o'clock. Puzzled by this change, I went over to the office of the Clerk of Works.

'What happened to the floodlights, George?' I asked. 'Why are they suddenly being turned off at ten o'clock?'

'It's Canon Blenkensop's orders, Sir,' the Clerk of Works responded. 'He came into the office last week and told me that from now on the lights must be out by ten. I thought it was a decision of the Chapter. Didn't you know about it?'

'I did not,' I replied, trying not to sound tetchy, 'and it hasn't been discussed in a Chapter meeting either . . .'

'Well what am I to do?' George Carpenter was understandably upset. He was a young man and had not held his post long.

'Did Canon Blenkensop give you any idea why he wanted the change?' I asked.

Carpenter shook his head. 'No! It was just an order and I thought it came from you.'

'But is there a reason why he might want to turn off the lights so early?'

The young man shrugged. 'Well the only thing I can think . . . I did hear that he and Mrs Blenkensop have changed their bedroom. They now sleep at the front of the house. Perhaps the floodlighting kept them awake at night . . .'

I was astounded. 'But we can't deprive the whole town of the beauty of the lighted cathedral just to suit one middle-aged couple. It can't be that . . .'

The Clerk of Works shrugged again. 'I'm sorry, Sir. I really don't know. I just do what I'm told,' he said.

There was nothing for it. I had to go and tackle Blenkensop himself. Full of righteous indignation. I went over to the Diocesan Office next to the Trinity Gate. Marmaduke was sitting on the doorstep washing himself and I had to step around him to get through the door. A secretary told me that Canon Blenkensop was in and suggested that I go straight up. His office was on the second floor.

When I knocked on his door, the Canon was standing looking out of the window smoking a pipe. As I entered the room, I was overwhelmed by the view of the west front of the cathedral. The office itself was comfortable, furnished with solid Victorian mahogany furniture from another age. On the walls were engravings in gold frames as well as several photographs of old rugby teams. I did not look at them closely, but no doubt they represented Reg Blenkensop's moments of glory when he was part of the Oxford University Rugby squad.

'Oh, it's you Provost,' Blenkensop's greeting was not exactly welcoming. He did not invite me to sit down, but I made my way over to the nearest armchair anyway. I was determined that this should be a civilised conversation.

'Sorry to bother you, Reg. But I did want to speak to you about an important matter.' Blenkensop made no response and continued to loom over me. 'It's about the floodlighting,' I said.

'What's wrong with it?' he asked truculently.

'Nothing's wrong with it. It works excellently and adds immeasurably to the beauty of the precincts at night. That's just the point. I understand from the Clerk of Works that you've given instructions for it to be turned off two hours earlier than usual and I've come to ask the reason why.'

'Four hours is quite long enough.'

'But I understand that they have always been on from six to twelve. You can't just make a unilateral decision like this. It must be discussed in Chapter and there must be a proper vote.'

Blenkensop continued to puff on his pipe. I found the smokey atmosphere very disagreeable, but I did not feel that this was the moment to discuss the Chapter's 'No Smoking' rules. Therefore I waited for an answer in silence.

Eventually, it came. Blenkensop frowned and knocked his pipe violently into an ash-tray. 'Look, Provost,' he said, 'perhaps you're not aware that I happen to be the Canon-Treasurer of the cathedral. It's my responsibility to allocate costs and the flood-lighting represents a sizeable expenditure. We simply can't afford it. So I took the decision to cut it for two hours every night.'

I was not going to put up with this. I smiled pleasantly. 'Oh if it's just a matter of money,' I said, 'you needn't worry about that.' I settled myself in the chair. 'Victoria's very good at fund-raising. Alf Flanagan has persuaded her to teach a course on Art and Antiques for the university. It's going to take place every Tuesday evening for ten weeks in the Provost's House, starting in January and the enrolment already stands at sixty. She's refused the usual fee for herself and was looking for some good cause to donate the money to. She loves the floodlighting and would be delighted to foot the bill for the extra two hours. You must let me see the breakdown of costs. If her course doesn't raise enough for the year, then she'll launch a separate appeal for the remainder amongst the ladies of the town.'

Reg Blenkensop went purple in the face. 'I don't want any interference from your wife,' he said.

I continued to smile nicely. 'Please sit down Reg. It's awkward to have a conversation on two levels, isn't it? You mean we don't accept donations? How unusual! We must be the only cathedral in England that doesn't. And if we don't need to, then surely we can afford the extra two hours of floodlighting?'

Blenkensop looked ready to murder me. 'It's nothing to do with the money,' he growled.

I looked puzzled. 'Oh I'm sorry; I misunderstood. I thought we couldn't have the floodlights on because it is too expensive. Is there another reason then?'

Blenkensop hesitated. 'Not really.'

'Fine,' I cut in. 'Then I shall tell George Carpenter to go back to the original schedule. I'm glad we've got that sorted out so easily. Now you must excuse me. I have an appointment at three . . .' And with that I rose from my seat and left the room. I closed the door quietly behind me, feeling rather pleased with myself.

As I descended the stairs, I came face to face with the secretary. She was carrying a neatly laid tray with a cup of coffee and a large plate of chocolate digestive biscuits. Reg Blenkensop clearly needed regular nourishment. I hoped the biscuits would sweeten his temper.

The next day Felix invited me to come round for a drink before dinner. He said he had more worries about the university. I walked to his house. He and his wife Emma lived in an elegant Victorian double-fronted villa near the precincts. They were probably quite comfortably-off since Emma was a food journalist for the BBC. She was also generally acknowledged to be the best cook at St Sebastian's.

She opened the door to me. 'Hello, Harry,' she said. 'I'm in the middle of rather a tricky soufflé recipe, so you must excuse me. Felix is waiting for you in his study.' She hurried off into the kitchen.

Felix was sitting in an armchair besides a pretty Regency table which was littered with papers. In the middle was a decanter with two glasses and a bowl of cheese straws. He motioned for me to sit down on a small sofa and poured me out some sherry.

'Thanks for coming over,' he said in an exasperated tone. 'It's very good of you; I know how busy you must be, but I really don't know what to do. Flanagan wasn't joking when he said that Sloth and his wife were fixing things up for the Higher Education Quality Control inspection. But they've made everything far, far worse.'

I sipped at my sherry and nibbled a cheese straw. It was homemade and was completely delicious. Felix picked up a document in a shiny plastic folder and sighed. 'These are supposed to be the Entertainment Faculty minutes. Of course we do keep minutes, but we haven't done all the things which we should have done as far as student assessment is concerned. So Sloth has been doctoring the original documents adding extra sentences here and there to deceive the inspectors.'

'That sounds appalling,' I said. 'But Flanagan seems to think you'll get away with it, so it's not a disaster.'

'Yes it is,' said Felix. 'The additions bear all the marks of Mrs Sloth. You know how she gets everything wrong. She can't even copy out the original material correctly. She's spelt all the names wrong and she's missed out words here and there so most of the sentences don't even make sense. Then she's managed to lose the minutes of three of the meetings altogether and the extra bits she's invented all refer to the wrong dates. Honestly her efforts wouldn't deceive a child . . .'

I stopped him mid-flow. 'Felix, I can't know about this. I'm the Visitor to the university. I can't be party to what is in effect a fraud.'

'But what am I to do?' wailed Felix.

'Discuss it with Sloth. Show him the doctored documents. Point out all the mistakes. Insist that they're all done again,' I said.

'It won't do any good. He just goes to sleep.'

'Then tell Flanagan.'

'He won't listen. You know he won't!'

'What are you asking me to do?' I asked.

Felix was clear 'I'm asking you for advice as a former colleague and as a friend. We're in trouble. The university is in danger. We could all lose our jobs!'

I took a deep breath. 'All right. This conversation has not happened. I won't discuss the matter again and I'm only going to make one suggestion. Have you thought of bringing in Pilkington?'

John Pilkington, former head of the Theology department, and now the university Dean, was a dour, narrow-minded man, who had never been a friend to either Felix or me.

'Pilkington?' Felix was astonished.

'He wants to keep his job as much as anyone and when I was at the university, I never noticed he was particularly scrupulous about telling the truth. But when all's said and done, he is efficient and meticulous.'

'You mean he could produce credible documents that show all that the Quality Control people want them to show . . .?'

'I don't want to know anything about it,' I said again.

Felix smiled. 'Well it's certainly an idea. You can't imagine his forgeries being full of inaccuracies,' he said.

Advent Sunday, the start of the Christian calendar, fell on December 1st that year. It was the time when all Christian people should examine their consciences in preparation for the great Christmas celebration of the First Coming and in awesome contemplation of the Final Judgement. Despite the solemnity of the season, relations had not improved in the precincts. Blenkensop had literally stopped speaking to me. Canon Sinclair, the Archdeacon and young Derek Trend continued to be civil, but I was aware they were all frightened of Reg and were careful not to be too friendly in front of him. Only the Precentor seemed happy.

70

As a result of my intervention, he had introduced a whole range of modern pieces into the musical repertory. One dischordant anthem followed another. We sang hymns with familiar words, which had been reset to strange melodies and the organ voluntaries at the end of services seemed to have no tune at all. The congregation was beginning to grumble and even members of the choir, most of whom seemed to like the Precentor, started to be restive.

The situation came to a climax on Advent Sunday itself. From year to year, everyone looked forward to the traditional old Advent hymns, 'On Jordan's Bank the Baptist's Cry' and 'Oh Come, Oh Come Emmanuel'. There was to be nothing like that in St Sebastian's Cathedral. Instead we had one hymn based on African rhythms and harmonies and another which had enjoyed its first performance only a year ago and was by an avant-garde Czech composer. The anthem was also unlistenable. Blenkensop smirked throughout the service and I realised that something had to be done.

I invited the Precentor for a pre-luncheon glass of sherry in the Provost's House and ventured to tackle the subject. 'You see, Percival, people like the old tunes. Of course I don't want the choir to have to sing nothing but Handel and Elgar, but there is a happy medium.'

'You mean you want traditional carol services – "Once in Royal David's City", "Hark the Herald Angels Sing" and an extract from the "Messiah"?' asked the Precentor sarcastically.

I took the question seriously. 'Yes, I'm afraid I do. People expect it. It's one of the reasons they come to church. It's all part of childhood and being English and sharing a common heritage in the Anglican Communion. I hope you'll continue to introduce some new music. It's good for all of us and things can't stand still or they stagnate.' I suddenly remembered that Alf Flanagan had said something like that to me when he was explaining the virtues of Brewing Technology. I dragged my mind back to the situation in hand. 'But we mustn't forget the traditions from which we've come. People miss the old favourites.'

I tried to speak gently and be understanding, but Precentor Samuel was not to be persuaded. 'I hoped for better things from you, Provost,' he said, 'But of course I will do as you ask.' He rose to his feet, curtly thanked Victoria for her hospitality and left the house without looking back.

Victoria shook her head. 'Dear me . . .' she said, 'The artistic temperament . . . Well there goes your last friend in the cathedral . . .'

To everyone's relief, Sir William had made a remarkable recovery from his fall. It turned out that he had only twisted his ankle and he accepted Matron's rebuke that he should be more careful. 'Not as young as I was!' was his own verdict. Meanwhile he enjoyed all the fuss the ladies made of him. Mrs Mackenzie, Pookie's owner, lent him a footstool so he could keep his foot up; her friend Mrs Germaney started knitting him a pair of fair-isle socks and old Mrs Blenkensop was willing to play blackjack with him by the hour.

Best of all, he had got on terms with the gardeners. Victoria described them to me. Apparently, they were terrifying young men with shaved heads, ferocious tattoos and truculent manners. Sir William was more than equal to them. It was not for nothing that he had spent twenty years in the army, training similar thugs. He took an interest in their lives, taught them horticultural techniques and helped them with their various youth employment forms. Soon they were offering to take Bess for walks and were asking the old man about his experiences at the D-Day landings.

One weekend he had even taken them to a clay-pigeon shoot at a local country hotel. The Priory had arranged a picnic lunch which they ate in the grounds, and Sir William instructed the lads how to handle a gun. They showed considerable talent and were full of admiration at Sir William's skill. It turned out that both of them had been brought up by lone mothers. There had been occasional, short-lived and unsatisfactory 'uncles', but neither of them had known many grown men. They had begun truanting from school at an early age and both of them had been through the dreary cycle of police-arrests, cautions and probation. The job at the Priory was their last chance before prison. It seemed that Sir William was succeeding with them when the whole panoply of the social services had failed.

A few days after my difficult encounter with the Precentor, the

Mandril-Fortescues came down from the Cotswolds to stay with us for a couple of nights. My wife had been to Cambridge and was an acknowleged expert on English antique furniture. Vanessa's formal education had stopped when she was seventeen and she had subsequently devoted herself to being a good wife and mother. Nonetheless, the two of them were excellent friends. Vanessa could not have been more enthusiastic about the beauties of the Provost's House and much enjoyed contributing to all the decorating plans.

I had less in common with James. He had spent his career in the City and had established a small financial consultancy in his retirement. He was a good churchman, however. He deplored all the recent liturgical alterations which had been made in the Church of England and was eager to tell me about the problems the village was having with their progressive lady-vicar. He also came with me to the cathedral week-day Evensong and I was thankful that the Precentor had accepted my suggestions. We had a couple of traditional Advent hymns and a very acceptable setting to the canticles.

One interesting piece of information did come out. The Mandril-Fortescue's younger son, Freddie, had taken his degree at Fandonegal University when Flanagan was Pro-Vice-Chancellor. We did not know the boy well, but I had a dim recollection that he was less academic than his elder brother and sister and that there had been an awkward incident when he was at Marlborough. He was on the outskirts of a drug scandal and he was lucky to escape being expelled. After Fandonegal, he had drifted about and was at present in a temporary job doing some research for a female Member of Parliament. I knew that James and Vanessa were still worried about him.

However, when he was at Fandonegal, one of his friends was a son of Lord Barridon. At that stage, Barridon was not married to Olive O'Shea; he was still formally attached to his second wife who was a hopeless alcoholic. Addiction ran in the family. The boy, Tristram had been expelled from Eton in his second year and had finished his education at a series of tutorial colleges. By all accounts Barridon had done his best for the child, but it had been an uphill task.

By the time he reached Fandonegal, he was a veteran of several expensive rehabilitation courses. He had more or less failed his 'A' levels and Fandonegal, under Flanagan, had been the only university prepared to accept him. James, who told me the story, was not enthusiastic. 'All the students seemed to regard Tristram as a bit of a joke. He did no work at all. Lay in bed all day and was obviously still taking drugs. He had much too much money and never bothered to go to any lectures. Freddie said he was hopeless.'

'How did he manage to graduate?' I asked.

'That's just the point,' said James. 'The Pro-Vice-Chancellor, O'Flannel, or whatever his name was, took an interest in the boy. He was given chance after chance. I honestly don't think that if he'd been anyone other than the Honourable Tristram Barridon that they'd have taken so much trouble. On one occasion the Pro-Vice-Chancellor even drove him to the hospital to have his stomach pumped. Anyway he was allowed to do his exams by himself in the university sanitorium and he emerged with a very respectable lower second class degree . . .'

'Do you think he got it by fair means?' I asked.

James laughed and shrugged his shoulders. 'How should I know? Freddie always maintained that this O'Flannel did the exams for him because he was anxious to keep in with his father . . .'

'Well Barridon now lives near St Sebastian's,' I pointed out, 'And Flanagan has just given his new young wife a most lucrative job . . .'

James and Vanessa returned to Gloucestershire on the Friday and that evening Victoria and I were invited to be guests of honour at the St Sebastian's Christmas feast. It was a black tie occasion, so I climbed into my ancient dinner jacket, trying to ignore how tight it had become. Victoria looked wonderful. Her dark slenderness was perfectly set off by the wine-red velvet dress and the triple string of pearls she was wearing.

We found ourselves at eight o'clock in the panelled Great Hall which was decorated with holly and mistletoe. The bizarre, super-life-like portrait of St Sebastian was lit up. Somehow, in the candle-light, it looked better than in the day-time. We were at the top table and I was placed next to Alf Flanagan on one side and Lady Barridon, otherwise known as Olive O'Shea, on the other. Victoria was on the other side of the Vice-Chancellor and had old Lord Barridon on her right.

Lady Barridon appeared like a Marilyn Monroe look-alike. She was certainly pretty with her short blonde hair, her painted red mouth and her pneumatic figure. No wonder Barridon had found a new lease of life in marrying her. But her conversation was dire. I heard in detail about her exhibition in Edinburgh two years previously. I learnt that she had been awarded an art prize by a small private gallery in Chichester where she occasionally exhibited. I asked her what the prize was and she loftily informed me at length that in the art world it was the equivalent of an Oscar.

She then told me all about her new job at the university; how she was going to persuade all her famous friends in the art world to donate to St Sebastian's. When I asked her why they would do that, she looked at me as if I were an idiot child and said breathlessly, 'They'll do it for Me!' Then she enumerated in elaborate detail how all these famous artists (none of whom I had ever heard) thought that she, Olive O'Shea, was the most important female artist since Barbara Hepworth. I objected that I understood that Miss O'Shea worked in water-colour while Barbara Hepworth was a sculptress. This was news to Lady Barridon and she was inclined to argue the point, but she was diverted by telling me that an owner of the most famous gallery in New York was always begging her to assemble an exhibition for him. When I asked the name of the gallery, she became vague.

Altogether, the conversation lasted without a break through the prawn cocktail, past the turkey-with-all-the-trimmings stage and through the Christmas pudding and brandy sauce. I was only rescued by Flanagan banging his fork against his glass, standing up and intoning, 'Ladies and Gentlemen . . . the Queen!'

With a certain amount of clattering, we all stood up and sat down again while port, madeira and sweet sauterne were poured out by the waiters. I thought several of them looked tired, but I consoled myself with the thought that at least they were subsidising their student loans with some extra earnings. Then I realised that they were almost certainly doing it for nothing – it was all probably part of Flanagan's so-called 'student work-experience'.

While this was going on, the conversation at the table turned to holiday plans over Christmas. Lord Barridon was polite enough to ask me if we intended going away after the festival. 'All those services must be very taxing . . . what?' he said.

Before I could frame a tactful answer, Olive cut across me. 'We're going to Nice. I've got lots of friends in the South of France and they've been begging me to go and stay with them for ages. We'll be gone a month.'

I was a little surprised. 'I thought you'd got a new job at the university here.' I said. 'Won't you have to be working?'

'I shall be working,' declared Olive loftily. 'I shall be cultivating my contacts. It's always such fun in France. Rhaoul Duval has cleared his gallery in Menton so I can have a little exhibition. His gallery is generally thought to be the most avant-garde on the coast. But of course, he'd do anything for me. He said it was a commercial decision. He couldn't afford to pass by the opportunity of showing my pictures for anything or anyone. Isn't that so, Toots?'

Lord Barridon looked a little bemused, but nodded his head. 'I like to stay in England,' he said, 'but Olive finds it a little dull here . . .'

'Oh don't be such a stick-in-the-mud!' declared the young Lady Barridon. She suddenly swept to her feet, overturning my empty water-glass as she did so. 'I hope you will all excuse us,' she said, 'but I need an early night. I've had a very tiring day and I feel a migraine coming on. It was nice to hear all about your work, Harry. Come along Toots.' And, without looking back, she stalked out of the Great Hall. Toots, otherwise known as the Right Honourable Baron Barridon of Horworth, obediently tottered out after her. I glanced at Victoria and, behind the Vice-Chancellor's back, she crossed her eyes.

With enormous noise and commotion, Alf Flanagan got back on his feet. Again he struck his glass with a spoon and cleared his throat. The company fell silent. I felt a chill of forboding. I suspected this could be a very long speech.

'Ladies and Gentlemen,' the Vice-Chancellor began. 'I want to welcome you all most warmly to this happy and festive celebration.' Standing, he made a striking contrast in his dinner jacket, pink cummerbund and and striped bow tie with the naked, athletic figure towering in the picture behind him.

'This is indeed an historic occasion,' he intoned. 'It is a time for looking-back and for taking stock. We have every reason to congratulate ourselves. When I came to this university over two years ago, St Sebastian's was in serious trouble. Our buildings were run-down; our accounts were in the red and we were suffering from a student recruitment crisis. Our political masters were worried. Questions were even being asked about the future viability of the institution. There was talk of tightening our belts, possible staff redundancies and some even mentioned the possibility of amalgamation with the dreaded Arrowsmith Teacher Training College.

'But I am delighted to tell you, Ladies and Gentlemen, that all this has changed. There is no such defeatist talk now. We have become one of the most popular universities in the country. We are overwhelmed with applications. In the most recent poll of student satisfaction conducted by the *Sunday Times*, we came second in the whole country. Only students at Oxford are happier and we all know they are the most dreadful swots.'

A ripple of obsequious laughter echoed round the room and a few brave souls began to clap. But the Vice-Chancellor had not finished . . . indeed, he had scarcely warmed up. He raised his right hand to hush his listeners. 'And how has this splendid state of affairs come about?' he asked magisterially. 'You might well ask! The answer is vision. Here at St Sebastian's we have a clear vision. We know what our customers want and we are determined to give it to them. As everyone in business knows, no one ever went broke pleasing the customers. No, indeed! And that has been my constant motto as I have built the foundations for the university's prosperity. You can't go wrong if you please the the customers.' I looked at Victoria who winced.

'And who are our customers?' Flanagan went on. 'They are the students, of course. Our wonderful students on whom we all depend. We have seen them in action tonight serving this delicious dinner and I'm sure we all want to congratulate them on their sterling performance. Let's all give them a clap.'

The young serving staff who were standing along the walls of the room looked embarrassed as all the diners applauded their efforts. The Vice-Chancellor waited for the noise to die down before he continued. 'I want to give you an illustration and I hope you will permit me to indulge in a little reminiscence. When I was an undergraduate many years ago, my tutors insisted that I follow a strict course of study. There was no freedom of choice. We were compelled to learn about subjects in which we had no interest and which proved to be of no relevance.

'I am proud to say that here at St Sebastian's we have broken with such constricting regulations. We are a modern institution. If I may say so, we are a real liberal arts university in the best sense of the word. Our students come to us seeking to expand their horizons. And we permit them to do so. We are not narrow-minded reactionaries tied to the traditional subjects. We are not pedantic intellectuals stuck in our ivory tower. We do not force our students into unnatural strait-jackets. We respect them to decide for themselves. Here at St Sebastian's we do not even chivvy them into stuffy exam halls. We have introduced a wide range of alternative modes of assessment that stretch their minds and test their real abilities. We are truly a twenty-first century university, perhaps the first in the whole country.'

Flanagan signalled to a nearby waiter to refill his glass. There was a brief pause, and then he continued. 'Our hallowed halls of learning are now filled with eager men and women who are pursuing subjects in which they have a real interest. We at St Sebastian's do not shrink from exploring new areas of learning. No, indeed! We are like the adventurers who set out from the stale old countries of Europe and discovered a brave New World on the other side of the Atlantic full of fresh opportunities and challenges.' I glanced at Felix and Magnus who were at a nearby table. Felix was sitting with his head in his hands, but Magnus, who was next to him, was gazing at Flanagan with bright-eyed fascination.

Flanagan did not shrink from difficult subjects. 'Soon we will be having an inspection by the Higher Education Quality Control Agency. I welcome their coming because I know what they will discover. They will perceive our excellence and they will marvel at it. And so they should! Ladies and Gentlemen, you see gathered together in this room some of the most able academics and administrators in the country. Men and women I am proud to call my colleagues. It has been a privilege to work with them. Together we have pursued our vision; we have stood firm; we have overcome difficulties and we are owed our success. Together, we have constructed what is generally acknowleged to be the most progressive curriculum in the British Isles. No wonder students are hammering on our doors to come in.

'But we are not complacent. No, certainly not! While we have been working on our innovations, we have also been sponsoring partnerships around the globe. Those students who live in foreign lands can now receive the unique benefits of a St Sebastian's education at places convenient to themselves. Ladies and Gentlemen, let me remind you, we are only following the great St Sebastian's tradition. Our founding fathers, in their wisdom, created this place to be a missionary college. In the nineteenth century our graduates went out to preach the Gospel in far-away lands. Things are no different today. Through our partnerships in Asia, Africa, Australia and America, we continue to follow our vocation of enlightening the world.'

Flanagan took a hankerchief from his sleeve and wiped his brow. He lifted up his glass. 'We have much to be proud of,' he boomed. 'Let me propose a toast. To St Sebastian's University! May we go from strength to strength!' There was a noisy scraping of chairs as we all got to our feet. 'In the past,' he declared, 'St Sebastian's outreach was to the heathen! Today it is to the ignorant. Let us enlighten them with our knowledge. Let the unique St Sebastian's brand of learning illuminate their minds!'

'To St Sebastian's,' we all chorused and the Hall reverberated with the sound of enthusiastic applause.

As we walked home, Victoria could not stop laughing. 'We never had speeches like that at Girton,' she said. 'You know, Flanagan is the wrong name for the Vice-Chancellor. He should have been called Frankenstein; after all, he's created a monster!'

CHAPTER FIVE

That Nightmare of a Cat

As Lord Barridon had predicted, Christmas was an exhausting time in the precincts. There were a great many additional services. It seemed as if every single institution in St Sebastian's had to have its own separate carol celebration. We had the police; the ambulance service; the Mayor and Corporation; every place of education and every civic society. The university was certainly not forgotten. One evening there was a sumptuous candle-lit Nine Lessons and Carols service. The youngest first-year student tackled the first reading and we worked up to the climax of Alf Flanagan unfolding the mystery of the Incarnation from St John's Gospel. It was quite a performance.

In addition Victoria and I felt we should do our duty by the secular customs of the festival. We ordered two large Christmas trees, one for my study and the other for the drawing room upstairs. Victoria spent a happy morning in Woolworths buying silver and gold decorations and yards and yards of tinsel. Both trees looked superb by the time she had finished with them. We had a large evergreen wreath on the front door and we decorated the house with holly and ivy for the traditional choirboys' treat.

This was a gargantuan tea-party to take place after Christmas Day Evensong. We recruited our cleaning lady, Mrs Thomas and her husband, the Chief Porter at the university, to do the catering and organise the games. They were quite unphased by it all.

It has to be said that all these celebrations went off very well. The Precentor, Percival Samuel, had accepted that we must have all the old musical favourites and every congregation sung them with a will. Indeed I was rather afraid the cathedral roof would blow off by the time the final notes of 'Oh Come All Ye Faithful' had been sung by the massed university students. As December wore on, I was relieved to notice that the Precentor's temper improved. Everyone likes being praised and it was clear that his efforts were generally appreciated. By the time Christmas Day itself arrived, he was his old self once more.

The cathedral had the usual two morning services on the 25th of December. A Matins at ten o'clock and a Sung Eucharist at half past eleven. All the Canons were present, robed and looking their best. Unfortunately, I had still not been forgiven by Reg Blenkensop. He turned his back on my greeting of 'Happy Christmas,' and sat in stony silence throughout the services. There was one consolation, however. Marmaduke did not appear. I heard afterwards that he had sneaked into the Blenkensop larder and had stolen most of their turkey. For once, sin was fittingly punished. He spent most of Christmas Day being very, very sick.

Following the marathon in the cathedral, Victoria and I checked that all was well in the Provost's House. Mr and Mrs Thomas had the preparations for the afternoon party well under control; I could not believe the quantity of sandwiches, cakes and jellies which were being manufactured. Then Victoria and I set off for the Priory to join Sir William and the other residents for Christmas lunch.

We arrived bearing gifts. Victoria had ordered a pair of slippers for her father from a small shop in the Burlington Arcade. They were in burgundy velvet and each one was embroidered with a small dormouse. I have to say, they were not cheap and, for the umpteenth time in our marriage, I was thankful that I had inherited a considerable private income. I gave my father-in-law a sizeable bottle of his favourite single-malt whisky. In defiance of all the Priory rules, when we arrived, the old man concealed it behind his shoes in the bottom of his wardrobe. Bess had a huge chewable bone which we found in the local pet shop. To ensure peace on earth and mercy mild, we also bought a similar, rather smaller version for Pookie. There was a nice bottle of port for Matron and small tokens for all Sir William's particular friends among the ladies. The gardeners had not been forgotten. Victoria had insisted on complicated Swiss pocket knives. I was not sure that this was prudent, but my wife was determined that they were a better choice than improving books.

When we arrived, Sir William was in a particularly good mood since he had been successful at cards the night before. After carol singing, the authorities had arranged that a local vicar would celebrate midnight mass for those who wished to attend. To Matron's dismay, Sir William had set up a rival entertainment in the shape of a racing demon tournament in the residents' lounge. It proved to be popular. The staff had great difficulty in getting them all to bed by one o'clock in the morning. The excitement was too much for old Mrs Germaney and she spent much of Christmas morning in bed to recover from palpitations.

'I say, Victoria,' Sir William greeted us. 'Had a splendid evening last night. A jolly good sing-song, carols and all that, and then we had a damned exciting competition afterwards. Mrs Blenkensop is quite a hand at racing demon.' Sir William, who was sitting in his tweed chair, pressed the lever and was evicted out of it.

Victoria kissed her father and put the presents on his bed. 'Matron told us all about it,' she said. 'I understand you and your lady friends were very late to bed.'

'They were jolly good sports. I won nearly every hand.'

'Really, Daddy! You must behave.'

'Behave? Of course I behaved. There wasn't any cheating.'

'No. But you really mustn't keep everyone up so late.'

'Nonsense! They had a damned good evening!' he said.

It was time for lunch. We all went into the Priory dining room which had been decorated for Christmas. There was a large tree in the corner with flashing green and red lights. Underneath were piles of boxes for the residents. Each table had a wreath in the middle and there were brightly decorated crackers at each place.

I sat next to Mrs Mackenzie who told me that Pookie and Bess were now best friends.

'I understand you had quite an evening,' I said.

'Oh Sir William takes it all very seriously. Mrs Blenkensop and I normally partner up for canasta. I think Sir William thinks that's a game for sissies and it's certainly been a lot more fun since he's been with us! He stirs us all up!'

'You've got to be careful,' I said. 'He's won an awful lot of money over the years playing blackjack. His last efforts in Atlantic City meant he could install central heating in his old home.'

Mrs Mackenzie laughed. 'Don't you worry about us, Professor Gilbert,' she said. 'His memory's not what it was and anyway we only ever play for matchsticks!'

As we were talking, I noticed that among the other visitors were Canon and Mrs Blenkensop. They were sitting at another table at the opposite end of the room. I watched them for a moment. All three were talking animatedly.

'I didn't notice that the Blenkensops were here,' I said to my neighbour.

'Oh yes,' she replied. 'They're often around. He's a very good son to his mother and she's devoted to him.' Mrs Mackenzie looked sad as she said this. Neither she nor Mrs Germaney ever seemed to have visitors.

Lunch went on for a very long time. Victoria and I had to leave at three o'clock before the mince pies in order to be in time for Evensong. The Blenkensops were also making a move. I walked over to their table.

'Do you want a lift back to the precincts, Reg?' I asked.

'Thank you Provost, but we have our own car,' he replied stiffly.

'Well would you like to come to the choirboys' party after the service? There seems to be an incredible amount of food.'

Blenkensop opened his mouth to say no, but Mrs Blenkensop cut across him. 'That would be lovely, Harry,' she said. 'Cyril Woodcock invited us last year and we greatly enjoyed ourselves.'

Reg looked sulky, but his wife, for all her meek appearance, was determined. 'Come on Reg, it'll do you good. You need to have more contact with young people. You're becoming much too stuffy. You can do your magic tricks . . .' I had never associated my difficult colleague with conjuring abilities, but it cast an interesting light on his character.

The cathedral Evensong was wonderful. The choir sang exquisitely and the hymns, canticles, prayers and lessons went without a hitch. I congratulated the Precentor afterwards and he blushed with pleasure. 'I'm glad you liked it, Provost. It has all gone well this year.'

Then it was time for the choirboys' party. We played games; we sang songs; under the supervision of Mr and Mrs Thomas we all ate a colossal tea. Then I felt it was time for a little break so I asked everyone to sit down. When there was a degree of quiet, I let them all into a big secret. They must not tell anyone, but Canon Blenkensop had a hidden talent. In his spare time he was a magician. I was a little afraid that my introduction would raise too many expectations, but I was wrong. My colleague's magic tricks were superb. I could not imagine how he did them. The boys gasped and giggled and applauded. It was splendid.

Then it was time for parcels from the tree. During the conjuring performance, Evan Thomas had climbed into a Father Christmas suit. Every choirboy was awarded his own individual present with an accompanying Welsh injunction, ('And it's a good boy, you've been this year I hope!') All the gifts had been carefully chosen by the Precentor and the floor of the drawing room was soon awash with discarded paper and string.

After that it was time for a second tea and the boys did not hold back. I could not imagine where they put all the food they ate. When they really could not swallow another mouthful, we let them loose in a wild game of hide-and-seek all over the house. By this stage the adults had given up. We all sat down among the debris in the drawing room and we silently wrapped ourselves round large glasses of sherry. I can never remember being so exhausted.

But the Precentor was tireless. We saw a different side to his nature. With the cathedral Chapter he was shy and awkward, but with his choirboys he was as loud and boisterous as any of them. At half-past-seven he gathered them all together. Under his guidance, we had three cheers for the Provost and Mrs Gilbert, three

cheers for Canon and Mrs Blenkensop, three cheers for Mr and
Mrs Thomas, three cheers for absent friends and, finally, three
cheers for St Sebastian's Cathedral and its incomparable choir.
Then at last it was time for them all to go home.

When we finally closed the door on the last of them, I said to
Victoria, 'That was terrific! And you know, Blenkensop was
quite human today.'

'Ah,' replied Victoria, 'that's because Marmaduke is incapac-
itated. I think that cat is a very bad influence.'

The next day we felt a little jaded. Mercifully little went on in the
cathedral in the period between Christmas and New Year and
Victoria and I had resolved to relax. We were having a late breakfast in the kitchen when the cats suddenly sat bolt upright. Then
we heard a letter being pushed through the front door. There are
no posts on Boxing Day so we knew that it must have been delivered by hand. Sure enough a white envelope with the address
written in green ink was lying on the doormat.

'It must be a late Christmas card,' Victoria surmised. 'No one
could have written a thank-you letter this early . . .'

Unfortunately it was not a graceful note of gratitude; rather it
was an irate complaint. Written in a florid hand, it read:

Dear Provost,

I am sorry to disturb you the day after Christmas, but I felt I
must express my disquiet about yesterday's party. Our son,
Rupert, is a pupil at St Sebastian's Choir School. When we
fetched him from the precincts late last night, he told us that
you display an obscene statue in your downstairs cloak-room.
Rupert described it to us, and we are shocked and appalled
that someone in a senior position in the Church of England
could possess such a thing.

As the Provost of our cathedral, you are the spiritual and
moral leader of our community. We simply cannot understand
how you could allow impressionable boys to be exposed to
such an object or indeed take pleasure in it yourself.

You also should be aware that Rupert came home grossly
over-excited after the party. He was sick in the night and I had
to stay up with him.

I am sending a copy of this letter to the Archbishop of Cannonbury. I am sure he will take it up as a serious breach of church discipline,

Yours sincerely

(Mrs) Gillian Holmes

Victoria began to laugh. 'Greedy little toad!' she said. 'What it comes down to is young Rupert ate too much. Don't worry about the statue. Magnus is an expert on the ancient world and if his pre-Minoan image isn't art, it's at least serious anthropology. Doesn't this woman ever go to museums or art galleries?'

'Perhaps the loo was a bad place to leave it . . .'

'Well I don't know where else it could go. I really don't want it in our bedroom and anyway the boys were all over there too when they were playing hide-and-seek . . . Anyway I don't think we should give in to this kind of Philistine bigotry.'

'Don't you think we should get rid of it?' I asked tentatively.

'No I do not! It was very generous of Magnus to give it to us and there's nothing obscene about it.'

I looked doubtful, 'Perhaps it should be in a less visited position?' I suggested.

'Oh all right.' my wife conceded. 'For the time being, I'll put it in the cupboard in the scullery, but it's not going to stay there for ever . . . Anyway, what are you going to do about that ridiculous letter?'

'I'll ring Percival Samuel,' I said. 'As Precentor, he must deal with these kind of communications once in a while.'

Percival answered the phone on the first ring. I told him the story and he sighed. 'Don't worry about it,' he said. 'The school has a complaining letter from that particular mother at least once a fortnight. Nothing is ever right. If it's not the music, it's the teaching and if it's not the teaching it's the food. If she would only leave him alone, Rupert could be a very nice boy. And considering he has a full scholarship and he is getting a completely free education, you would have thought that the parents might show a bit of gratitude. But no! Something is always wrong. I'm sorry she's turned her attention to you, Provost. My impression is everyone had a splendid time last night. I certainly did and I was going to telephone you later this morning to thank you.'

'That makes me feel better,' I said. 'It's good of you to say so. I really do not want to corrupt the morals of your nice boys . . .'

The Precentor laughed. 'With a seriously old fertility statue? I don't think so. If you only knew what sites they look up on the internet, then you'd have cause for concern.'

'But don't you block all the pornography on your computers?' I asked.

'We do in school, of course,' Percival reassured me. 'But what they get up to at home is another matter.'

'Anyway,' I said, 'what am I to do with this letter? What should I say to the anxious Mrs Holmes?'

'Tell her the truth.' The Precentor was very downright. 'Say that the statue is of an ancient fertility goddess. Point out that the Choir School is intending to take Rupert's class on a visit to the British Museum next term and he is likely to see several similar examples there. If she really wants to protect him from this sort of thing, then she must let the School Secretary know as soon as possible that Rupert should not be included in the expedition. Then, if you feel very energetic, you might download pictures of similar statues from various world-famous museums. That will stop her in her tracks. Then say you're sorry that Rupert was sick, but that it is a valuable lesson in life to learn when you have had enough.'

'All right,' I said. 'You sound very experienced about this sort of thing. Do you often receive these kinds of letters?'

The Precentor sighed. 'I would say about three in an average week. However little education she herself may have had, the modern parent believes that she knows best. Most of my mothers seem to spend all their time on the telephone comparing notes with one another and insisting that their little paragon of boyhood has been hard done by.'

I laughed. 'I don't envy you your job,' I said.

Despite his triumph at the Choirboys' Treat, there had been no thaw in my relationship with Reg Blenkensop. He continued to look straight through me and ignore whatever I said.

Marmaduke was fully restored to health by the end of Boxing Day and there was no improvement in his behaviour either.

One lunchtime, just before the New Year, I was waylaid by one of the cathedral ladies. She formed part of the regular volunteer cleaning corps, whom Victoria persisted in referring to in private as the 'Holy Dusters'. In fact they did an excellent job and it would have cost the Chapter a lot of money if they had to be replaced with professional cleaners.

She was in a state of considerable distress and was clutching one of the cathedral needlepoint kneelers. It was in a dreadful condition. It was smeared with blood; it had been heavily clawed so many of the threads were hanging loose and much of its stuffing was falling out.

'I found this when I was polishing in the nave,' she said. 'There was a half-eaten blackbird beside it.' She wiped her nose with her handkerchief. 'I'd have felt bad whichever kneeler it was, but as it happened I embroidered this particular one in memory of my dear mother when she died eight years ago. It took me six months.'

There was nothing I could say. I commiserated with her and promised that if she could mend it, the cathedral would of course pay the cost of the materials. She was not to be consoled. When we parted she was still lamenting and vowing vengeance on (I quote) 'that nightmare of a cat'.

On the afternoon of New Year's Day, Magnus rang up to wish us a Happy New Year. We had not seen him over the holidays since he and Pushkin had been spending Christmas with his Aunt Ursula. She was a lady of immense age who had brought Magnus up and who continued to live independently in Norfolk. Victoria invited him round for a drink.

He was in fine form though he was not pleased to hear of the complaint about his statue. 'Silly cow!' he said of Mrs Holmes. 'I expect she has no idea what young Rupert gets up to when he's alone in his bedroom with his computer.'

'That's exactly what the Precentor said,' I remarked.

'Well he would know. Believe me, the young all have a detailed knowlege of every possible sexual perversion from bestiality to paedophilia and beyond. If my students spent a quarter of their time on their Hebrew grammar that they do poring over the Internet, there might be some hope for Semitic scholarship in the future . . .'

Victoria disappeared into the kitchen to find some clean glasses while I finished off a letter I was writing. Meanwhile Magnus picked up a copy of *The Times*.

I was startled by him saying 'No!' very loudly.

'What's the matter?' I inquired.

'Haven't you read the paper yet?' he asked. 'Look at this!'

He handed over the page and there, in the middle, was a picture of a familiar face. Underneath was printed 'New Baron: Professor Alf Flanagan Joins the Opposition Front Bench in the House of Lords'.

'I don't believe it!' Victoria had come back into the room. 'Let me see!'

There was no mistake. Alf Flanagan was listed among the new barony creations in the New Year Honours. It was a political appointment. He was being rewarded for his services to higher education and he was to be the new Party Spokesman for universities and colleges.

Victoria, as the daughter of a baronet, was familiar with the ways of the world. 'Someone important in the Opposition is sponsoring him. You don't get that kind of honour just for beavering away and being a thoroughly dutiful good egg.'

Magnus and I looked at each other. 'Lord Barridon!' We said in unison.

Victoria nodded. 'I should think so. It's a little thank-you for bailing out the druggie son and heir. And probably the nice little earner that was thrown in the direction of the glamorous Miss Olive O'Shea didn't go amiss either.'

I shook my head. 'I suppose it really does work like that . . .'

''Fraid so, Harry,' said Victoria cheerfully. 'Yet again, it's nothing to do with the greatest good for the greatest number!' she grinned as she looked at me.

Magnus was abstracted. 'Of course . . . that explains it!' he said.

'Explains what?'

'I need my drink,' Magnus insisted. 'It explains Flanagan's behaviour. I couldn't understand why he was so cavalier about

89

the Quality Control Inspection. It would have reflected very badly on him if St Sebastian's had failed. And he knows as well as anyone how incompetent both Sloths are . . .'

Victoria handed over a large whisky and soda. She nodded. 'Yes . . . it all makes sense. He's known this was in the pipeline for at least a year and, of course, once he's left, the University of St Sebastian's will be nothing to do with him. His reputation will be completely intact.'

'But he can't go straightaway,' I said.

Magnus laughed. 'You won't see him for dust! I shouldn't think any of us will meet Lord Flanagan ever again.'

Later that evening, I was sitting at my desk working on my sermon for the next Sunday matins. As I typed away on my computer, a message flashed up that a new e-mail had just arrived. I was bored with my own efforts so I looked up my new mail straightaway. It proved to be a letter from Flanagan addressed to all members of the university staff. It had been copied to me as Visitor.

Dear Colleagues,

You may have read in the newspapers that I have been invited to become a Life Peer and shall be taking up a seat in the House of Lords as Opposition Spokesman for Higher Education. I am of course very surprised and honoured by the summons. At the same time I am very aware that it merely reflects the success of all we have achieved at St Sebastian's University over the past couple of years. Each and every one of us has played a part in pioneering a programme of education that can serve as the model for all institutions of higher learning in the United Kingdom and beyond. We should all be proud of what we have accomplished, and my elevation to the Lords is a symbol of the fact that St Sebastian's is now the outstanding university of the twenty-first century.

I am, of course, very sad that I shall be leaving you all. I have greatly enjoyed my time here as your Vice-Chancellor and I will miss the many friends I have made. I am afraid that I shall be compelled to leave St Sebastian's almost immediately to take up my seat – certainly before the students return at the beginning of term. My sponsors insist that my advice is urgently needed and that there are some essential tasks to be undertaken within the next few weeks. This means that I will not be able to say good-bye in person to everyone, but this in no way detracts from the value I place on our relationship.

I am also aware that the university is currently facing a major inspection by the Quality Control Agency in the next few weeks. Indeed, it is a great disappointment to me that I shall be missing it. However, I am totally confident that our plans for this visitation are at the highest state of readiness. As you may know, Mrs Jenny Sloth was recently appointed to a new post, that of Quality Control Officer. She is doing a splendid job, gathering together all the necessary documents and ensuring that all our procedures are watertight. With the institution under the overall control of our dear Registrar Sloth, I know I can leave with a clear conscience. I much look forward to reading the inspectors' final report when it is issued. I know how glowing it will be.

London is not far away and I want to return very often to this ancient city. I hope you will invite me back frequently. I shall, of course, be hearing the latest news from Olive O'Shea, the university's talented hospitality director. The Barridons own a flat in Dolphin Square which lies empty while Olive labours for St Sebastian's. They have been generous enough to lend it to me while I look around for something more permanent. Although I shall be very busy, I shall forever be interested in the welfare of the university and its concerns will always be close to my heart.

With all good wishes now and in the future,

Alf Flanagan

The next day the Vice-Chancellor's elevation was the front page story in the *St Sebastian's Gazette*. In a lengthy interview, the Vice-Chancellor described the numerous progressive innovations he had made since he had arrived at the university and he outlined the policies he would be advocating in the House of Lords. Again it was made clear that he would be leaving for London immediately.

The Times newspaper announced Flanagan's new title. Despite all his professed fondness for the city of St Sebastian's, he was not going to be associated with it formally. Instead, his elevation was gazetted under the title of Baron Flanagan of Fandonegal. 'Quite right!' was Victoria's comment. 'After all, it was to the Honourable Tristram Barridon's time at Fandonegal that he owes his promotion.'

'That's not fair,' I objected. 'Presumably what finally pushed Lord Barridon over the edge was the generous salary St Sebastian's University was persuaded to cough up for his wife.'

'I don't think so,' said Victoria. 'Olive's wages are simply Flanagan's way of getting the university to pay his London rent. You should regard it as a pension for him.'

At that moment, the telephone rang. It was Felix. 'Harry,' he said, 'have you seen the e-mail Flanagan sent out?'

'I read it too. What about *The Times* and *St Sebastian's Gazette?*' I asked. 'It seems that he's leaving straightaway.'

'Well the quality inspectors are coming in February. He couldn't afford to hang about,' Felix pointed out.

'He was very laudatory about the Sloths,' I said.

'Fine words butter no parsnips! We all know they're hopeless. Jenny Sloth's made a mess of everything. She's lost more documents than she's found. And as for that dozy individual her husband. He seems to be asleep most of the time. Do you think the inspection can be delayed? After all, there should be a Vice-Chancellor in charge on these occasions.'

'I have no idea, Felix. I'm only the Visitor. I suppose it's up to Council to decide what should be done.'

'Aren't you the Chairman?'

'No, I'm not even a member. The Visitor is essentially a figurehead, or the final arbitrator if there's an appeal. But he's not supposed to take executive decisions.'

'But the Council has always been hopeless. They never do anything except rubberstamp Flanagan's decisions.'

'They'll have to act now,' I said. 'They've no alternative.'

Felix paused. 'Look, Harry,' he said. 'I'm serious. There's a vacuum at the top without Flanagan. The most senior person in the university is the Registrar. Sloth is as bad as his wife. He gets everything wrong. You know he's a narcoleptic – he's usually asleep during meetings. He can't be left in charge.'

'It's not up to me, Felix.'

'Oh come on, Harry, you've got to face facts. You'll have to intervene. We'll fail the Quality Control inspection if you don't, and then the whole place will be in serious trouble. Come on, you're a clergyman. It's a matter of Christian charity.'

I thought this was a bit thick coming from Felix. He was, after all, Jewish.

'I'm sorry, Felix. I can't. The university statutes won't allow it and anyway, I've got my hands quite full enough with the cathedral.'

Felix sighed and we said our good-byes.

I put the telephone down and it immediately rang again. This time it was Magnus. 'Did you see Flanagan's e-mail?' he asked. 'Really that man goes too far . . .'

'He probably always has . . .,' I said.

Magnus was not to be halted. 'I was in the middle of writing a really damning review of a new Hebrew grammar. It's written by some rabbi who teaches at the University of West Wales of all godforsaken places. It's intended for beginners, but that's no excuse. It's grossly over-simplified, full of errors, completely unscholarly. No wonder the young can neither think nor remember if they're fed pap like that . . .'

I was used to Magnus's comments on his fellow-Hebraists' work. If he had ever written a good review I had never heard of it. 'Magnus, I hate to interrupt, but I'm busy. I've got a sermon to write. What can I do for you?'

'Well . . . Flanagan's just sent us all a farewell letter.'

'I know. I've read it,' I said.

'So who's supposed to take his place? It can't be that cretin Sloth. I was actually ringing to suggest that you take it on.'

'I can't. I'm just the Visitor,' I said.

'But you could be Acting Vice-Chancellor. At least for a short time. You don't have much to do.'

'I have a colossal amount to do,' I said indignantly. 'The cathedral is not all plain sailing, I can tell you. Remember I've never been an administrator. I was an academic. Being Vice-Chancellor is definitely not my sort of thing. This is for the University Council to decide.'

'But you know they can't make up their minds about anything.'

'Well they'll just have to.'

'I think,' said Magnus gloomily, 'that for the first time in history, we are about to witness the demise of a British university.'

A couple of days after I had spoken with Felix and Magnus, I received a formal letter from the Chairman of the University Council. After Flanagan's bombshell, there had been an emergency meeting. The Chairman wrote that the session had been dedicated to sorting out interim arrangements until a new Vice-Chancellor could be appointed. It had been unanimously agreed that Registrar Sloth would take over as Acting Vice-Chancellor.

Because of the impending visitation from the Higher Education Quality Control Agency, it was felt that measures must be put in place to emphasise the stability of the institution. A new appointment sub-committee of the Council had already been set up. One of its tasks was to draft a job description of the Vice-Chancellorship and to place an advertisment for candidates in all the serious national papers. It was anticipated that interviews would take place in the Spring. The Council recognised that the person appointed would in all likelihood have to give his or her existing institution adequate notice. (At this point, I wondered why someone had not insisted that Flanagan had served out his notice in accordance with the terms of his contract. Presumably Lord Barridon had been brought in again to insist that the needs of the Upper House were greater than those of St Sebastian's.) In any event it was recognised that the new Vice-Chancellor would probably not be in post for at least a year. In the meantime, Sloth would occupy the role.

Later in the day I had a telephone call from the Registrar himself. He sounded almost awake. The last time I had spoken to him was when I was still employed by the university and we had parted on less than friendly terms. However, all this past history was now forgotten. He needed my help and he could not have been more civil.

'Harry,' he began, 'there is a pressing matter that I must discuss with you. As you no doubt know, we are due to have a visitation from the Quality Control Agency in February. I understand that there will be a delegation consisting of four members who are planning to stay a full week from Monday morning to Friday evening. We have already booked them into the White Hart Hotel, but we wonder if there might be a possiblity that, as Provost of the cathedral and Visitor of the university, you could entertain them in your house perhaps on their first evening. The university will of course pay for any costs. We can provide the food and drink. Students in the Catering department will prepare dinner, and they will also act as waiters and waitresses. We can also supply all the dishes, glasses and cutlery. They'll do all the washing up, too. I realise this is a last minute request and we don't want to inconvenience either you or Victoria, but I can't tell you how grateful we would be . . .'

I realised that the time had come to bury the hatchet. 'Yes,' I said. 'I'd already offered our services to Flanagan and it would be nice to have a big dinner party in the Provost's House dining room. It's much too big just for Victoria and me.'

'So what will you need?'

'Well I must ask Victoria, but, if we can get her, may I invite Emma Glass to prepare the food? She is very well-known in culinary circles and she's a wonderful cook. I'm sure she'd produce something memorable.'

I could hear Sloth thinking about this. He hesitated and then made up his mind. 'You're right. She's excellent. I had a meal in her house once and it was the best food I think I've ever eaten. But she will need some help serving and washing up and so on.'

'Oh yes,' I said. 'We'd be very grateful if the Catering department could send in some students. But there's no need to worry about dishes and so on. Both Victoria and I have inherited several sets of plates over the years and far too much silver. It'll go better with the style of the house than modern university pieces.'

The Registrar sniffed. Too late I remembered that when we were colleagues he had made no secret of his resentment of my privileged background. Still in the circumstances he had no choice. 'That would be very generous, Harry,' he said stiffly. 'I only hope the students don't break it all when they do the washing up.'

'Don't worry about it,' I said.

'Well thank you. That's a real weight off my mind. I'll be

in touch nearer the time. Now I'm afraid there's one more thing . . .'

'Oh . . . ?' I waited.

'If you can possibly spare the time, we would like you to be involved in the visitation. I know it's a lot to ask because you're so busy with the cathedral. But as the university Visitor, it would be most helpful if we could include you in some of the discussions. After all you were a professor here for eleven years, so you know all our ways.'

'I never served under Flanagan,' I pointed out. 'There have been a great many changes recently.'

'Yes . . . well . . .,' said Registrar Sloth.

I took pity on him. 'All right,' I said, 'I'll look in my diary and see when I'm free.'

'That's really kind. Your being around would add weight to the proceedings. I'll get my secretary to e-mail you with the schedule right away. I realise I should have asked you earlier about this, but things have been terribly hectic. And now that Flanagan's gone . . .'

'Oh yes. I meant to congratulate you on your appointment as Acting Vice-Chancellor.'

There was a pause. Then Sloth sighed. 'Quite frankly, Harry, I'd rather they'd chosen someone else. Between you and me I'm not sure I'm up to it. Flanagan was always very confident and kept telling me not to worry, but I can't seem to find all the papers we need anywhere. The inspectors want a full record for the last ten years and I don't know where they are. And as for all these new degrees and diplomas that Flanagan introduced . . . There doesn't seem to be any paperwork at all . . . I just don't know what to do.'

I tried to make sympathetic noises, but Sloth was in full flow.

'Jenny and I are working as hard as we can to fill in the gaps. But the whole thing's very problematic . . .'

I took a deep breath. 'Why don't you ask John Pilkington to give you a hand? He's very efficient and I'm sure he'd get everything sorted out for you.'

Sloth thought about this. 'Funny you should say that . . . Felix Glass made the same suggestion yesterday. You're right. John is very reliable. It's a good idea. Thank you.'

That evening Victoria and I arranged to go to see *La Bohème*. It was a performance by a travelling company in the local theatre. I am not particularly musical, but Victoria loves opera and, as Provost, I felt it was my duty to support local cultural initiatives. I had seen the piece several times before and I always found Mimi's death unbearably sad. It made me feel very fortunate to live in twenty-first century Britain with its efficient National Health Service.

So we were in a melancholy mood when we arrived home at about eleven. As soon as we had shut the front door, we were aware of a lugubrious feline wailing somewhere in the house. We rushed upstairs and, when we had turned the lights on, our first feeling was that the cats must have caught someone's pet white rabbit. There was white fluff everywhere. Then we saw our poor Siamese Brutus lying limply on the bed. Next to him, Cleo was wailing and, between cries, was licking at his coat. The counterpane was disarranged and there was blood all over it. Then we realised that the while fluff was not from a rabbit. It was from Brutus's coat.

'My poor Brutus,' Victoria said as she stroked his head. 'You've been in a fight.'

'Do you think the two of them had a quarrel?' I was horrified. They had always been very good friends. 'Cleo's never bitten him before.'

Victoria shook her head. 'Don't be silly, Harry. Cleo wouldn't do this. It's that damn cat Marmaduke. He got into the house somehow. He's probably stolen all their food and he's beaten up Brutus. He's a horrible beast.'

I brought in a bowl of warm water from the bathroom; Victoria went downstairs to find some salt to dissolve in it. Very gently she started to bathe the wound.

'It's nasty,' she said. 'He'll have to go to the vet first thing in the morning. Poor old fellow! You'll be all right. We'll get you well very soon!'

I went downstairs to see what had happened. Victoria was right. The cats' dishes had been licked completely clean and the cat-flap latch was unlocked. Probably Mrs Thomas had knocked it when she was cleaning. Marmaduke had seized his chance and had broken in to claim new territory.

I went back upstairs to report. 'Damn Blenkensop,' I said. 'Why can't he control that animal? If there was any justice in the world Marmaduke would be in prison with a conviction for burglary and grievous bodily harm. But instead he and his horrible owner are tyrannising over the entire precincts of St Sebastian's Cathedral. And I can't seem to do a damn thing about it.'

The next morning we took Brutus to the vet. She was sweet with him. She told him he had been very brave, but that in future he must work on his right hook. She washed out the wound with antiseptic, gave him a shot and prescribed a course of antibiotics. I had serious doubts that we would ever get them down him, but we promised to try.

Later in the day I ran into Blenkensop. He was locking his bicycle to the railings outside the Monk's Gate. 'Reg,' I said, 'I must have a word with you.'

'Yes, Provost,' he said icily.

'There was a terrible cat fight in our bedroom last night while we were out at the opera. There was fur everywhere. Marmaduke must have got into the house.'

Blenkensop looked at me sharply. 'You saw him?' he asked.

'No. As I say, we were out. But there was white cat-fur everywhere, and Brutus was bitten. We've just come back from the vet.'

'Then I can't see how you can be certain it was my cat. Marmaduke is ginger. If there was white fur everywhere, your cat must have been attacked by a white cat. Did you find any orange hair?'

'No . . . It was Brutus' white fur, not another cat's,' I said. 'He's a gentle creature. He doesn't know how to defend himself. It's obvious your cat attacked him.'

'I'm sorry, Provost, but what proof do you have that it was Marmaduke?'

'It couldn't have been anyone else,' I insisted. 'You know what he's like.'

Blenkensop put his bicycle clips in his pocket and stood stiffly. 'Before you make serious accusations of this sort,' he said in a very nasty tone of voice, 'you should at the very least have substantial proof. I don't appreciate wild speculations based on no evidence. Indeed I do not! Now if you'll excuse me, Provost, I have some important matters to attend to.' And with that he walked off in the direction of the Diocesan Office without looking back.

CHAPTER SIX

What an Inspector Has to Do

Once the New Year began, I was very busy. I was the chairman of various cathedral committees and they all met early in January. In addition, we had our first Chapter meeting of the year. By this time, I had heard from the Archbishop about the vexed question of admission charges. He advised delaying the decision until there was a full audit of diocesan finances in the summer. I circulated his letter to my colleagues before the meeting and the subject was discussed at length. Although Reg Blenkensop continued to be vociferous in his demand for the change, the Archdeacon felt it more prudent to follow the Archbishop's advice. So when it came to a formal motion, there was one vote in favour of charges (Blenkensop), three against (the Archdeacon, Sinclair and the Precentor) and one abstention (Trend). I was very relieved when we agreed to shelve the subject until the autumn.

I also had committments beyond the cathedral. Previously the Archishop had asked me to be a member of a Church consultancy committee on medical ethics. It happened that bills on both abortion and euthanasia were being discussed that year in Parliament.

The committee felt under pressure to make its voice heard and I had to attend frequent meetings in London. Victoria was also busy writing a series of articles on eighteenth-century snuff boxes for an antiques magazine. Generally, she would accompany me to town to do research in the London Library and round the various auction houses while I was closeted in Church House.

At the end of the month, I was also due to go to a three-day conference of Deans and Provosts at Wellington Cathedral. I did not look forward to staying in the prescribed university hall of residence with its shared bathrooms and enforced camaraderie at breakfast. To make the idea more bearable, Victoria agreed to join me for a little weekend break in a nearby country house hotel directly afterwards.

The conference was more amusing than I had expected. I caught up with several old friends and I discovered that life in our great English cathedrals was not all milk and honey. Every one of the deans or provosts to whom I spoke had the equivalent of a Reg Blenkensop in his life. It seemed that Christianity does not necessarily make people behave well. One of the most popular sessions was entitled 'Dealing with Difficult People'. The speaker pointed out that they might be even worse if they were not Christians, but of course that was an unverifiable proposition. When the time came for questions, I felt like putting up my hand and asking for special tips in dealing with difficult cats, but I thought this might sound frivolous.

I was very glad to see Victoria when the three days came to an end. The Country Lake Hotel was located in a beautiful area of natural forest near Wellington. Our room was on the top floor overlooking a lake and there were green rolling hills in the distance. It was furnished with a comfortable large four-poster bed and a variety of mahogany storage pieces. There was also a sofa where the newspaper could be read in comfort and a splendid old rocking chair. Heavy gold curtains framed the windows and the bathroom was sumptuous.

We arrived late on Friday and we were both tired. The next morning we decided to have breakfast in our room. Victoria was sitting in her dressing gown when room service arrived – the daughter of the house entered carrying a large tray with a pot of coffee, croissants and toast, home-made jam, boiled eggs, and fresh orange juice. As Victoria poured out the coffee, she started giggling.

'I've been dying all week to tell you about a conversation I had, but I thought I'd save it until you had time to enjoy it. Guess who I had coffee with on Wednesday?'

'I have no idea!' I said. 'Who did you have coffee with on Wednesday?'

Victoria could never resist telling a story. She was a good mimic and she acted out the different voices. 'Well . . .,' she said. 'I was doing some shopping in Marks & Spencer and I felt that I'd earned a cup of coffee. Normally, it's a place I avoid because I invariably run into one of the Holy Dusters and have to embark on a long conversation about the academic progress and health of their various grandchildren. 'And how is young Justin getting along . . . Really? . . . Top in his common entrance exam, was he? . . . You must feel proud. And how is young Melinda's glandular fever? . . . Oh I'm so glad to hear that . . . And you've just heard that she got three grade 'A's in her mock A-levels tests . . . How splendid! . . . And where is she planning to go to university?' I can't imagine why these ladies think I should be interested, but "noblesse oblige" . . . I do know my duty as Mrs Provost!'

'Anyway, I was so tired, I thought I'd risk it. Well the café was very full and after I had collected my cappuccino and biscuit, I looked round for somewhere to sit. I swear to you that the only free place was at a table for two and sitting in the other seat was Maureen Pilkington!'

We both laughed. Maureen Pilkington was the wife of John Pilkington, who was now dean at the university. Neither Victoria nor I had had much to do with Maureen, who was exactly as one would expect the wife of John Pilkington to be. However, we had dutifully attended her annual theology staff party and Victoria had been merciless afterwards about her ideas of food and interior decoration.

'Well . . .,' continued Victoria, 'when I saw the situation, I nearly abandoned my tray and fled the shop there and then. But then I thought that I had paid much too much money for my coffee and I was jolly well going to drink it, Maureen Pilkington or no Maureen Pilkington. So I sat down opposite her. And I have to say she was extremely pleasant and welcoming.'

'She wanted to tell me all about John. Apparently he's been recruited to manufacture the paperwork for all the new degrees that Flanagan set up. Basically, it's to deceive the Quality Control People.'

'Surely she didn't approve of this?' I asked. The Pilkingtons were devout Methodists and even their worst enemies would acknowledge their show of upright integrity.

Victoria smiled. 'She didn't know what to think. She kept saying, "It's very shocking isn't it, Victoria, that things have come to this." But she was more like a naughty child, enjoying it all vicariously. Apparently John is astonished by the mess he's found. He couldn't believe the chaos in the Registrar's office. Maureen said that she wasn't in the least surprised. She'd never thought much of Robert Sloth. She said he was lazy and slipshod. She clearly believed that John would have been a far better Registrar and should now be the Acting Vice-Chancellor.'

'I have some sympathy with that position,' I commented. 'It would be hard to be more hopeless than either of the Sloths. They really are in a class of their own.'

'Anyway,' continued Victoria, 'she now seems to think that I am a person of influence, as I am married to the university Visitor, and she was anxious to tell me how clever John is being. Apparently when John saw the shambles, he took over completely. Maureen said that one of the major problems was that no-one had ever arranged for external examiners to be appointed for the new degree courses. Flanagan said it wasn't important and Sloth never got around to doing it. But the difficulty is that the Quality Control people have to fail the university unless an infallible system of externals is in place.'

'So what is John doing about it?' I asked.

'Maureen told me that he had no choice. She flushed bright pink and said, "You'll think it very dreadful of him Victoria, but he really had no alternative." He's made up a series of names for examiners who do not exist and has manufactured their reports for the last five years!'

I shook my head. 'I was afraid they might do that,' I said. 'It's both dishonest and dangerous.'

'That's not the worst of it,' Victoria was overcome with mirth. 'Maureen didn't see that it's funny. She thought John was merely

103

being bold and creative, but it turns out that that man has a whimsical subconscious worthy of Dickens!'

'John Pilkington?' I was astonished. 'He's about as whimsical as Marmaduke. What on earth has he been doing?'

'Honestly,' said Victoria, 'Maureen told me the names that Pilkington has made up. He's obviously put down the first thing that came into his head. I wrote them down so I could tell you. I didn't want to forget.'

She picked up her diary which was lying beside the bed. 'Let's see,' she said. 'The external examiner for the Dance department is a Professor Lightfoot. He has served for the past seven years, but for the last two they have also brought in a Dr Beryl Glitter. She specialises in the Artistic Dance division. Then they have a Dr Driver who checks the standards for the diploma in Professional Golf and his assistant, who managed all by herself last year, is one Ms Penelope Puttick. Then you'll be interested to know that for the last two years a Dr Small-Beer has guaranteed the standards of the Brewing Technology department and, at the same time, Professor Stella Starr was appointed to look after Celebrity Studies. Then, as a piéce de resistence, the supremo for the licence in Catering is a Dr Morris Eatwell and the Drama department is examined by Professor William Playright.'

I was astounded. 'But they'll never get away with it!'

'That's what I told Maureen.'

'And what did she say?'

'She didn't understand what I was talking about. Neither she nor John saw the intrinsic improbability of every examiner having a name appropriate to the subject. When I pointed it out to her, she wasn't a happy bunny . . .'

'So what are they going to do about it?' I asked.

'There's nothing that can be done now. They submitted all the papers to the inspectors at the beginning of last week.'

'You're not making this up?'

'Really, Harry, that's what she told me.'

'But it's asking for trouble. All the Quality Control people have to do is check to see if these people exist. What's Pilkington thinking about?'

'I don't know Harry. But there's nothing that can be done about it now. It's too late. Perhaps the inspectors won't notice.

Maureen said they've given them piles and piles of documents. Perhaps all those ridiculous names will be lost in the morass. After all, the inspectors will only be at the university for a week.'

I gave a sigh. 'We can only hope . . .,' I said.

As soon as we returned to St Sebastian's from our weekend away, it was time for Victoria to think about her class in the Provost's House. As Flanagan had predicted, all the old ladies of the precincts and beyond had signed up for the course and on the first Tuesday evening more than eighty people crowded into the drawing room. We had to borrow some stacking chairs from the cathedral. Victoria was planning to talk about a different subject each week. She started off with antique snuff boxes and she gathered together some examples of our own to illustrate the lecture. She had also prepared a set of slides.

We were rather touched that Sir William insisted on coming. He said that he had never heard Victoria speak in public and he was interested in what she had to say. On his own initiative, he hired a taxi and Mrs Mackenzie, Mrs Germaney and old Mrs Blenkensop accompanied him. It was not very easy conveying them all up the stairs, but with the aid of other members of the audience, the task was accomplished. All four old people enjoyed themselves hugely. 'Jolly good show!' was Sir William's verdict on the proceedings when we said good-bye to them all at nine o'clock. 'We'll be back next week!'

The weather took a turn for the worse in February. By the date of the inspection, the Green Court was covered in a thick coating of snow. As usual, the British railway system failed to rise to the occasion. Our guests were due to arrive in the city by five o'clock. This would give them plenty of time to settle themselves in the White Hart Hotel, freshen themselves up and be at the Provost's House at half past seven. In the event, it was rather more complicated.

Emma Glass had appeared early in the afternoon accompanied by Felix who was burdened with an enormous bag of groceries. She began preparations immediately. Meanwhile, Felix read quietly in my study and helped out whenever he was called. Several students on the university catering degree turned up at half-past-five and, under Emma and Victoria's supervision, helped lay the table and arrange the flowers. I was pleased to see that my wife had chosen to use my grandmother's dinner service. It had been her parents' wedding present. It had been specially commissioned from the Royal Worcester factory and was elaborately painted and gilded after the fashion of the time. The classical proportions of the dining room suited it perfectly.

The Sloths arrived early. Unusually, the now Acting Vice-Chancellor looked wide-awake. He quivered like an anxious hamster. We settled him down in the drawing room with a weak whisky and soda to steady his nerves. Jenny looked her usual complacent self. She wore a printed silk dress in an unfortunate combination of colours. Pinned to her shoulder was a large amethyst brooch. It looked as if it had once beonged to a particularly dreary old aunt who was in perpetual mourning for one dead relative after another. As soon as the Sloths arrived, Emma Glass joined us from the kitchen. 'Everything's under control!' she said.

A good quarter of an hour passed before a taxi swooped into the Green Court and stopped outside the house. I opened the front door before our guests could ring the bell and I urged everyone to come in from the cold. The head of the team was an Oxford don, Harold Ewing, a Professor of Jurisprudence whom I had once met at a talk-dinner at the Acropolis Club. He was very affable, pretended that he remembered me and introduced me to the other members of the team. The next one through the front door was a Dr Hermione Fairweather from the University of Wessex. Her speciality was French Literature and Philosophy. She was followed by a Mr Brian Senior who was a partner in a large Cambridge accountancy firm. And last, but not least, was a Miss ('Not Ms!' as she was determined to inform me) Dorothy Upton. For many years Miss Upton had been Senior Copy-Editor at Oxford University Press, but was now Reader in Information Retrieval at the University of Brambletye.

After shaking hands, Victoria led them upstairs into the drawing room and urged them to warm themselves by the fire. Everyone was introduced. We were served drinks by two good-looking student waiters who also passed around the most delicious home-made canapés. Yet again, Flanagan had been right. Good food and drink does make a difference and very quickly everyone relaxed.

Professor Ewing sat on the sofa with Dr Fairweather beside him. She downed her drink in a couple of gulps and had no hesitation in demanding another. 'Ghastly journey,' she said. 'It took two-and-a-half hours from London. The excuse was snow on the line. I ask you! What do they expect in weather like this?' She reached in her handbag and took out an ebony cigarette holder and a packet of Camel cigarettes. 'Mind if I have a smoke?' she asked. I did, but did not feel it would be polite to say so. One of the waiters quickly produced an ash tray and a lighter. Engulfed in cigarette smoke she told us that she was half way through a book on Voltaire, but that her duties as an inspector had interrupted her research. I asked if she had seen Leonard Bernstein's opera *Candide*. She smirked and said she thought it was a pointless frivolous work. Then she embarked on a long denunciation of the modern musical theatre.

Brian Senior sat on the opposite side of the room. He had been monopolised by ex-Registrar Sloth who was explaining the problems of modern university administration. I noticed, however, that although he smiled and nodded in the right places, he was far more interested in the handsome young serving staff. His eyes followed them around the room and he summoned one in particular more often than was strictly necessary. Meanwhile, the fourth of our visitors was chatting to Felix Glass and Jenny Sloth. Dorothy Upton was a compact little woman in her late fifties. Her hair was grey and looked as if it had been cut round a pudding-basin. She had a high-pitched giggle, very dark eyes and delightful dimples in her cheeks. I thought how pleasant she looked until Felix showed her the coming menu. She balanced her glasses on the end of her nose and read it with the most intense attention. I realised that underneath the frivolous exterior, she was formidable.

At eight o'clock exactly, one of the waiters struck a gong and announced 'Dinner is Served!' We all got to our feet and clattered downstairs to the dining room.

Victoria indicated where everyone was to sit. She took one end of the table and I the other. Once we had found our places, I said a short Latin grace. I sat between Dr Fairweather and Miss Upton. Victoria had Professor Ewing and Brian Senior. The Sloths and the Glasses fitted in-between. The first course was a marvellous parsnip concoction, more purée than soup. It was feathered with cream and was accompanied by tiny twists of hot French bread and a very dry sherry.

Throughout, Hermione Fairweather told me about the conference she had attended in Paris during the winter vacation. She had given a paper on the influence of Voltaire on Foucault (or it could have been the other way round). This was to be published in an avant-garde journal of linguistics. I then asked her about her current research. She moaned and said she had just applied for a grant from the Arts and Humanities Research Council. If she were awarded it, she could spend six months in France and escape from her present 'crushing teaching load'. I felt it more tactful not to ask precisely how many hours a week she did in fact devote to her students.

While she droned on, I could hear at the other end of the table Sloth telling Professor Ewing about the recent changes at St Sebastian's. He explained that Flanagan had just been elevated to the House of Lords and that he was currently taking his place as Acting Vice-Chancellor. 'I'm afraid you may find us rather at sixes and sevens, but I hope everything will be satisfactory.'

'Well you've certainly sent us plenty of literature to look at!' said Harold Ewing as he took another sip of his Tio Pépé.

The main course consisted of a succulent Boeuf Daube which was accompanied by a magnificent selection of vegetables and potatoes. It was unbelievably rich and winey and French. Victoria's brother Billy had sent a case of Mouton Rothschild for Christmas, and earlier I had opened several bottles. This was poured from a couple of wine decanters that I had been given as a leaving gift from Sweetpea College. When there was a break in Ms Fairweather's disquisition, I turned my attention to Miss Upton.

She was enjoying herself. She ate the food with relish and she started telling me about her time at the university press. She was very amusing about the personalities involved. However, we were interrupted by Harold Ewing asking me how St Sebastian's University had changed since my retirement.

Before I could speak, Sloth intervened. 'Harry's only been gone three years, but the university has altered enormously. We've modernised. I think I can say with confidence that we're now the most progressive liberal arts institution in the British Isles.' I looked at Felix who took a deep breath. Sloth was not to be hushed. 'We offer a whole array of new subjects which are all proving very popular. You'll find all the information in the papers we sent you.'

Harold Ewing turned to Felix. He looked puzzled. 'Yes,' he said, 'I saw that you are the Head of the Entertainment Faculty and that you have an established Chair. Is it true that you are the Immanuel Kant Professor of Entertainment? I thought it might be a misprint.'

Felix was embarrassed. 'I wish it were. As it happens I am a philosopher and I'd like to be able to say that I am the Immanuel Kant Professor of Epistemology. But alas, although I am allowed to teach Philosophy, it's the entertainment subjects that I administer.'

Victoria giggled as Felix went on to explain how he had acquired such an incongruous title. He turned it into a joke, but nonetheless it was obvious that he found the situation galling.

Dr Fairweather shook her head. 'Quite unbelievable,' she said 'But times change, and I suppose we must change with them.' She looked across at Professor Ewing who nodded. The waiter refilled her glass as she told us about their last inspection. They had to interview film students who were doing a joint project about the history of European pornography. 'Quite revolting, wasn't it?' she said to Professor Ewing.

'Quite,' he replied. 'But an inspector has to do what an inspector has to do!'

There was a short pause after the beef for everyone to digest. To my fury Dr Fairweather insisted on smoking between courses, but at least conversation was lively and animated. Then it was time for the pudding. One of the waiters brought in an exquisite tarte aux poires. Ten halved pears lay downwards in a beautiful yellow custardy syrup, the whole encased in a golden French pastry circle. It was served with thick crème fraîche and the young attendants poured sweet sauterne wine into the waiting dessert glasses. It was a confection fit for angels.

As if this were not enough, the tarte was followed by a selection of French cheeses with celery and grapes. I have always had the inclination to be tubby and I knew that this dinner was not doing me any good, but it was irresistible. The vintage port which accompanied the cheese had come from the Castle Dormouse cellars. I understood why my father-in-law would only bring it out if he particularly liked the company.

As we all dallied with the last crumbs, I looked round the table. There was no doubt that every one was having a good time. When I caught Emma Glass's eye, I slightly raised my glass to her. She was a real artist.

Then just as we were ready to go back to the drawing room for coffee, Robert Sloth rose unsteadily to his feet. When all was said and done, he was the Acting Vice-Chancellor and he was determined to assert himself in front of our visitors. The candle-light reflected on his bald head. With a slightly drunken expression on his flushed face, he raised his glass.

'You are all very welcome here in St Sebastian's,' he said. 'Very welcome indeed! May our partnership together be as happy and harmonious as this delicious dinner has been! Happy and harmonious!' he repeated. Professor Ewing bowed across the table in silent acknowledgement.

Bloated and content, the company made its way upstairs. All signs of the previous drinks had been cleared away. The fire had been banked up and our two cats were toasting themselves, curled up together on the chaise-longue. Hermione Fairweather recognised the best seat when she saw it. With an imperious movement, she swept poor Cleo and Brutus onto the floor and settled herself in the posture of Madame Récamier. With slightly more restraint, our other guests assembled themselves on the other chairs. Meanwhile coffee was poured from a Queen Anne silver coffee pot which Victoria had inherited from her maternal grandmother. Everyone was offered sugar and cream. Then the good-looking young waiter distributed Emma's own-recipe chocolate truffles. I noticed that Brian Senior summoned him back three times.

As the cathedral clock struck half past eleven, Professor Ewing looked at his watch. He announced that he had ordered a taxi to take them all back to the White Hart. With difficulty, the other members of the inspection team extricated themselves from their seats and followed their leader downstairs. Many appreciative remarks were made and we all shook hands at the door. Snow was still falling and the cathedral looked magical under the floodlighting; luminous gold against the icy white. I was glad I had won that particular battle with Blenkensop. The taxi was waiting and, once they were all aboard, it skidded away round the Green Court and through the Monks' Gate.

After they had gone, Sloth put his arm around my shoulder. 'Jolly good of you to do this, Harry!' He sounded more than a little tipsy. 'Wonderful start to the proceedings! Now we just have to hope that our good friend John Pilkington has done his work thoroughly We can only pray they won't look too carefully at all the documents. We've certainly provided enough paper to sink a battleship . . .' I thought of the dimpled Miss Upton who seemed so delightful. Somehow, with her glasses perched on the end of her nose, she looked more than a match for my erstwhile head of department. I wondered if St Sebastian's really was going to get away with it all.

The snow showed no sign of abating. There were flurries on both the Monday and the Tuesday. By the time Wednesday dawned, the roof of the cathedral was covered with nearly a foot of white powder. The temperature hovered just around the freezing mark, so when the sun broke through there were tiny unpredictable avalanches down into the Green Court.

I had promised to meet the inspectors at eleven o'clock. So I wrapped myself up in my old tweed overcoat and dug out my wellington boots. As the cathedral clock struck the half hour, I was trudging across the Green Court leaving a splendid set of footprints behind me. The town was very quiet and I met almost no one I knew, but the university was conducting business as usual.

The inspectors had established their headquarters in the Registrar's old office. When I arrived, all four members of the team, together with Sloth, were all seated around a table. Miss Upton was pouring out cups of coffee. Both the table and Sloth's old desk were covered with untidy piles of paper. While we sipped at our hot drinks, there was general chatter. Then Professor Ewing made a very polite little speech about the exceptional hospitality they had received at the Provost's House.

Just before we were due to begin, Robert Sloth took me outside and shut the door. He was positively gleeful. 'It's all going terribly well, Harry,' he said. 'Yesterday they interviewed a selection of students from the new degree programmes. Of course we were careful which undergraduates we asked, but they did us proud. Without exception, they were all highly complimentary about their chosen subjects. Senior, that accountant chap, who spent the longest with them, told me he was very impressed. I think it's going to be all right, Harry! I really do!'

I smiled. When I was a member of the university staff, Sloth and I had crossed swords on several occasions. But now it seemed we were playing for the same team. 'That's good to hear,' I said.

'I asked them what they wanted to talk to you about.' The Acting Vice-Chancellor was anxious to be helpful. 'They were interested in the idea of a Visitor. I think they want to know how you see the role. They'll need to know about the grievance procedure, disciplinary cases, general appeals and all that.'

'Don't worry, Robert,' I said. 'I'm familiar with the regulations.' I remembered back to the time when I myself had to face grievances from my colleagues. Despite the obvious injustice of the proceedings, the Visitor then had been completely useless. It was only when I threatened to bring in the Archbishop that he decided things had gone far enough.

'I know we can count on you,' said Robert Sloth.

I went back into the office and took my place at the table. Professor Ewing handed me the particular statutes which referred to the Visitor. He asked whether I had had any appeals to consider recently. I replied that since I had only been Provost and consequently Visitor since the autumn, it was not surprising that my authority had not yet been invoked. The other three nodded gravely. Meanwhile Dorothy Upton, who was sitting on my right, was carefully reading through the regulations. We all waited in silence until she had finished.

'There is a spelling mistake on page five, paragraph two, line three,' she said. 'And regulation 6.7 appears to be in conflict with 9.4.'

We all shuffled through the papers. She was right about the misprint. Professor Ewing took out a red pen and corrected it. Then we compared the two regulations. We all looked wise as

Miss Upton read them out and explained the contradiction. This morning there was no giggling. She could not have been clearer or more precise. Really she was wasted in this job. If she only had devoted herself to drafting parliamentary legislation, the British court system would soon find it had nothing more to do.

When she had finished her exposition, we all sighed. 'Ah, yes,' Ewing said. 'I see what you mean!' Then ensued a half hour discussion in which we looked at the rules relating to the powers of the Visitor at other institutions. At this point Miss Upton demonstrated her mastery of information retrieval. She opened up her laptop computer and within seconds all the relevant information was downloaded from the central Quality Control Agency. Eventually Ewing crossed out a couple of sentences from the St Sebastian's regulations, and made copious notes in red ink in the margins. Then he looked up at Sloth. 'We shall want this altered,' he said. Sloth smiled wanly and nodded his agreement.

Ewing was satisfied. He leaned back in his chair and said, 'I think that's it, Provost. Everything else seems in good order. Thank you for coming.'

Sloth led me down the stairs. He was triumphant. 'You see what I mean, Harry,' he said. 'I think we'll pass with flying colours.'

'I hope so.'

'We've only got to tackle the question of examinations and the role of the externals and then we'll be done.'

'I heard that a university can't pass this kind of inspection unless the team is satisfied that the arrangements for external examiners are in apple-pie order . . .' I spoke tentatively.

'Oh I think we can put our trust in John Pilkington,' said Sloth as he turned back to return to the office.

As I walked towards the exit of the Old College, I bumped into Magnus. He looked self-conscious. 'Have you been with the inspectors?' he asked.

'I have . . . It seemed to go all right.'

'Did you meet a Miss Dorothy Upton?' He was curiously diffident.

'Yes of course. She's one of them. She also came to the house for dinner on Sunday night.'

113

'What was she like?' he asked.

'Why this sudden interest?' I was puzzled. 'I thought she was delightful – very jolly and approachable. But it's clear that she's like a terrier after a rat if there's a problem with a document.'

Magnus sighed heavily. 'I knew her when she was an undergraduate. She was reading Semitic languages at Somerville when I was doing my doctorate. We were generally thought to be a bit of an item . . .' He blushed. 'My aunt Ursula was very keen on her.'

I was interested. I had no idea that Magnus had a lost love. 'What went wrong?' I asked.

'She thought I was sloppy in my approach to Aramaic tenses. Her work was always impeccable. She got the highest congratulatory first that the department had ever given and she could not reconcile herself to what she called my "slovenly approach".'

'Golly!' I said.

'I've always been rather sad about it,' confessed Magnus.

It was snowing harder when I stepped out into the street. I put on the black fur hat that Victoria had bought me several years ago when we had gone to Moscow for a theological conference. As I picked my way home, I thought about my role in this charade of an inspection. I could not make up my mind.

Perhaps it was my duty to tell the Quality Control team the truth about Flanagan's flagrant disregard of all rules, regulations and procedures. After all I was a Christian clergyman and, as a general principle, clergy should tell the truth. As Visitor, surely it was also my prime responsibility to ensure honesty and fair play within the institution.

On the other hand, if I did tell the inspectors the real facts, it was not impossible that they would close the place down. It would not be just Magnus and Felix and the other academics who would lose their jobs. The cleaners, gardeners, cooks and porters would also face dismissal. The university was the largest employer in St Sebastian's, even bigger than Arrowsmith College. The consequences of its closure would be appalling for the whole area. As Provost of the cathedral, arguably my responsibility encompassed the welfare of the whole city. How could I let all these people down?

I was facing a serious dilemma. Despite forty years of research into the history of ethics, I was in a complete muddle. I had no idea at all where my duty lay.

Late on Friday morning Magnus rang me up in a state of agitation. He told me that extraordinary things were happening at the university and he wanted to discuss them. I was busy through the afternoon, but I arranged to meet him after Evensong in the town. We would find each other in the Mitre, an old-fashioned tea-shop which was run by two of our most faithful 'Holy Dusters'.

By this stage, the snow was beginning to melt and the streets were covered with greyish slush. Magnus was already occupying a table near the window when I arrived. He had poured himself a cup of tea and was eating a sizeable sticky bun. 'I've got news for you,' he announced after I had taken off my wellingtons and had greeted the shop's two proprietors. 'It's all very strange,' he said. 'No one understands it, but apparently the Quality Control Inspectors left early.'

'When did they go'? I asked. 'I thought they were staying until late this evening.'

'So did everyone else. But this morning, after being incarcerated with Pilkington for a couple of hours, they suddenly packed up their papers and left.'

This did not sound good, but I tried not to let my misgivings show. 'Perhaps they finished early. Sloth gave me the impression on Wednesday that it was all going very well.'

'Who knows?' said Magnus. 'It's just so unexpected. Yesterday I plucked up courage and made contact with Dorothy Upton. I took her to tea at Flanagan's and it was just like old times. She told me quite distinctly that they were staying until this evening. It's not like her to leave without saying good-bye.'

'I'm sure she'll get back in contact,' I consoled my old friend. 'After all she teaches at Brambletye University. It's not far from here. You only have to send her a letter.'

'But something must have happened,' persisted Magnus. 'I ran into Marigold Campbell, the Vice-Chancellor's secretary, just as they'd left. She was very agitated. She told me that Sloth is in a frightful state and Pilkington has gone off on sick leave.'

'Why? Was he suddenly struck down?' I asked.

Magnus shook his head. 'All Marigold would tell me is that he emerged from his interview looking shattered. He disappeared while Marigold was preoccupied with making arrangements for their sudden departure. Then, very soon afterwards, he telephoned from the medical centre to say that the doctor had ordered him to be off work for at least a month. He'll be sending in the medical certificate this afternoon.'

'Oh dear!' I said. 'It all sounds very odd. What can be wrong with him?'

'Marigold also told me that the four of them flatly refused to stay for lunch. They were barely polite. They told her to order a taxi and then they left, just like that. They didn't even say goodbye to Sloth.'

'How's he taking it?' I wondered. 'Something extraordinary must have happened. He was convinced that it was all going so brilliantly . . .'

'Perhaps Pilkington suddenly realised that he was sickening for leprosy,' Magnus grinned. 'That's why he shot off to the doctor and why the inspectors fled for their lives. The whole university will have to be in quarantine.'

I shook my head. 'I think there may be a more prosaic explanation,' I said.

The next day, late in the afternoon, I caught the train from St Sebastian's for Oxford. I was due to preach on Sunday morning at St Jerome's College. An old Cambridge friend was currently the chaplain there, and he had invited me to come and give a sermon in the chapel. I was to stay overnight in the college guest room and we would have dinner together.

I checked in at the porters' lodge and was led up a winding staircase to a comfortable room overlooking the quadrangle. Lights glimmered from the buildings opposite and I could see students going to and fro. I felt nostalgic for my own time as an undergraduate. Then I unpacked my bag and met my host at a small Italian restaurant across from Christ Church. At nine o'clock we said "Good-night" to each other and he went home to his wife.

Making my way back to St Jerome's, I was surprised to hear someone calling my name. I turned round and saw Professor

Ewing. He was trying to control a large Airedale who was straining on a lead. 'Harry,' he said, 'I thought it was you. I didn't expect to see you in Oxford.'

I explained that I was due to preach at St Jerome's the following day. 'I think we ought to have a chat,' he said. 'Have you got time to come back to my rooms for a drink?'

As we made our way through the dark Oxford streets, Ewing apologised for the abrupt departure of the inspection team the previous day. 'It was quite terrible,' he said. 'Most unfortunate. I've never experienced anything like it. But we had no alternative.'

Professor Ewing was a Fellow of Balliol. When we arrived at his staircase, the Airedale was unleashed and he shot up the stairs to sit outside his master's rooms. The set itself was magnificent, panelled in oak and lined with books. There were also numerous engravings of the Inns of Court and a few legal caricatures. He motioned that I should sit in a tattered leather armchair next to the gas-fire and he poured me a generous glass of whisky. Then he paced the floor as he described his team's final disastrous encounter with St Sebastian's University.

'Late Thursday afternoon,' he said, 'we were due to look at the external examiners' reports. Dorothy was a little late for the session. She came in flushed and smiling. Apparently she had just had tea with an old flame in the university restaurant and it had all gone rather well. She was in an exceptionally good mood and, looking back on it, I think her judgement must have been a little unbalanced by her social engagement. Anyway she said that she had been amused by the names of some of the examiners and she read them out to us.'

'Well, Hermione Fairweather can be a bit abrasive as I'm sure you noticed at that marvellous dinner your wife so generously gave to us. But she's very shrewd. She thought that it was all too much of a coincidence. It couldn't be the case that the examiner for the Dance department was called 'Lightfoot', and that a Dr Driver oversees professional Golf. Or that a Professor Eatwell examines for the Catering department.'

'I see,' I said. 'Yes. It does sound a little far-fetched.'

'I have to say, Harry, that up to that moment everything was going very well. I had been worried about this particular inspection. You won't know, but I was a member of the team that had examined Fandonegal University five years ago. It was all very iffy. The whole place was dominated by an obvious crook called Flanagan. Our team was very suspicious of his documentation, but there was no proof of foul play, so there was nothing we could do about it. But when I heard that Flanagan was now Vice-Chancellor of St Sebastian's . . .'

'Not any more . . .,' I interrupted,

'Well let's just say I thought it would be prudent to have Dorothy Upton as one of our number.'

'Why Miss Upton?' I asked.

Professor Ewing smiled wryly. 'She was the copy-editor of my first book twenty-five years ago. I was just a lecturer then and I was commissoned to do a Dictionary of Jurisprudence for Oxford University Press. I spent nearly two years writing it, but it took at least a year more to complete the copy-editing. Dorothy kept sending me pages and pages of queries. I think there must have been over a thousand.'

'I understand she got a very top first in Semitic languages,' I said.

'Oh she was quite the brightest undergraduate of her day. Nothing gets past her. You should see her do *The Times* crossword! So, you see I was determined to include her when we visited St Sebastian's. Anyway, after Hermione had pointed out the unlikelihood of all those names, she insisted that she did a thorough check. We postponed the session until Friday morning, and she spent all of Thursday evening on her computer. I don't understand how this information retrieval business works. But she told us the next day she couldn't find anything about any of these so-called examiners. She was very much concerned that they did not exist.'

'Oh dear!' I said again. 'So you asked Pilkington when you saw him?'

'We did. We went through everything. And I'm afraid I was compelled to be quite severe. At first he denied it all and tried to bluff his way through. He got on his high horse and said he was insulted that his integrity was called into question. But Dorothy wouldn't have it. She showed him conclusively that there were no such people as Driver and Puttick and Starr and Playright . . . Playright indeed! Did the man think we were morons?' Ewing took a long draught of his whisky.

'Then Brian Senior took over. He's a lawyer as well as an accountant. He said that the documents of the Quality Control Agency were official. If Pilkington had deliberately falsified the records, he was putting himself in danger of a perjury charge. It wasn't just a matter of losing his job. It would go far beyond the university.'

'How did he react to that?' I asked.

'He collapsed completely and the whole story came out . . .'

'What did he say?'

'He blamed the previous Vice-Chancellor for everything. Well of course, I could believe that. When Flanagan set up his new degree programmes, he ignored all the established regulations and procedures. Believe it or not, no examiners were ever appointed. Pilkington then said that he was instructed by your Acting Vice-Chancellor to write all the reports himself. Which he did. He said he was only obeying orders.'

'That isn't an excuse, as we all know . . .,' I said.

'Indeed it is not. The upshot is that we can't trust any of the university's documentation. What it comes down to is that we have no confidence whatever in any of St Sebastian's quality control procedures. And we are submitting a report saying just that. . . .'

There was a pause while Ewing took a deep breath. 'Anyway,' he continued, 'it's the worse case we've ever come across. Over the last six years, we've inspected nearly a hundred and thirty universities and colleges. One hundred and twenty-eight to be precise. The procedures of the vast majority achieved our "Full Confidence". A sad fourteen were only awarded "Limited Confidence", but no institution up until now has received the ultimate condemnation of a "No Confidence" verdict. St Sebastian's will be the very first.'

'That's dreadful!' I did not know what else I could say.

Ewing shook his head. 'The institution will be given three years to improve. In the meantime, the University Funding Council will be informed of the result.' He leaned forward. 'I have to tell you, Harry, they will insist on a full investigation. The Council could shut off funds altogether if it feel the situation is bad enough. Your predicament is dire,' he concluded. 'I know you've nothing to do with all this. You've only just become Provost. But it is your university and it's in need of urgent attention!'

119

CHAPTER SEVEN

A Colossal Dolt

My sermon at St Jerome's seemed to go down quite well and I was given a very nice lunch in the college dining room afterwards. A taxi to the station was ordered for half-past two so I had no trouble catching the three o'clock train. I sat down comfortably in my corner seat and prepared to enjoy the *Sunday Times*.

We had nearly reached Reading when I was interrupted by my mobile telephone. A text message had arrived. It was from Felix Glass and he wanted me to call him back as soon as possible. As it happened we were going through a series of tunnels. The signal was very bad so it was a little while before I got through. Felix answered on the second ring and he sounded distraught.

'Harry,' he said. 'There's been a disaster. Yesterday evening the inspection team from the Quality Control Agency sent Sloth an e-mail. He was as hopeless as usual. He didn't pick it up until this morning. They told him that they were unable to award the university either the Full Confidence or the Limited Confidence classification in their assessment of the university's procedures. This was because they had No Confidence at all in any of them

120

'. . . Sloth contacted me at lunchtime; he just sent on their e-mail with a covering note. Emma didn't think I should telephone him on a Sunday, but I felt it was a crisis, so I rang him up.'

'What did he say to you?' I asked.

'He was very cagey. He wouldn't tell me exactly what happened, but he admitted that the problem centred around the examinations. Apparently, after talking to Pilkington for a couple of hours, they made a gigantic fuss and walked out without even finishing the inspection. Reading between the lines, I think they discovered that the supposed external examiners don't exist. They're merely figments of John's imagination.'

I thought there was no point in concealing the truth from Felix. The whole sorry story was going to come out and it would be all around the university within the next few days. 'I know all about it,' I said. 'I've just been preaching at St Jerome's in Oxford. Last night, by chance, I bumped into Harold Ewing. He buttonholed me and wanted to talk . . .'

I then recounted my conversation with Ewing. I explained that the suspicions of the inspection team were aroused by the names Pilkington had chosen for the examiners. They subjected him to the third degree and eventually he broke down. The whole appalling truth was revealed.

'You mean it's all Pilkington's fault?' Felix sounded despairing.

'Well . . .' I tried to be fair. 'Not really. In the end it all comes down to Flanagan. If Flanagan had not been so determined to start up all these new programmes so quickly, there might have been a chance that all the proper procedures would have been followed. Real external examiners would have been appointed and all the paper-work might have been in order.'

'Sloth's not exactly guiltless either,' observed Felix. 'As Registrar he was meant to see that our degrees were correctly assessed and examined. It's part of his job description. He didn't do it and he went along with Flanagan's plan of doctoring all the papers. Then he appointed that idiotic wife of his to execute the whole conspiracy.'

'I suppose I'm responsible too,' I suggested humbly. 'Asking Pilkington to prepare the final review was my idea. I made the recommendation both to you and to Sloth.'

'Yes you did!' said Felix.

'I do feel responsible,' I continued. 'There's no doubt that John is efficient and meticulous. I was sure he'd do the job thoroughly. What I hadn't reckoned on was his complete lack of imagination. When he chose the names of the examiners, he put down the first thing that came into his head. And of course they were all connected with the particular subject he was writing about.'

'What names did he use?' asked Felix.

'Oh it was unbelievable! The Dance examiner was a Professor Lightfoot; Golf was the responsibility of a Dr Driver; Professor Eatwell managed the Catering; Brewing was looked after by a Dr Small-Beer and the Drama external was a William Playright!'

'No!' said Felix. 'That's incredible!'

'I'm sure Pilkington did his best. It was certainly a very complete job, but inadvertently, he blew the whistle on the whole shooting-match . . .'

'He's a colossal dolt!' was Felix's verdict,

'You haven't heard the end,' I said. 'Harold Ewing told me they have no alternative. They have to report St Sebastian's to the University Funding Council. There's bound to be a huge inquisition. They'll want to know exactly what's been going on and, as you know, they have the power to shut off all the money which keeps the place going . . .'

'It just gets worse and worse . . .,' wailed the first holder of the St Sebastian's Immanuel Kant Chair of Entertainment.

The first person I met when I arrived back at the Provost's House was Marmaduke. He was sitting in our front garden and for the first time in our acquaintance he looked nervous. I soon discovered why. Using my latch-key I opened the front-door and Bess tried to push pass me. She clearly intended to round up the ginger-and-white beast and teach him some manners. However, before she had the chance, she was called to heel by Sir William. This gave Marmaduke the opportunity to flee for his life. He was half-way across the Green Court before he paused for breath.

'What are you doing here?' I asked my father-in-law. I was fond of Sir William, but I was tired after my journey and was looking forward to a quiet little chat with Victoria.

'Daddy's upset,' said Victoria. 'I told him to call a taxi and come over. He's just arrived.'

'I need a drink,' said Sir William.

I left my bag in the hall and the three of us trooped into the study. Cleo and Brutus had already positioned themselves on the top of the tallboy to keep out of Bess's way. However, I thought I could detect definite smirks of satisfaction on both their faces. They were not displeased at seeing Marmaduke humiliated.

Victoria poured out whisky for all of us and I asked the old man what had happened. 'Kev's been arrested!' he said.

My mind was not working properly. 'Who on earth is Kev?' I asked.

'Kev and Steve are the gardeners at the Priory,' said my wife impatiently. 'Daddy takes an interest in their welfare. You remember, he took them clay-pigeon-shooting.'

I nodded. The shaved and tattooed young men were decidedly memorable. 'What's he done?' I asked.

'That's the point,' boomed Sir William. 'He hasn't done anything. He was working overtime in the gardens this afternoon, tidying up and so on. Then suddenly a couple of policemen turned up and, without a by-your-leave, they hustled the lad into their car. It was a thoroughly bad show!'

'But he must have done something to arouse their suspicions,' I persisted.

'Well I made Matron take me to the police station. I had a word with the desk sergeant. He was a disgrace to the force, slouching about in his seat, his tie all over the place. I made him stand up properly and call me "Sir". As I told him, it's my taxes which pay his wages.'

'But what about Kev?' I tried to get the old man to focus on the matter in hand.

'Well once I'd explained who I was, he realised he'd better look a bit sharp. Kev was just keeping a bag for a friend. He had no idea what was in it, but it turned out that the friend had just done a house burglary and he'd stored the loot there.'

'Well then Kev is guilty of receiving stolen goods, William,' I said. 'That's quite a serious criminal offence.'

'Nonsense!' said my father-in-law. 'He didn't know what was

in that bag . . . He was just doing a favour for a pal. It could have happened to any of us!'

'Well what did you do about it, Daddy?' asked Victoria.

'The police had shut him in one of their cells. I insisted on seeing him by himself and then I sat with him while he made his statement. I know he's telling the truth. He wasn't involved with that burglary.'

'Kev is helping Daddy redesign the flower beds at the back of the Priory,' Victoria told me. 'He's a good worker and the Priory can't afford to lose him.'

'The problem is that he's on his final warning,' said Sir William. 'Last time he came before the Magistrates, they told him that he would go to prison if he ever came before the courts again.'

'So what will happen now?' I asked.

'His case'll come up by the end of the month. I'll go and give a statement on his behalf. I'll make sure Matron does too!' Not for nothing had Sir William commanded a regiment.

'Perhaps you could get all your lady-friends to sign a petition!' suggested Victoria.

'Damned good idea!' said Sir William. He relaxed in his chair and he addressed himself to his whisky. Then he looked up. 'He's a helpful, reliable lad and I'll get him on the straight-and-narrow if it's the last thing I ever do! You never know when a boy like that may be useful!'

After we had driven my father-in-law back to the Priory, Victoria and I sat together in front of the study fire. I told her all about my encounter with Harold Ewing and my telephone conversation with Felix.

'Tell me! Do you feel guilty about the university because you didn't tell the investigating team straightaway what was going on?' asked Victoria. 'Or are you really upset because you recommended Pilkington to do the evil deed and as a result the university was found out?'

I knew that she was teasing me, but it was a serious question. I sighed. 'I don't know. Of course I should have told Ewing what was happening, but the thought of the university failing the inspection was too horrible to contemplate. I'm right about that.

Once the Funding Council comes in, it's not impossible that the whole institution will be amalgamated with somewhere else or even be closed down altogether. There may be job losses . . . Unemployment will increase in the town . . . There're all sorts of ghastly possibilities . . . It's a real mess . . .'

'Poor Harry!' said Victoria. 'Real life is not as simple as all your philosophers would have us believe, is it?'

The following week passed without any more mishaps. Kev's case was due to come up before the court in a fortnight. Since his encounter with Bess, Marmaduke was avoiding our front garden. Canon and Mrs Blenkensop were taking a short holiday in Italy and Victoria's Tuesday lecture – this time on Welsh porcelain – was generally enjoyed. I heard nothing more from the university. Then, on the following Monday morning, a letter arrived on offical writing paper. It was from Robert Sloth in his capacity as Acting Vice-Chancellor and was dated the previous Friday. It read as follows:

Dear Harry,

I am writing to you formally as the Visitor of the University. By now you will no doubt have heard the verdict of the Quality Control inspection. Throughout their visit, everything appeared to be going very well. As you will recall, the team was particularly impressed by the comments made by students about their courses. Although a small number of minor recommendations were made about our procedures and regulations, there was every reason to think that we would receive the classification of 'Full Confidence', which is the agency's highest accolade. Indeed, the team leader, Professor Harold Ewing, indicated at noon on Thursday that this would be the likely outcome.

However, on the following day, Friday, the inspectors talked with the Dean, John Pilkington. The interview lasted for more than two hours and the discussion centred on the arrangements for external examiners. Unfortunately, they discovered a number of anomalies. I am sure the matter could have been sorted out calmly and amicably, but instead of discussing the problem quietly with me, they abruptly cut short the whole inspection. They ordered my secretary to telephone for a taxi and they left St Sebastian's by the 1:30 train.

I had a partial explanation from Professor Ewing in an e-mail on Saturday, but it was not until yesterday that I received an official letter from the inspectorate. After listing a number of criticisms, it delivered its official verdict. I regret to inform you that St Sebastian's has received the classification of 'No Confidence'.

This is, of course, a great disappointment and may have some serious implications for the future. I was most grateful to you and Victoria for allowing the university to host a dinner party in your house. With such a splendid start to the inspection, it is regrettable that we have not had a better outcome. In any event, it appears that we will now be faced with a further investigation. Professor Ewing, again without discussing the matter with me, has been in touch with the University Funding Council. Today I have received a letter from the Chief Executive Officer. He informs me that the Council is commissioning a team of three consultants. All three will be visiting the university in the very near future. They intend to conduct a thorough review of all of our procedures and they have indicated that they will be expecting to interview a number of members of staff.

The main purpose of this letter is to tell you about the result of the Quality Control inspection. However, I wonder if I could trouble you once again in your role as Visitor of the university. The three consultants are due to come to my office for the first time on Wednesday morning at eleven o'clock. I appreciate that this is very short notice, but I would be so grateful if you could be there to welcome them. Despite our experience with the Quality Control team, I still believe that first impressions are very important. It would be such a help if you could shake their hands and perhaps say a few words of encouragement about St Sebastian's.

I cannot disguise from you that, as a result of this recent inspection, the whole institution may be under serious threat. As you may know, the Funding Council has the power to withdraw funds altogether if it is not satisfied with its consultants' findings. We are standing at a crossroads. This is a critical moment in the history of our university and I would be most grateful if you would come to our aid in our hour of need,

126

May I ask you to inform my secretary as soon as possible whether we can expect you on Wednesday morning.

With best regards,

Yours ever,

Robert
'(Dr Robert Sloth, Acting Vice-Chancellor)'

This was not a plea I could ignore. So on Wednesday I set off for the university as arranged. However, I was determined to have a word with Magnus beforehand. We planned to meet in his office at ten. As the cathedral clock struck the hour, I mounted the steps of the Old Building and headed off for his room. When I knocked on the door, he opened it wearing a maroon velvet smoking jacket and a black cap with a tassel. 'Good grief,' I said.

'Rather fetching don't you think? It was a present.'

'A present?' I asked. 'From whom?'

Magnus looked a little self-conscious. 'I've just come back from Brambletye. Dorothy Upton invited me to give a lecture on Hebrew internet sources to her students on Friday and I stayed for a long weekend. Brambletye's a nice old place. I'd never been there before and we found this jacket in an interesting old clothes shop.'

I was amused. 'So you've been to stay with Miss Upton and she bought it for you?'

Magnus nodded. 'She remembered that years ago I said I wanted one.'

'And did you give her something in return?' I persisted.

Magnus looked even more uncomfortable. 'Well . . . I made a small outlay at an antique jewellery stall . . .'

I sat down abruptly. 'Magnus! Are you engaged to Dorothy Upton?'

'No, No!' Magnus hastened to reassure me. 'We agreed that we are both better suited to the single life. But we have decided to renew our friendship . . .'

'So what did you give her?' I asked.

'I came across a little Victorian brooch which spelled out her name in coloured stones?'

'What kind of stones?' I had never heard of such a thing.

'Oh a diamond for the "d", an opal for "o", a ruby for "r", another opal for the second "o", then a topaz for the "t", a hessionite for "h" and a yellow sapphire for "y".'

'Good heavens!' I said. I was impressed. Then I had a sinking thought. 'Please don't tell Victoria about this. She'll want one too. What precious stone begins with a "v"?'

Magnus looked complacent. 'You know Dorothy said she's never forgotten me! She makes a point of reading all my book reviews. She says it's nice that at least there's still one person in the world who has proper standards!'

'It sounds like you two are very well suited,' I observed.

'She's a bit less critical now in her old age. I still find it a bit galling that she can do the crossword faster than I can!'

I found this very hard to believe. Magnus invariably polished off the *Times* puzzle in less than ten minutes. 'She's obviously an exceptionally brilliant woman,' I said.

Magnus nodded 'Yes, she is! That's why she likes me! And she always got on very well with my Aunt Ursula,' he added. 'She's agreed to come with me to Norfolk to visit her over the next vacation.'

I thought it was time to change the subject. 'I have to say, Magnus, your jacket's a bit tight across the shoulders.'

'Just a bit snug . . .'

'And the cap comes down over your ears.'

'I wouldn't want it too tight. It would give me a headache. Anyway, sit down Harry and I'll get you some coffee.' Magnus handed over a biscuit tin with a picture of a zebra by George Stubbs on the top. Inside were a few crumbly chocolate digestive biscuits. 'So,' he said, 'you're here to greet the consultants.'

'It appears so,' I agreed. 'Sloth wants me to make a good first impression and, as he put it, "Say some encouraging words". Do you know how long they plan to stay?'

'I understand they're supposed to make several visits. This is the first. Sloth sent out an e-mail with a list of people they want to see. They're beginning with all the heads of departments, but it's going much further than that. It looks like they intend to examine everything.' Magnus handed me a mug of coffee and sprawled out on his sofa.

'This mess is all Pilkington's fault, you know,' he said. 'I always knew he was a mindless idiot, but I never cast him as a whistle-blower. But he jumped into this catastrophe with both his big feet. It's unbelievable!'

'How is he?' I asked.

'No one really knows. I saw Marigold yesterday. She said that John and his wife have gone to stay with Maureen's sister in the Lake District to recuperate. She runs a bed and breakfast up there and it's presumably empty at this time of year.'

'When is he coming back?' I asked.

'Well it's anyone's guess. Everyone's heard the story by now so it'll be very humiliating for him. The rumour is that he's thinking of changing careers.'

'Just because of the inspection?' I asked.

Magnus reached into his tin and took out the remaining biscuits. He started dunking them in his coffee. 'Apparently John has been talking about training to be a Methodist minister. He's already a lay-preacher so it wouldn't take too long.'

'Things are that bad?'

'Marigold insisted that she heard Sloth shout at him when she was arranging the taxi for the inspection team. She heard him say that he would make sure Pilkington stopped being Dean.'

'Sloth shouted?' I was astonished. 'Sloth can barely raise his voice from its normal sleepy langor. Are you sure?'

'That's what Marigold said!' Magnus maintained.

'It wasn't entirely his fault.' I was trying to be fair. 'After all, it was Sloth who should have made sure that external examiners were appointed at the proper time.'

'Well if it comes to that, the great Lord Flanagan of Fandonegal shouldn't have forced everyone into introducing all these new courses at such a breakneck speed . . . Still I'm not going to weep for Pilkington. He's always been a pain in the neck. In my view, the whole thing serves him right, the stupid clod.'

'Do you know why John thinks that he's been called to the ministry? Was it a long-time ambition, do you think?'

Magnus was amused. 'I think it was more of an instant Damascus Road experience. But instead of the Call of the Lord, it was the Shout of the Sloth.' Magnus sniggered. Then he looked

129

at me slyly. 'Now he can be just like you, Harry. Except I believe Methodists wear taller dog-collars!'

I left Magnus's office at five to eleven. I had to pass the chapel on my way to see Sloth. There was a great deal of unusual bustle in the corridor. Groups of people, all very nicely dressed, were milling around. I could not imagine what was going on until I realised that a wedding was about to begin. I had never seen a gay commitment ceremony and I was curious about this innovation at St Sebastian's. I tried to look inconspicuous and waited to see what would happen.

I was not disappointed. Accompanied by much camp laughter, the company drifted through the chapel doors and settled themselves in the pews. It was not a big gathering – after all it was a week-day – but everyone looked as if they were enjoying themselves. Then the organ struck up Mendelssohn's wedding march; there was the sound of shuffling as the congregation rose to its feet and a procession came round the corner.

It was led by a diminutive little black boy carrying a silver cross. It was bigger than he was. Then came the choir; there were ten more small boys, all walking in perfect step, all looking angelic in starched ruffs and surplices. After the choir there were two devastatingly handsome young men. They were both very blond and could have been models for the young Narcissus. Dressed in white shirts and trousers with gold sashes, they were scattering a trail of yellow rose petals. I felt sure that our cleaner Mrs Thomas would not have approved. The two principals came next. They were both in immaculate morning coats with full-blown yellow roses in their button-holes. One was young – not much older than the two narcissi and equally good-looking. The other was older; he was perhaps a little fleshy, but still very well-preserved and prosperous. Both were smiling. To bring up the rear was the celebrant. To my amazement, he was a real-live bishop in full white-and-gold pontificals. He had soft white curly hair and appeared exactly as a bishop should – unworldly, charming and innocent.

I was mesmerised. I did not recognise the bishop and was curious who he was. Given the current homophobic climate in the Church of England, conducting a gay wedding was a brave thing to do. He seemed quite unperturbed. As the little procession turned into the chapel, there was the sound of clapping. Then there was quiet. The Mendelssohn was finished and the organist played an introductory chord. The boyish voices siezed the note and, with a piercing sweetness, they started singing, 'Somewhere over the Rainbow, Skies are Blue . . .'

I have to confess that I thought the whole thing delightful, but I did wonder how much it cost. Flanagan's money-making schemes were incredible. I looked back nostalgically to my own wedding day. It was a somewhat different occasion in the Dormouse Village Church. My father-in-law gave Victoria away. The choir and organist did their not-very-good best and the reception was in the Great Hall of the castle. Even in the middle of July, it was bitterly cold and the guests shivered in their summer finery. I had been terrified that Victoria would call it off at the last minute and my predominant memory was my relief that I had finally persuaded her to marry me.

Because of the gay wedding, I was a little late. Sloth was flustered and was waiting by the door when I arrived. Seated around the table in his office were three men in grey suits. Although one was bald and only two wore spectacles, somehow they were indistinguishable. Sloth did his best to introduce us and we all shook hands. Stacked on the table were piles of documents, a laptop computer, a printer, and a digital tape-recorder which was already running. Another chair was hastily pulled up and I sat down.

'The Provost was previously a professor here in the Theology department,' Sloth announced. 'So he knows St Sebastian's intimately. By virtue of his present office in the cathedral, he's now acting as the university Visitor.' The men in suits nodded. Bravely Sloth carried on. 'I don't know whether you want to know about the role of the Visitor . . .' This suggestion was met with total silence. So, turning to me he smiled. 'Perhaps you might like to say something about your time here,' he said.

I cleared my throat. 'Yes, yes,' I began, 'I was here for over ten years . . .'

'The Provost made a distinguished contribution to his department. His academic speciality is Christian ethics,' Sloth interrupted. I thought back to my previous encounters with Sloth in

131

this very room. On those occasions he did his best to ensure my dismissal from the university. I faced one disciplinary procedure after another and he made no secret of the fact that he disliked and despised both me and my academic work. It is strange how circumstances alter memories.

The inspectors listened with a glazed expression as I told them about the various courses I had taught over the years. I struggled to present the university in the most positive light, but I had to admit that things might have changed in the three years I had been away. I tried to be sprightly, but the three grey men could not have looked more bored. Eventually I came to a halt.

'Thanks so much for that,' said Sloth. With an anxious expression, he looked at the inspectors. 'Is there anything you might care to ask the Provost before he leaves us?' he asked. There was another deathly hush.

'No questions?' asked the Acting Vice-Chancellor desperately. Further quiet. 'Well, in that case, we must say goodbye,' he said. The three men stood up and we shook hands again.

Sloth walked me to the door and took me outside. He shook his bald head. 'This is not encouraging, Harry. It hasn't been an easy morning. I know the Quality Control inspection was a disaster, but at least the inspectors were friendly. This group has hardly said a word. When they arrived, I offered them coffee. They said no. Then I invited them to lunch. They said that they had brought their own sandwiches and would eat them while they worked. They just sit like sphinxes waiting for the heads of department to arrive. They're due to see each one at half-hourly intervals and tomorrow they've scheduled the heads of the faculties. They're all getting a full hour . . .'

Sloth wiped his forehead as he voiced his indignation. 'And they've made it clear that they don't want me to be present while the interviews are taking place. They're even insisting that everything is tape-recorded. Honestly, it's as if they don't trust us!'

I prepared to go. 'Let me know if I can be of any more help,' I said.

My erstwhile colleague smiled wanly and told me he'd be in touch if I were needed. 'Thanks, Harry,' he said as he walked back towards his office. 'You've been a real trooper!'

The next afternoon I had a frantic telephone call from Felix. He was coughing and sneezing over the line. He asked if he could come to see me straightway. I was due to go to a meeting with the Clerk of Works about a patch of damp which had suddenly appeared in the cathedral crypt, but I told him that I could spare half an hour. A few minutes later he arrived carrying a file bulging with papers. I showed him into my study and he collapsed onto the sofa. 'You look like you need a drink,' I said.

'I've got a filthy cold,' he sniffed. 'Could I have a large whisky, please?'

I sat opposite in an armchair as Felix blew his nose. 'Harry,' he began, 'the situation's desperate. I saw the Funding Council Consultants earlier. They met the other two faculty heads this morning and it was my turn this afternoon. It was terrible. They grilled me about our partnerships. I didn't know what to say. I stressed that all these arrangements were made by Flanagan, and that I had had no choice but to go along with his plans. That didn't seem to impress them.'

Felix took his handkerchief out of his pocket again. He looked flushed and feverish. 'I've got an awful cold on top of everything,' he said. 'Emma thought I should stay in bed, but I told her I had to go to this interview. I really wish I hadn't . . .'

'They have doubts about the partnerships?' I asked.

'Not just doubts. They were outraged. Especially about our arrangements with the Florida Pussy Galore College. Honestly, Harry, the whole place is going to close down.'

I tried to be soothing. 'Felix, you must calm down. It can't really be as bad as all that,' I said. 'What is the Pussy Galore College?'

Felix shuddered. 'Don't ask! The university has a partnership with it . . .'

I realised that I needed to begin at the beginning. 'Look,' I said, 'I don't really understand how the partnerships work. Explain them to me.'

Felix took a deep breath. 'It's a very lucrative scheme of Flanagan's. The principle is that some Mickey Mouse college goes into partnership with St Sebastian's. They teach their own students and sometimes they send the students over to us for a term or so. In either case the college pays handsomely for the

133

privilege. The university monitors and examines all the work and the students get a St Sebastian's degree at the end of it.'

'What's wrong with that?' I asked.

'Well nothing, if there were a proper system of moderation and examination in place. But, as we all know, there isn't. But worse still, the university is given a sum of money from the Funding Council for every student it takes onto a degree course.'

'So it's not only the Pussy Galore College which pays for these Florida students to get their degrees in Artistic Dance, it's also the British Funding Council. Is that right?' I was not sure that I had fully understood.

'Exactly,' said Felix. 'I don't think the Funding Council had any idea what was going on at St Sebastian's. They just fired off cheques whenever they were asked. Now they've just found out and they're not amused. The consultants told me that they're going to shut off all funding for the partnerships immediately. In other words, they'll all have to be self-supporting if they exist at all.'

I tried to look on the bright side. 'I'm sure the Pussy Galore College could afford to pay a little more to make up for the loss of Funding Council money.'

Felix was almost in tears. 'The Pussy Galore College is only the tip of the iceberg. We've got scores of partners, obscure missionary seminaries, strange third world teacher-training establishments, dance and drama schools which are barely registered even in their own countries. You name it, we give it degrees. At present we receive more than three million pounds a year from the Funding Council for them all. St Sebastian's will be crippled without that money.'

'Surely there are other income streams coming into the university?' I asked. 'You aren't just dependent on these rather shaky partnerships. What about all the normal resident undergraduate and post-graduate students?'

'Yes we'll still get money from them . . . Though of course we're in trouble with the Quality Control Agency. If we can't get our assessment procedures right, we won't be able to give degrees to anybody. But the immediate problem is the Funding Council. If we lose the partnerships' money, there will be a gigantic hole in the university budget. There will inevitably be job losses and redundancies and who knows what else . . .'

'I'm sure some interim compromise can be sorted out,' I tried to console him.

'But that's not the end of it . . .' Felix could not be pacified. 'These consultants are going to look at everything. They're complete ferrets. They're going to discover all the appalling programmes Flanagan set up . . . I know they won't approve any of them . . . No one could . . . Nothing was done properly . . . Honestly, it's a complete disaster . . .'

He gazed outside through the windows. The sky was grey and rain was falling in heavy drops onto the Green Court. Felix's expression was anguished and his nose dripped. 'Harry,' he said, 'you're a senior clergyman. You know all about signs and wonders. Your religious tradition is based on them. There's only one thing that will save the university now and that is a theological miracle of very substantial proportions!'

Things went quiet at the university. The Funding Council consultants continued to do their work, inspecting, interviewing and listening. Apparently they remained as inscrutable as ever. Meanwhile I was not having an easy time at the cathedral. The damp patch in the crypt proved to be more serious than was first thought and was going to cost a lot of money to put right.

By the Tuesday of the following week, I felt I needed a break. After yet another gloomy session with the Clerk of Works, I slipped out of the precincts and treated myself to a cup of coffee at the Mitre café. It was a charming place. Situated in a mediaeval building next to the Trinity Gate, it had low ceilings and heavy oak beams. The walls were decorated with delicate watercolours of the cathedral, all executed by the two proprietors. Cream and blue linen curtains hung at the windows and the plates and cups were all in the traditional blue willow pattern.

It had been run by Miss Betty and Miss Mildred Monkton for over twenty years. They were regarded as a St Sebastian's institution with their white hair and blue overalls. I knew them quite well because they were both regular attenders at services as well as dedicated 'Holy Dusters' in the cathedral. They could also bake the most delicious sponge cake I have ever tasted.

I was just settling down to my cake and coffee in a comfortable corner table. I had opened my copy of *The Times* and was just about to begin on the obituaries, when the two ladies stood before me. They were clearly distressed. 'Could we speak to you for a moment, Provost?' asked Miss Mildred.

There is no peace for the wicked. I put down my newspaper, stood up and pulled out a couple of chairs for them. With many fluttering apologies for disturbing me, they sat down.

'We don't know what to do!' said Miss Betty. 'We just got this letter this morning. There was no warning or anything . . .'

It was from Reg Blenkensop, the Canon-Treasurer of the cathedral, and was on official writing paper. It gave the sisters notice that the rent on the Mitre premises was to be increased five-fold. If this were not agreeable to the Misses Monkton, Canon Blenkensop would be grateful if they would regard the document as a notice to quit. The cathedral already had the firm offer of another tenant.

'I don't understand,' I said.

Mildred took out a handkerchief and wiped her eyes. 'I rang up Canon Blenkensop's office this morning. His secretary told me that the offer was from McDonald's.'

'And who is Mr Macdonald?' I asked

'No, Provost. It's not somebody called MacDonald. It's that awful American hamburger chain. The ones that are always advertising on the television. Well of course they can afford enormous sums of money. So we've got to go . . . We've been here for more than twenty-five years.'

I was astonished. 'But the Canon doesn't have the power to evict you,' I said. 'That's a matter that only the Chapter can rule on.'

'That's not what Canon Blenkensop's secretary told us. She said that it was the Canon-Treasurer who makes these sorts of decisions. The cathedral needs a great many repairs and the Chapter can no longer let out its premises on charitable rents.'

'Charitable rents!' I was horrified. 'You are not a charity. You are a successful small business paying a very fair commercial rent.'

Betty smiled damply. 'That's what we always thought, Provost. We'd feel dreadful if we thought we weren't paying our way . . .'

'Look,' I said, 'you're members of the cathedral family. The Mitre is an important part of the town. We all know and love it.

No one can bake a victoria sponge like you.' I looked longingly at my cake which was sitting uneaten on the plate in front of me. 'Now you mustn't worry,' I continued. 'We're not going to have a fast-food chain next to the Trinity Gate. Revenue from rents is important. But your future is not in jeopardy. Canon Blenkensop simply doesn't have the authority to make these sorts of judgements. The other Canons won't countenance such an idea. And neither will I.'

'But what about the rent?' Betty lamented.

'It may have to be raised a bit. I can't promise that won't happen. But it certainly won't go up five-fold. The cathedral regulations stipulate that rents can only be increased in line with the retail price index. So it simply can't be more than that.'

The sisters looked profoundly relieved and grateful. 'Thank you, Provost,' said Miss Betty. 'You don't know how worried we've been. It would break our hearts to leave St Sebastian's, but we couldn't afford to stay without the business.'

'I'm going to get you a fresh cup of coffee,' announced Miss Mildred.

The next Chapter meeting was on that Friday. I did not warn Blenkensop in advance. Instead I looked up the regulations to make sure I was on solid ground and, when I found that I was, I planned to humiliate him publicly.

In the event, it was unnecessary. I passed round copies of Blenkensop's letters to the sisters under Any Other Business. Once he understood what was threatened, old Canon Sinclair turned white with fury. Despite his Parkinsons disease, he rose to his feet and lambasted the Canon-Treasurer. This time there was no talk of the unpleasantness of Chapter disagreements. Sinclair had known the two women since they were children. Their father had been the Chief Verger of the cathedral and their mother had arranged the flowers for more than fifty years. It was a disgrace even to contemplate evicting them, whatever the commercial advantage. And to attempt to do it under false pretences was nothing less than wicked.

It was a splendid display of righteous anger and I enjoyed every moment of it. As soon as the Chapter meeting was closed, Reg slunk away to lick his wounds.

The trial of the Priory's errant gardener was scheduled for the next Monday morning. It was to take place in the Crown Court, a grim Victorian building located next door to Arrowsmith Teacher Training College on the other side of town. Under Sir William's instructions, Kev had already pleaded guilty so there was not going to be a jury. My father-in-law had demanded that both Victoria and I attend. 'The judge needs to see that the boy has the support of the Church,' he said.

Sir William had spent the previous weekend persuading all the Home's inmates to sign a petition for leniency. He himself was scheduled to plead mitigating circumstances. When we offered to give him a lift in from the Priory, it was curtly refused.

'Quite unnecessary!' said my father-in-law. 'Matron is driving the bus!'

We parked our car in a convenient car park and waited in the entrance hall. It was a horrible place. Other young men besides Kev were also being tried that morning. There was an air of desperate optimism among the small family groups which were hanging around. I noticed that there was one lone, middle-aged woman sitting by herself. She had badly-dyed blonde hair and there was a pathetic shabby-smartness about her appearance. She was about the right age and she looked miserable. I had nothing to lose so I walked up to her. 'Are you by any chance Kev's mother?' I asked.

She was startled, but I explained who I was and introduced Victoria. At that very moment, Sir William and his party came through the door. Besides Steve, the other gardener, there was Mrs Mackenzie, Mrs Germaney and old Mrs Blenkensop, as well as three other ladies I did not know. 'Matron's still parking the bus!' Sir William informed us.

Last of all came Kev. He was dressed up for the occasion in a suit which was slightly too big for him. 'Got it at Oxfam!' announced Sir William. 'Jolly good, don't you think!' Topping it, to Victoria's amusement, was Sir William's old school tie. It had been lent for the occasion. 'Nice to find a good use for it,' was Sir William's explanation.

I presented Kev's mother to the ladies and they all made little sympathetic noises. I noticed that it was old Mrs Blenkensop who gathered her up and insisted that she sit with the Priory group in the public gallery. Kev was whisked off by a police officer and Sir William was conducted to the witness room. Finally, Victoria and I waited for Matron and the three of us joined the others. With so many supporters, it was quite a squash up there.

We waited with the court officials. Kev sat at the back with the policeman in the dock. He looked scared and smaller than usual. I realised that he was not very old. At half past ten the judge arrived and we all stood up. He was dressed in a black gown with a red sash. The court officials bowed and the judge took his seat.

First to speak was a representative from the police. He described the iniquity of the crime that had been committed by Kev's friend. Quite rightly, he was already serving a prison sentence. He pointed out that, although it was commendable that Kev had pleaded guilty, he had a considerable criminal record. Receiving stolen goods was a serious offence and should not be treated lightly. In his opinion a custodial sentence would be the only appropriate punishment.

The ladies were horrified. Mrs Mackenzie gave a hastily suppressed little squeak and there was much sighing and shaking of heads. Kev's mother wiped her eyes and Kev himself looked even smaller. I realised that he had been through all this before. The judge looked at his notes. He asked no questions.

Then Sir William was summoned. He looked grave and determined. Supported by his stick with its silver dormouse handle, he asked permission to make a statement. The judge bowed his consent.

Having explained who he was (name, title, regiment, rank, occupation and current address), he gestured towards the public gallery. 'It is clear, Sir,' he said, 'that young Kevin has a great deal of support from the residents of the Priory, where he works in the capacity of gardener. And that's because he does a jolly good job!'

There was a little murmur of assent among the ladies which was hastily hushed. 'I took the liberty, Sir,' continued Sir William, 'of organising a small petition on young Kevin's behalf. It was signed by every member of our community, residents and staff, every single one. No exceptions. Kevin is an excellent worker and a very helpful young man. We are all anxious that he should be given another chance.'

Again there was a small flutter of approval which this time had to be reproved by a court official. Then Sir William embarked on the nature of the crime. He was very breezy about it. 'When all's said and done, he was only keeping a bag for a friend. He was doing a favour for an old comrade. Of course he should have asked what was in the bag, but that's the kind of mistake any of us could have made, Eh What!'

Then Sir William described how Kev had helped him with the Priory garden. 'Splendid boy!' he said. 'I'd like to have had him in my regiment! He'd know how to fight for Queen and Country! Not like most of the lads you get nowadays!' He pointing at Kev with his stick. 'In my opinion we need more like him! He's a good worker and a helpful young man! No point in sending him to prison! He'd be a damned nuisance there! We need him in the Priory garden.'

He turned to the judge. 'Sir,' he said, 'what it comes down to is we're all counting on you to restore him to us. We are expecting to take him home with us in time for luncheon.' He gave a brief salute and left the witness box. There was much nodding and a gentle ripple of applause from the public gallery.

Then there was a pause in the proceedings. Kev was led away and the judge repaired to his chambers. The rest of us took the lift upstairs to the canteen for coffee. Matron and I made everyone sit down and we organised the refreshments. The ladies all clustered round Sir William twittering their congratulations. He looked grim. 'It all depends on that judge fella,' he said. 'I never did trust lawyers . . .'

Within half an hour, we were summoned back to the courtroom. Again we all stood as the judge entered. With considerable gravity he announced that he had listened carefully to what had been said. He recognised that the young man was a good worker and had earned considerable respect from the residents of his place of employment. However, receiving stolen goods was a very serious offence. For someone with Kevin's record, a custodial sentence was to be expected.

He turned to Kev. 'Therefore I have decided to sentence you to a year in prison . . .'

There was a gasp of horror from the public gallery and a small 'Oh no!' from Mrs Mackenzie . . . but the judge was still speaking.

'. . . It will be suspended for two years! You have been excep-tionally lucky to be given this extra chance. Make sure you do not betray the trust that has been placed in you.' The ladies looked at each other. It took them a moment to understand what had been said. Then there was another spontaineous burst of clapping. The judge rose; the court officials bowed and the trial had come to an end.

Outside the courtroom Kev was mobbed by the old ladies. Matron invited Kev's mother back to the Priory to have lunch with everyone. She looked awkward, but she was persuaded into the bus by Steve and Mrs Blenkensop. Sir William was the last to climb into vehicle. 'Excellent day's work!' he pronounced to Victoria. 'Now the lads can get the bulbs planted for the autumn. Not a moment too soon in my opinion!'

CHAPTER EIGHT

A Corrupt Place

The Funding Council consultants continued their visitation at the university. They were obviously doing a thorough job because they seemed to be interviewing literally everyone. But I heard nothing more. My own preoccupation was with the cathedral. Nearly every day I had a meeting with the Clerk of Works to discuss various options for dealing with our underground damp problems. Reg Blenkensop, as Canon-Treasurer, was often present on these occasions. He continued to ignore me, but he kept up an elaborate conversation with George Carpenter. As it happened, the Clerk of Works was also a rugby player although not at such an exalted level as Blenkensop. I had to endure a great deal of reminiscence about the glory days of the Oxford University team in the very early 1960s. In between, Reg was always complaining about the criminal expense of repairs. There were endless not-so-subtle hints that the only solution to our problems would be to impose admission charges. Secretly I was afraid he might be right.

One Monday morning I received a call from Penelope Ransome. She was a senior lecturer in Women's Studies and was the president of the trade union at St Sebastian's. Several years previously, when I was facing my own difficulties at the university, she had given me considerable support in that capacity. I was delighted to hear from her. She said that there was an urgent matter which she needed to discuss with me. It could not wait so we arranged to meet at the Mitre at four o'clock that afternoon.

I arrived early and was greeted warmly by Miss Mildred and Miss Betty. There was a nice table free near the window, so I sat down and ordered tea for both of us. Several minutes after the cathedral clock had struck the hour, my guest arrived in a flurry. I think the Misses Monktons found her appearance disconcerting, but they were too well-bred to mention it. I had forgotten how Penelope presented herself. Dressed in grubby blue-jeans, Dr Martens boots and a phosphorescent lime green jumper, she was sporting large silver earrings. In the old days, her brownish hair had been streaked with emerald green, but now she was transformed into a dazzling platinum blonde. What had not changed was her mascara. It was still dotted all over her cheeks rather than on her eye-lashes.

I stood up when she entered. 'Golly, Harry,' she said, 'I've never seen you in a dog-collar before. Am I supposed to call you Provost?' Before I had a chance to reply, she flopped down in a chair and put a bag bulging with papers on the table. 'What a day!' she said.

Miss Mildred came over in her neat blue overall to ask if the new visitor would like anything to eat. Penelope looked hungrily towards the cake tray. 'Are you having something?' she asked.

I was quite stout enough, but I could see that this was an occasion when temptation was not going to be resisted. 'Try the victoria sponge. It's nectar and ambrosia,' I said.

'Oh goodie!' said Penelope. 'I need it. I really do.'

Miss Mildred brought over two very large slices of cake and Penelope and I smiled at each other. 'What's going on?' I asked.

The words tumbled over each other. 'Harry, you won't believe what St Sebastian's is like now. It's completely changed since you left. We had the most appalling Vice-Chancellor. A complete nightmare! But anyway he's gone – to the House of Lords would you believe! He's become the opposition spokesman for higher

143

education. Honestly! One doesn't know whether to laugh or cry! But the point is he's left the place in a total shambles. When he was with us he went into partnership with the most dubious institutions. And he introduced degree programmes and diplomas in the most ridiculous subjects.'

'I understand he attracted a lot of students,' I observed mildly.

'Oh he attracted them all right. He just didn't educate them. It was a complete exercise in dumbing-down. The most popular undergraduate subject in the university now is Celebrity Studies! I ask you . . . Celebrity Studies! We even give university certificates in pole-dancing as part of the Artistic Dance programme. The place is littered with nubile models from a partnership college in Florida. No one bothers to check if the students can read or write. As long as they can writhe around a pole, they get their certificate. We've become a laughing stock in the world of higher education . . .'

'But I believe it's very lucrative . . .' As a professional ethicist, I always try to see both sides of any question.

'Oh yes . . . Flanagan knew how to make money. It was only by the grace of God we're not educating half the American Mafia. He was determined to combine with some gambling establishment in Las Vegas and introduce a degree programme in casino management for them.' I had heard about that particular scheme. To Victoria's amusement, my father-in-law had been instrumental in its destruction.

'Anyway,' continued Penelope, 'the whole thing is a total disgrace. None of these courses or partnerships have been properly vetted, and it appears that a team of investigators from the University Funding Council has just uncovered what's going on . . .'

'Yes, I know,' I said. 'I spoke to them on their first day. Sloth thought I would make a good impression.'

Penelope giggled. She remembered my conflicts with Registrar Sloth in the past. 'Times have changed!' she chortled.

'So what's going on?' I asked again.

'Well,' said Penelope, 'last week I was summoned to see the Registrar. That bald creep is now the Acting Vice-Chancellor, if you can believe it. You know what he's like – most of the time he's asleep. Well, he told me that all the idiotic partnerships that Flanagan set up are going to be shut down. Apparently they're illegal. There's no justification for the British taxpayer subsidising fly-by-night colleges abroad. Well that seems reasonable to me. I just can't understand how the old Vice-Chancellor got away with it as long as he did. But the upshot is that the university is faced with a loss of rather more than three million pounds every year.'

I felt slightly sick. 'I heard this was happening. Why did he tell you?' I asked.

'I'm in charge of the union and he has to consult me if he wants any employment changes.'

'I see,' I said.

'As Acting Vice-Chancellor,' Penelope continued, 'He's now in charge of finances, and he showed me the budget for next year. Council had planned for a surplus of nearly half a million pounds. But without the partnerships, instead we'll be in deficit by at least two and a half million. So Sloth wants to solve the situation by getting rid of staff. And he's insisting that everything is sorted out by the end of April. He wanted the union to know what's happening.'

'By April? That's impossible! We're already in March.'

'That's what I told him. Anway, he said that the University Council is setting up a redundancy committee this week, and they're planning to make at least ten people compulsorily redundant.'

'Ten people compulsorily redundant!' I echoed. 'That's disgraceful. Surely the union won't stand for it.'

'We won't,' Penelope reached into her bag and took out a large red looseleaf folder. I recognised it as the old Staff Handbook. I used to keep one in my desk. 'They're also planning to ignore the proper redundancy procedures,' she said. 'But we're determined not to let them.' She turned to the relevant pages in the handbook and read out the statutes regarding redundancy. 'You see Harry,' she explained, 'the university is compelled to take every step possible to avoid compulsion. Compulsory redundancy is the absolutely final resort and is only acceptable if nothing else can be done.'

'What are the alternatives?' I asked.

'Well,' said Penelope, 'first the Council is obliged to introduce a voluntary severance and an early retirement scheme. All vacant posts should be frozen. If a vacancy does occur which really has to be filled, every effort must be made to appoint someone already on the staff from an area under threat. I explained all this to Sloth, but he just wouldn't listen.'

'But if it's in the Staff Handbook . . .? Surely . . .' I shook my head.

'I took mine in with me when I went to see him. But he paid no attention. You know what he said? He insisted that the Staff Handbook hasn't been revised recently and is therefore out of date. Consequently the statutes are irrelevant.'

'That can't be right,' I said.

'It isn't. He's the Registrar. It was his responsibility to update the handbook. He was meant to revise it and distribute the new versions round the staff at least once a year. But he didn't. And anyway there aren't any more in print. So after my meeting with Sloth, I checked it out with Morris O'Murphy – he's still our regional union officer by the way – and he told me the statutes remain in force unless they've been replaced by new ones. He sent an e-mail to Sloth explaining this in simple language, but inevitably he hasn't received a reply.'

'Appalling!' I said.

'Harry, you're now the Visitor. That's why I've come to you. We're not asking you to act yet, but we want to keep you informed. Next week we're going to have a union meeting to explain the situation to our members . . .'

As Penelope was speaking, her telephone rang. She delved in her pocket and took out a shiny pillar-box-red Blackberry. 'It's Morris,' she said. 'Do you want to speak to him?'

Several years ago at the end of my time at the university, Morris had also helped me through my ordeals. Both Victoria and I were very fond of him. We had kept up by Christmas card, but I had not spoken to him since I left the university. Penelope handed me her phone. 'Hello, Morris,' I said, 'It's Harry Gilbert!'

There was noisy shouting and rattling in the background. 'Hi Harry. I heard from Penelope that you're now Provost. Welcome back!'

'I can barely hear you,' I said.

'I'm on the train going to a hearing in Manchester. I'm dealing with some fifty-eight-year-old professor who's got involved with one of his first-year students. Silly bugger! He denies the whole thing, but she kept tapes of their recent encounters. They're quite sensational . . . Anyway, has Penelope filled you in?'

'She just told me,' I said.

'Typical of your university. St Sebastian's never follows the rules. They make up procedures as they go along. And it's even worse now that that dozy ignoramus Robert Sloth is in charge. God help us all!'

'Are you visiting St Sebastian's? Why don't you came and see us?' I asked.

'I'll be there for a set of meetings on Thursday and Friday,' he said.

'Look, Morris. We're living in the Provost's House now and we've got plenty of room. Come and stay with us. I can't take sides in this dispute. As the Visitor, I officially have to be neutral. But Victoria would love to see you.'

'Are you sure? That's really kind!' There was a pause. 'Look, Harry. Let me take you both to that splendid Indian restaurant we went to after your case. Wasn't it called something like the Red Fort?'

'The Taj Mahal,' I said.

'That's the one! The union'll pay and I'll let you in to all the gory details of what your university is up to.'

I felt confident about asking people to stay. I knew Victoria was anxious to have visitors. Since the New Year, on and off, we had had workmen in the house. My wife was good at organisation and had planned the whole thing like a military operation. Because of her classes and because she did not want me disturbed, she had insisted that the drawing room, our bedroom and bathroom, the dining room, the hall and the study be painted while we were away for our summer holidays. But all the other bedrooms, bathrooms and domestic quarters were finished. They looked superb and I knew Victoria wanted to show off her handiwork.

Morris came on the appointed day. He had arrived in St Sebastian's early in the afternoon and had been closeted for a couple of hours with Sloth and Penelope. Because of his suitcases, he took a taxi from the university to the precincts and, when he arrived at six o'clock, he was just polishing off a packet of crisps.

'I needed some refreshment. That Registrar of yours hasn't been improved by becoming Acting Vice-Chancellor. It's hard to believe that anyone can be so dense!' he remarked.

He and Victoria were delighted to see one another and he was most impressed by the Provost's House. 'Well,' he said, 'this certainly puts your old colleagues' noses out of joint.'

Between the three of us, we manoeuvred his two suitcases, his bulging brief case and his two tatty carrier bags into the hall.

'How long are you planning to stay, Morris?' asked Victoria.

'Oh these are just a few papers and my laptop . . . and the remains of one or two snacks. I've got to keep my strength up. I've had a very stressful couple of days . . .' He stared round at all the portraits in the hall. 'Who are all these geezers?'

'They're all former Provosts,' I replied

'Wow! . . . Are you going to have your picture painted too? They all look pretty solemn. You might liven them up a bit!'

'No one's suggested it yet,' I admitted.

I took Morris to see his room. He was overwhelmed by the bathroom. Victoria had converted a neighbouring dressing-room and she had found an original Victorian bathroom suite in the cellar. The bath was enormous and the lavatory resembled a vast mahogany throne.

'I'll be too nervous to use it,' said Morris. 'I'll feel as if the butler is about to come in at any moment . . .'

'Don't worry,' I reassured him, 'the poor old Church of England can't even afford to provide us with a tweeny, let alone a butler.'

Morris was as stout as I remembered him, but this did not deter him from insisting we have what he referred to as 'a slap up meal' at the Taj Mahal. 'Treat's on me,' he insisted. Before we went, Victoria provided him with a large mug of tea and a tin of biscuits and he disappeared into his room for an hour's nap. 'I need it after dealing with your Dr Sloth,' he said.

As the cathedral clock struck seven, he reappeared. He had changed from his jacket and was sporting a navy blue sweater with a union badge sewn on the shoulder. He was also wearing a UCU pin in his collar. With a great deal of ceremony, he took two more pins out of his pocket and presented them to us. Victoria immediately took off her grandmother's pearl locket and stuck the pin into her lapel. She admired herself in the looking glass over the fireplace. 'Perhaps I could start on a new career,' she suggested. 'I'd love to have worked for a trade union. I've always been happier outside the tent pissing in, but for some reason I always find myself inside the tent pissing out. Can you explain it? . . .'

I was not sure whether I should be seen supporting the union so I put my gift discreetly in my pocket. 'It doesn't really go with a dog-collar,' I said.

We walked to the Indian restaurant which was located three doors down from the Mitre tea-rooms. On our way we passed Marmaduke. He was busy hunting some unfortunate creature in the Precentor's garden. Completely absorbed in his activities, he took no notice of us.

The Taj Mahal smelt enticingly of curry. I had already reserved a table in the corner, and Morris sat down between us. A young waiter bought us menus and we ordered three pints of lager and six spicy poppadums. Morris helped himself to two and then he embarked on an account of Sloth's inadequacies.

'I know he's just started, but he's the worst Vice-Chancellor I've ever come across. And there's quite some competition for that title, I can tell you . . . Most of the time I wonder if he's got any idea what I'm talking about. He gazes vacantly out the window when I ask him a question. Three or four times I actually caught him dropping off to sleep.'

'He suffers from slight narcolepsy,' I said. 'It's not his fault . . .'

'It's not my fault that I can't run a mile in four minutes, but then I shouldn't volunteer to do the fifteen hundred metres for Britain in the Olympic Games,' pointed out Morris. 'He was less than satisfactory as a Registrar, but his efforts as Vice-Chancellor can only be described as pathetic.'

'Did you have to deal with his wife as well?' asked Victoria slyly.

'That woman! . . . She's a basket case . . . She was meant to come up with all the financial papers for our meeting, but she'd lost them . . . She thought she might have put them all out with the recycling!'

Morris finished his beer and motioned to the waiter for another. As he reached for his third poppadum, he pulled a set of papers from the bag he had brought with him. 'Now I've got to show you this,' he said. 'It's from the union barrister.'

The document was a brief about the redundancy procedures at St Sebastian's. 'The guy who wrote it is a London Queen's Counsel. Sharp as mustard! Anway, the gist is that for once there's nothing wrong with the university's procedures as set out in the statutes and Staff Handbook. The problem is that the university has completely failed to follow its own regulations . . .'

'What have they done wrong?' I asked.

'It would be quicker to tell you what they have done right. The answer to that would be 'Nothing!' They've violated every rule in the book in setting up a redundancy committee. For example, there were supposed to be three academic members on the committee elected by Senate. But Senate has never met. So Sloth thought it would be adequate to telephone every university employee, academic and academic-related, to see if they'd be willing to be co-opted. But no one likes to help sack their colleagues, so he only managed to find one volunteer.'

'Who was that?' I asked.

'I've never met her. Someone called Olive O'Shea. She's something to do with public relations. Anyway she should be ashamed of herself, whoever she is . . .'

Victoria and I looked at each other. 'She's Lady Barridon,' Victoria said. 'She and her husband got Flanagan his peerage.'

'Well she still ought to be ashamed of herself. She's no lady – she's a scab!' Morris laughed at his little joke. 'Anyway, she hasn't done Sloth much good. The day after she agreed to serve, she disappeared to New York. Apparently she's gone for six weeks . . . So what it's come down to is Sloth has set up the committee without any members of the academic staff on it.'

'Does that matter?' asked Victoria.

Morris was shocked. 'Employment law's all about procedure. What he's done is in direct contravention of Statue 38.2. It'll never stand up in an employment tribunal!'

'Did you tell Sloth this?' I asked.

'Of course I did. But did he listen? He did not! He just said there wasn't time to find anybody else. And since they made an attempt to co-opt suitable people to sit on the committee, that was good enough. The university had done its duty . . .' Morris seized the final poppadum and crunched his way through it.

'But it's not enough to try . . .' I shook my head.

'Of course it isn't,' continued Morris. 'The upshot is that there is now a redundancy committee which is improperly consituted.'

At this point the waiter came to take our order. Morris demanded the full Taj Mahal Special Feast. He emphasised that it was to be for four people rather than three.

As soon as the waiter had departed, he continued. 'But that's not all. Sloth wants to rush this thing through as quickly as possible. He's actually appointed his wife as chairperson of the committee.' Morris pulled another document out of his bag. 'Look at this,' he said. 'The stupid woman's worked out a set of criteria for redundancy. Every person in each department's going to be ranked on the basis of these criteria. The person with the lowest score is going to be sacked.'

During my time as an academic nothing like this had ever happened. I was shocked. 'You mean every academic is going to be awarded a score, like gymnasts in an athletic competition?'

'Exactly like that. The heads of each department are responsible for doing the assessment and filling out the forms.'

'But they're not going to be objective . . . They'll mark up their friends and downgrade their enemies!' Victoria had no illusions about the ways of the world.

'I know . . . it's a disgraceful system . . .'

'Sloth must be mad,' I pronounced. It was the only charitable explanation I could find.

'That's not the worst of it,' Morris continued. 'He insists that the committee makes its recommendations for dismissal by the end of next week when Council meets. That doesn't give any time for those who are selected to challenge their scores.'

'But that's against natural justice . . .' I was horrified.

'Of course it is!' agreed Morris. 'Penelope and I pointed out that it's a fundamental principle that the process of redundancy must be just and fair. It's obvious that denying individuals the right to make a case against the scores they've been allocated is grossly improper.'

'What did he say to that?' I found it hard to believe what I was hearing.

'He shrugged his shoulders and said they would have a chance to complain later. Jenny Sloth is supposed to meet with each person who is under threat individually . . .'

'But all this should happen in advance,' I pointed out. 'Proper consultation should take place before the redundancy committee makes any recommendation. And anyway shouldn't there be a voluntary severance and an early retirement scheme in place before the university even starts to think about compulsory redundancy?'

The food arrived. There was an incredible quantity. The young waiter had considerable difficulty fitting all the dishes onto our table. Morris helped himself to a huge stuffed paratha and started making inroads into it.

'Sloth doesn't understand employment law, or management or anything else,' he pronounced through mouthfuls. 'He's got total tunnel vision. He simply can't think beyond balancing his budget.' Victoria and I watched fascinated as the paratha disappeared and Morris reached for another. 'But I can tell you, Harry. We won't put up with it. We really won't. Whatever he thinks, Sloth's got a fight on his hands . . .'

Morris was up by half-past seven the next morning. He was full of enthusiasm when Victoria suggested a cooked breakfast and he consumed every crumb. 'I really feel set up for the day,' he said. Victoria packed him a few sandwiches to keep him going. He was, after all, facing a full union meeting with all the St Sebastian's members and he did not have good news for them.

The following Tuesday evening was Victoria's last class. The series had been a huge success and, unlike most evening classes, the number of enrolments had increased over the term. To celebrate the final session, Victoria organised that coffee and cakes be served in the drawing room. These refreshments were prepared by the Misses Monktons and were much appreciated.

In addition, the more able-bodied members of the audience were invited to go round the house in groups of fifteen or so to see the re-decorated bedrooms and kitchens. Victoria was always very conscious that the Provost's House was a treasure that belonged to all the people of the town. It was not just a private residence. Everyone was so grateful and enthusiastic that Victoria promised that there would be another series starting after Easter. 'Book us in!' said Sir William, as he gathered the little party from the Priory into their taxi.

I heard nothing more about the university until a couple of days later. I was due to give an afternoon talk to the St Sebastian's Mothers' Union on 'The Permissive Society' and I was sitting in the study adding a few finishing touches. Suddenly the door-bell rang. I was not expecting anyone, but as Victoria was out shopping I went to the front door. Magnus was standing outside. 'Hi, Harry,' he said grinning. 'I've got something to show you.'

In his hand was the latest copy of the *Times Higher Education* magazine. On the front page was a large photograph of St Sebastian's Cathedral and underneath was the headline: 'St Sebastian's Slammed'. I led Magnus into the study where he flopped down on the sofa. I sat at my desk and skimmed through the article. It was based on an initial draft report issued by the Funding Council consultants. It was not complimentary about the university and its arrangements.

'This is ghastly,' I said. 'How in the world did the *Times Higher Ed*. get a copy of this? It's only a draft so it must be confidential.'

Magnus stretched himself out. 'Did you say something about coffee?' he asked, 'And perhaps a few bikkies?'

I went off to the kitchen and returned with two mugs of coffee and a box of shortbread biscuits. Magnus helped himself to three and began dipping them into his coffee. He smiled like a snake. 'Good, isn't it!' he remarked.

'Magnus,' I said, re-reading the article, 'it's frightful! If the reporter has got it right, then the Funding Council consultants fully endorse the Quality Control team's criticisms of St Sebastian's. Its lack of coherent procedure is a serious weakness. The Registry has failed to keep adequate records for a considerable period of time. There has been no systematic financial planning. Many degree courses have never been validated. The Senior Management team has no comprehension of standard good management practice and is out of touch with both the Council and Senate. The personnel department has no appreciation of staff needs and fails to provide adequate support . . . It's a disaster from first to last.'

'I've been saying all that for years,' Magnus commented. 'No one ever listened to me, but they'll have to do something now . . .'

I was surprised to find no mention of the previous Vice-Chancellor in the article. After all, the current crisis was largely his fault. 'Why didn't they say anything about Flanagan, d'you think?' I asked.

'Because he had the very good sense to jump ship before all his sins were uncovered. He was safely ensconced in the House of Lords by the time both the Quality Control inspectors and the Funding Council consultants started poking around.'

'It doesn't seem fair,' I said. 'Still, Felix was quite right. He said those consultants were like ferrets. It's clear nothing got past them.'

Magnus giggled. 'Sometimes there is a particular satisfaction in being right,' he said. 'I always knew St Sebastian's was a corrupt place. Look how they treated you! Look how they treated me, for that matter! It's nice to see them get their just desserts!'

I was suspicious. 'Look, is there something you're not telling me?' Magnus looked at me slyly over his spectacles. 'Did you have anything to do with leaking the report?'

'Me?' He was all innocence.

I tried to look stern. 'Come on, you'd better tell me . . .'

Magnus scattered crumbs over the carpet as he explained what had happened. 'I wanted to photocopy several pages from a Hebrew grammar for my class,' he said, 'but that wretched woman Jenny Sloth was hogging the photocopier. She was reproducing something confidential for Council and she told me very rudely that I'd have to come back later. So I, obedient and anxious to please as ever, went away. But when I returned twenty minutes later, I found that she'd left the original document still in the tray . . .'

He took a sip of his coffee and drew breath. 'Well, what would you do?' he asked. 'As soon as I saw that it was the consultants' draft report, the temptation was irresistible. Of course, I couldn't actually steal it . . . I'm a friend of the Provost of St Sebastian's cathedral and the padre at school taught us that theft is very wrong. But to use the photocopier to create my own personal copy was the work of a moment . . . and then I replaced the original where I found it in the tray. I got away just in time. As I turned the corner, I heard the silly woman come out of her room to go back to the machine. I'm sure she was very reassured to find it still there!'

'Well, you can imagine how thrilled I was when I read it. It was everything I've always been saying! Tremendous stuff from soup to nuts! Nobody knew what I'd done. I was completely safe. After I had relished every sentence, I wiped off all the fingerprints with my handkerchief, put it in a white envelope and dusted that off. I typed the address so no one would recognise my handwriting and I sent it off anonymously to the *Times Higher Ed*. . . . So here we are! Front page news! Rather explosive isn't it?'

'Really, Magnus. It wasn't very responsible. This is going to do the university a lot of damage. And after all, it's only a draft report. They may have nicer things to say in the final document when they make their recommendations.'

'Now come on Harry,' Magnus was unrepentant. 'I know you're a clergyman, but there's no need to be stuffy. In the first place, St Sebastian's deserves it. Sloth and that wife of his should have been put out to grass years ago. And secondly, you know as well as I do that if I hadn't leaked the report, someone else on the Council would have done so. It was only a matter of time . . .'

Later in the day I had a phone call from Penelope Ransome. She sounded desperate. 'Harry,' she said. 'There's a ghastly article in the *Times Higher Ed*. today. It quotes the Funding Council's draft report and says that the university management is incompetent and should be removed. Sloth summoned me to his office. He's certain that I sent it to the newspaper because we've been complaining to him about the redundancy committee. I told him I didn't know anything about it.'

'Are you on Council?' I asked. 'How does he think you got hold of the report?'

'He can't think! You know that! He suggested that someone who's on Council leaked it to me and then I contacted the journalists. It's completely untrue. I didn't even know the consultants had finished at the university and the article is the first I knew of the report.'

'I don't think you've anything to worry about,' I said. 'If you didn't leak the document, then there's no way he can prove that you did.'

'But he doesn't accept my word for it. He can get my username and password from the Computing department and he's going to read all my e-mails. He's on a fishing expedition and he insists that he has the right to do this.'

'Well obviously that's a disgrace. Your e-mails are private to you and your correspondents, but if you haven't spoken to journalists, there's still not a problem.'

Penelope's voice became increasingly shrill on the other end of the telephone. 'There is, Harry. I wasn't responsible for this leak, I promise you. And I have no idea who was. But as president of the local union, I've sent out confidential e-mails to members all year. And I've received confidential e-mails back. There's been lots of correspondence about Sloth and his awful wife. And now he can read everything.'

'Well,' I said, 'I can see that it's embarrassing, but being rude about one's employer is not an illegal act. Even if you said something positively libellous, you'll always have the defence of truth. So there's nothing he can do about it.'

'I don't trust him. He's a vindictive bastard.'

I was curious. 'Penelope, does he really have the right to do this? You haven't committed a crime. I shouldn't think you're a terrorist. I'd be surprised if you were part of a giant paedophiliac network. Can he really get into your e-mails just because he suspects you of speaking to a journalist?'

She sounded almost tearful. 'He says the article is putting the university into disrepute. That's gross misconduct and technically a sacking offence. I phoned Morris just after I left Sloth. He's preoccupied with a mediation case up in East Anglia, so I didn't feel he was really concentrating. But he did say that tapping my e-mails was an illegal violation of my human rights. As Acting Vice-Chancellor, Sloth is only justified in breaking into staff correspondence if there's a suspicion that they've acted illegally. Morris has contacted him informing him of this. But you know what he's like. It won't make any difference.'

156

I tried to be consoling. 'Sloth himself is in trouble after the Quality Control's investigation and now the Funding Council's report. If the article is accurate, he can't survive much longer. Someone will have to put him out of his misery. So I don't think you need be too concerned. He has other things to worry about.'

'But, Harry,' wailed Penelope, 'you've no idea what I wrote about him on my computer. Among other things, I described him as a bald moron. He won't like it! Really he won't!'

The following week, I had a telephone call from Morris O'Murphy. He insisted on seeing me urgently within the next few days. I had already committed myself to a talk-dinner at the Acropolis Club on the following Wednesday night. Through the winter and spring, various eminent members gave lectures on their specialist subjects and there was a communal dinner beforehand. The occasion was always pleasant and this time my old friend Charles, the Bishop of Bosworth, was to be in the hot seat. He was going to talk on 'Whither the Church of England?' I felt he would probably need all the support he could muster.

Since I was going up to London anyway, I arranged to catch an earlier train and I invited Morris to meet me for tea in the club. We arrived together at the Pall Mall entrance at four o'clock and I ushered him inside. This was not the first time I had entertained him at the Acropolis. Several years previously, when I was having my difficulties at St Sebastian's, we had had lunch together in the ground floor dining room. Then we had discussed how to save my job. This time we were going to talk about how to save the university.

Morris had made an effort to conform to the rules. At our previous lunch, he had been astonished to discover that the club insisted on a jacket and a tie. Since he had arrived without either, he had had to be kitted out with a selection of leftover garments by the porters. The result was most peculiar. Today there were no problems. He was wearing dark green corduroy trousers, a green tweed sports coat and a natty green and white polka-dot tie. 'Very elegant, Morris,' I said smiling.

'Like the boy scouts,' he said, 'you've got to be prepared for all eventualities in life!'

We went up the magnificent staircase. It was presided over by a vast portrait of George IV who had been the reigning monarch when the club was founded. As we entered the drawing room, we passed a group of three women, all wearing dog-collars. They were chattering merrily together. 'Did you see that?' Morris asked as we sat down. 'Are they allowed in here?'

'One of them has to be a member,' I said.

'But did you notice that they're all vicars?' He was fascinated.

'They're like the Vicar of Dibley on the television – only there are three of them! I thought this was a gentlemen's club . . .'

'It was, but recently the members decided to admit ladies as well. After all, Morris, even the Acropolis believes in equal opportunities nowadays!'

'Bugger me! I thought it was just a working men's club, only posh!' The waiter arrived to take our order. We asked for cups of tea and four toasted tea cakes. I thought Morris could probably eat three.

Almost before the attendant had left, he had reached into his inside pocket and pulled out a crumpled document. 'This is what I wanted to talk to you about,' he said.

'I hate to tell you this,' I said. 'But we can't look at any papers while we eat.'

'What?'

'It's a club regulation.'

Morris looked around the room. 'This place is a madhouse,' he said. 'You have to wear a jacket and a tie. You can't look at documents when you eat. They won't allow mobile telephones anywhere. The members fall asleep on the sofas. Some of them have probably been dead for a couple of days, but everyone is too polite to mention it. There are gaggles of lady-vicars nattering together and the place is haunted by a cat who takes the best chair.' He sighed and put the papers back in his pocket.

Looking around the beautiful room, which was decorated in the original 1830s colour-scheme, I could see what he meant. The scene was very much as he described it. I had not noticed the cat, but he was indeed asleep on a large padded sofa next to a bust of Spinoza. According to the annual report, the club employed him to keep the mice down in the kitchens and cellars.

Not surprisingly, he preferred the conviviality of upstairs. Some of the chairs were very comfortable.

Morris had positioned himself near the window overlooking Pall Mall. 'Look, Harry,' he said, 'I don't want to break any of the sacred club rules, but do you think you might be able to read the material I brought if you hid it behind a newspaper?'

'I'll look at it as soon as we've eaten our tea cakes,' I promised.

Morris rolled his eyes. 'Damn strangest place I've ever been in!' he pronounced.

Despite his complaints, Morris was enjoying himself. He drank three cups of tea and he commended the tea cakes. 'I like them swimming in butter,' he said. 'These are excellent!' I wondered if I should order another, but he was anxious to show me his document.

It turned out to be a further instalment of the paper Morris had shown me when he had stayed at the Provost's House. This time the barrister went further. It was entitled: 'Injunction against St Sebastian's University' and it ran to eight pages. There was no doubt that Sloth had seriously bungled the whole redundancy process. One university statute after another had been ignored or violated. On the final page the document concluded: 'It is clear that the university has carried out the redundancy process in breach of its statutes and has acted *ultra vires*.' The whole opinion was signed by one Solomon Shapiro QC, 12 Stone Chambers, Clements Inn.

It took me some time to unravel the impenetrable legal language and to understand the flow of the argument. Mr Shapiro was demonstrating that the university had acted against its own regulations and that therefore the whole process could be halted by an injunction in the High Court. Morris explained that the union was determined to follow this recommendation. This would prevent the Acting Vice-Chancellor continuing on his chosen path. 'The union's legal department has already approved taking out the injunction,' Morris said, 'and the Executive Committee has authorised it.'

'How much is all this going to cost?' I was familiar enough with the law to know that it was very expensive.

'At least forty thousand pounds. Maybe more. Initially, we'll seek an interim injunction. But then there has to be a hearing in the High Court. All the barristers have to be paid. These things don't come cheap.'

'And the union's prepared to spend that amount of money on St Sebastians?' I was amazed.

'We don't approve of compulsory redundancy when there are alternatives,' said Morris sanctimoniously. Then he laughed. 'Actually, we hope that in the end it won't be our money. It'll be the university's. They're in the wrong and that means they'll have to pay our costs. And this is just the beginning. If they're stupid enough to contest it in the High Court – and I wouldn't put anything past Sloth – the bill could run to hundreds of thousands of pounds.'

These sums of money made me nervous. 'Is the union certain it will win?' I asked.

'Well you can never be absolutely sure. Our lawyers are pretty positive. There's no doubt Sloth has made every mistake in the book, but there's no certainty in this business. Sometimes you can come up against a rogue judge . . . but the odds are very much in our favour.'

I felt out of my depth. 'Why are you telling me all this, Morris?'

'Because you're the university Visitor. It's hard to believe it when you think of the situation you were in a few years ago. But now you're a person of influence. We want you to tell Sloth not to challenge the action . . . or, better still, to draw back even before we go to the High Court.'

I took a deep breath. 'Morris, I don't think you understand. I'm the Visitor. That means I'm a sort of neutral *eminence grise*. I'm not even on the Council and this ultimately must be a Council decision . . .'

'Oh come on Harry,' Morris was impatient, 'you know as well as I do that the St Sebastian's Council has just been a rubber stamp for years. It got into the habit of doing whatever Flanagan told it. And it'll do the same for Sloth. That's why we need you to talk to him.'

It was an accurate assessment of the situation. I sighed. 'What exactly is going to be my task?' I asked.

Morris leaned forward in his seat. 'It's crazy, but the injunction will have to be served within the next few days. Sloth is determined to make at least ten people redundant even before the Funding Council consultants issue their final report. So we've got to get in there first. It's idiotic to sack people before the long-term plans for the university are known.'

I could see what he meant. It would be characteristic of Sloth to destroy the very departments which the Funding Council was in fact prepared to finance.

'St Sebastian's would also be mad to embark on a lengthy legal battle. But you know what Sloth is like. He never listens to reason. He won't even understand how much it's going to cost and if we try to tell him, he'll go to sleep.'

'I agree he's very obstinate . . .,' I began.

'I know,' Morris nodded. 'That's just the trouble. I'm sure he thinks that it doesn't matter if he gets into a complicated legal fight with the union. If he understands it at all, he's probably decided that if costs are awarded against St Sebastian's, the university can find the money by making a few more people redundant. The next thing you know, there'll be no academics left at all . . .'

I nodded. The scenario sounded all too probable.

'So we're counting on you, Harry,' Morris continued. 'You've got to pull him back from the brink before it's too late . . .'

I felt despondent. I could see that I was not going to have an easy couple of months. Morris, however, had cheered up. As we were talking, he had noticed that the waiters were uncovering the drinks table nearby. He looked longingly towards it. 'Harry,' he said, 'you don't think we could have a little something from over there. I don't want to be greedy, but I've had a hard day. And all those nuts and olives would be particularly tasty with a small glass of Scotch . . .'

CHAPTER NINE

Absolute Accuracy is Essential

Holy Week began in the first week of April. I was always glad to see Lent coming to an end. I do not have the temperament for penetential gloom – although I am well aware that there are plenty of things I should be gloomy and penetential about. Consequently, Palm Sunday always felt like the light at the end of the tunnel. To add to my relief, the Precentor had chosen a good mixture of traditional and modern hymns and anthems, all of which were appropriate to the festival.

It was a particularly busy time in the cathedral. In many ways St Sebastian's was old-fashioned. Not only did we go through all the offices, but we had the full three hour service on Good Friday with seven meditations on the Words from the Cross. There was also a splendid rendering of Bach's 'St Matthew's Passion' in the evening, performed by the local choral society with professional soloists. Altogether it was an exhausting twenty-four hours. On the Saturday we had a midnight Easter Vigil and, of course, there was the full programme of services on Easter Day itself.

Because I was preoccupied, I rather lost track of what was happening at the university. Normally, I would have had regular bulletins from Magnus, but he had gone to visit his Aunt Ursula in Norfolk. He was a little nervous about it as he was taking Miss Upton with him. The two ladies had got on very well together nearly forty years previously, but as Magnus observed, that was no guarantee of present harmony. However, as soon as the Easter Bank Holiday was over, we received a postcard from him. It showed a view of Norwich Cathedral. The message on the back was reassuring. Dorothy Upton and Ursula Hamilton still liked each other.

The classes on antiques began again the next week. This time, Victoria decided that the series would be about collecting old silver. It was a popular choice. The Secretary of the university Continuing Education department informed her that over a hundred people had registered. We realised it was going to be a tight squeeze in the drawing room. We asked the Clerk of Works to instruct his men to bring even more chairs than usual over from the cathedral.

The old people remained faithful. Matron herself professed an interest in the subject so it was she who drove the Priory party over in the minibus just before seven. The days were growing longer and it was still light when they all arrived. I had reserved a special parking place in front of the house, so that no one would have to walk too far. Even so, it was not easy to extract the residents with all their sticks and handbags. There were eight old people all together. As usual Sir William was accompanied by old Mrs Blenkensop, Mrs Germaney and Mrs Mackenzie. An unexpected and not altogether welcome addition was Pookie on a lead.

'He's a bit under the weather,' explained Mrs Mackenzie as I helped her out of the bus. 'I hope you don't mind. I didn't want to leave him by himself. He'll be a good boy . . .' Before I could find something civil to say in response, I noticed a ginger figure crouching nearby. Marmaduke had emerged from the undergrowth. He sounded like a kettle boiling over and it was clear that he was about to spring at the unfortunate poodle. With enormous presence of mind, Sir William, who was standing next to me, stepped forward and started hitting at the cat with his stick. Marmaduke was stopped in his tracks. He spat and he swore, but he realised that he was outmatched. Growling in fury, he turned tail. Trying to look dignified, he stalked away across the Green Court. I noticed that after about twenty yards, he broke into a run.

Mrs Mackenzie was all of a flutter. We took her and Pookie into the hall and sat her down on a chair. Mercifully, the little dog was untouched. He did not seem to be a particularly intelligent creature and had no appreciation that he had been in danger of his life. Mrs Mackenzie lifted him onto her knee and stroked his head. 'My poor Pookie,' she said. Pookie licked her hand.

Mrs Germaney was particularly outraged. She could not believe what had happened. 'It was an act of unprovoked aggression!' she kept saying. 'Who does that cat belong to? Surely not to you, Provost! Somebody ought to do something about him!'

I was able to reassure her that he was nothing to do with me. Our own two were safely tucked up on our bed. 'Marmaduke is rather a trial to us all,' I said.

Mrs Blenkensop did not shrink from hard facts. 'I'm afraid,' she said, 'it's my son's cat.'

Mrs Mackenzie continued to stroke Pookie fondly. 'He should be locked up, shouldn't he darling? What a nasty creature!' She consoled him.

Mrs Blenkensop did not disagree. 'Yes,' she said, 'he's a complete menace. I keep telling Reg he should be neutered.'

I was astonished. 'You mean to say he's never had the operation? He's still a tom cat?'

Old Mrs Blenkensop nodded. 'Oh yes,' she said. 'Reg doesn't approve of neutering animals. He thinks it's unnatural. My daughter-in-law's more sensible and she'd have had it done, but Reg likes things his own way. You've probably discovered that by now . . .' She glanced at me over Mrs Mackenzie's head.

'It's a disgrace!' pronounced Sir William. 'Even the RSPCA tells people to neuter their pets. What's the man thinking of? Someone should take control of the situation!'

'No wonder our two are so terrified of him,' I said.

Time was moving on and Matron took the lead. The lecture was scheduled to begin. She shepherded her charges up the stairs and they all settled down to enjoy Victoria's talk and slides. It must be said that Pookie behaved impeccably throughout.

I worked downstairs in my study while my wife did her piece. When I heard the audience making a move, I went to the front door to say goodbye. The little group from the Priory came down the stairs last. Victoria asked them if they would like a cup of tea before they left. 'It'll calm everyone's nerves,' she said.

Sir William seated himself between Mrs Blenkensop and Mrs Germaney on the large Victorian sofa; Matron and the other residents sat in armchairs in front of the fire. They had all had a good time and were full of praise for the session. After asking a few questions, they were soon engaged in a cosy discussion as to the best way to polish silver.

While this conversation was going on, Mrs Blenkensop who was seated near me apologised about Marmaduke. 'I'm sure he's terrible in the precincts,' she said. 'Reg won't hear a bad word about him, but I know he's a dreadful cat. I've heard rumours about his activites.'

It was hard to disagree with her. I tried to compromise by suggesting that he was very handsome. 'Handsome is as handsome does!' pronounced Mrs Blenkensop crisply. 'You know,' she continued, 'I've got to go in and feed him next month. Reg is at a college reunion in Oxford and Henrietta is seizing the opportunity to stay with her sister in Somerset while he's away.'

'Reg must have been quite a star when he was up at the university,' I said.

'You mean at games?' she asked. 'He's a nice boy, but he was certainly no great shakes intellectually. His sister was the clever one. I always had a struggle making him concentrate on his books.'

'Still the rugger . . .,' I said. 'It's really quite something to win a blue. I certainly was nowhere near it in any sport . . .'

Mrs Blenkensop looked surprised. 'He never won a blue . . .,' she said. 'My husband did. He was a wonderful sportsman. Reg was big and strong enough, but he lacked finesse. He was in the first team at school, of course, and he played for his college, but he never made it into the first university team. It was a disappointment to his father . . .'

'Well children must forge their own paths,' I remarked.

'That's what I always told my husband,' pronounced old Mrs Blenkensop.

After we had waved the Priory party off, I talked to Victoria about what I had learned. She shook her head. 'Poor Reg. He's never managed to escape from his father's expectations. Think about it . . . a sister who was brighter than he was and a dominating father who was satisfied with nothing less than outstanding sporting success. That's not much fun for a boy.'

'Old Mrs Blenkensop's nice,' I pointed out.

'Yes, she is,' Victoria agreed. 'She was very kind to Kev's mother after the trial. And there's no doubt that Reg is devoted to her. But he must have been very damaged by his father. It's sad that he has to pretend to his colleagues that he did better at Oxford than he did.'

'Why do you think he won't have Marmaduke neutered?' I asked.

Victoria shrugged. 'Who knows? No doubt the psychiatrists would say that he projects his uncertainies about his own masculinity onto that cat.'

I put on a Viennese accent. 'You mean it's all to do wiz zee muzzer.'

'Actually, in this particular case, I suspect it was zee fahzzer who was the problem,' retorted Victoria. 'Anyway I always said that cat was a bad influence.'

The more I thought about Reg Blenkensop, the sadder I found it. He had certainly always given the impression that he had played rugby for Oxford. And there was no doubt that this had contributed to his image as an athletic and powerful figure. I had always felt somehow physically inferior beside him. Yet his whole persona was built on sand. Clearly he was not as self-confident and impregnable as he seemed.

Later in the week, I had a chance to speak to him by himself. As I was walking into the town, I came across him chaining his bicycle to the railings. 'I saw your mother this week,' I said. 'She's a great friend of Victoria's father and she's coming to the lectures at the Provost's House. She said you'll be in Oxford next month.'

Blenkensop decided to be civil. He was excited about his trip. He told me that this was a five-yearly event. He was planning to meet up with all his old rugby friends for Sunday lunch the day after the college feast.

'That'll be fun,' I said. 'It must have been hard following in your father's footsteps. I understand he was a very brilliant rugger man. I always think it's difficult trying to live up to one's parents' expectations.'

Blenkensop flushed. For a moment we looked at each other. Something passed between us. He knew that I knew.

'You must excuse me, Provost,' he said abruptly. 'I've got an important appointment at eleven.' And without another word, he turned on his heel and strode off in the direction of the diocesan office.

The university was closed over the Easter period so I was not too worried about my commission from Morris. However, once things started up again, and particularly after Victoria's class, I knew I would have to bestir myself. Through his secretary, I tried to make an appointment to see Robert Sloth.

I told her that I had heard some disturbing rumours. Firstly, I was aware that the Funding Council consultants had not been altogether complimentary about the St Sebastian's administration. Secondly, that many of the partnership were likely to be dissolved and that this would have unfortunate financial implications. Thirdly, that I understood the Acting Vice-Chancellor intended to cover the projected shortfall by a programme of staff redundancies. As Visitor of the university, I felt it my duty to hear from Dr Sloth himself what was happening.

There was no response to my message. Clearly Sloth did not like my questions. Nothing daunted, I telephoned again two days later. This time I insisted on speaking to the great man himself.

I was kept waiting for several minutes and when he finally came on the line, he was less than forthcoming. He conceded that the consultants' draft report had been disappointing, but he insisted that the tone of the final document would be very different. He also admitted that there was a problem with Flanagan's partnerships and that 'minor adjustments' would have to be made to the budget. He was not, however, prepared to discuss future staffing arrangements. Initially, he pretended that the projected redundancies were merely gossip and had no foundation in fact. He was disconcerted to find that I already knew all about the establishment of the redundancy committee.

We fenced around these points for a good ten minutes. In the end I lost patience and pulled rank. 'Robert,' I said, 'It's my duty as Visitor to know what's happening in the university and it's your duty as Acting Vice-Chancellor to keep me informed. Consequently, I propose making a formal visit next Wednesday afternoon at two o'clock. I hope that will be agreeable to you. I have already checked with your secretary that you are free at that time.'

He had no defence. He did his best to put me off, but I cut through his excuses. I told him that I looked forward to seeing him and I rang off. Then I put the engagement in my diary.

However, two days before my appointment at the university, I received a distraught call from Penelope Ransome. She asked if I could see her immediately. As it happened, I had a free hour at two o'clock and I invited her over to the Provost's House.

When she arrived, she looked even more untidy than usual. She told me that she had just been to the doctor to renew a prescription. He had insisted on taking her blood-pressure and had been appalled at the result. Penelope was going to have to take a serious course of medication and what was needed was rest and relaxation. Given that the university had just delivered a bombshell, these remedies were unlikely to be available.

I sat her down in an armchair in front of the fire and went to make us both some coffee. When I returned, she was wiping her eyes and was clearly miserable. 'What is it?' I asked.

Silently she rummaged around in her shopping bag and brought out a document. It was a letter from the personnel department and it stated in the bluntest possible terms that she was one of the ten university employees who had been selected for redundancy. Her contract would terminate at the end of the month.

I read the missive. Then I took a handkerchief out of my pocket and handed it to her. 'This is ridiculous,' I said. 'Why have you been chosen?'

She reached into her bag and took out another typed leaflet entitled 'Criteria for Reduncancy'. 'It's all in here,' she said.

'Explain to me how it works.'

Penelope took a deep breath. 'As I told you, Sloth established a redundancy committee which is chaired by Jenny. Somehow they've decided on ten criteria to evaluate every member of staff.

Things like whether their area of expertise can be taught by anyone else, whether they attract post-graduate students, whether they have an international reputation and whether they contribute to the administration of the university.'

'So the whole thing is meant to be objective?' I suggested.

'Supposedly,' sniffed Penelope. 'It's the heads of department who have been told to rank each staff member. You get three points for excellent; two points for average; and one point for poor. Then they add up each person's points. Whoever is lowest is put at risk. Then all these people in the different departments are compared with one another, and those with the lowest scores of all get this horrible letter telling them they'll be sacked.'

Penelope tried to pull herself together. She blew her nose. 'Look at my assessment, Harry. I only got thirteen out of a possible thirty.'

'That can't be right,' I said. 'You work very hard for the university. Look at what you've done for the union.'

Penelope sounded bitter. 'That doesn't count. You get no points for the union at all . . .'

I was shocked. 'That's a disgrace! It's an important element in staff welfare. Anyway, even without it, I just don't believe your score. You publish a lot and I know you're a successful teacher. Your classes always attract lots of students.'

'I know. Thirteen is ridiculous. I teach as much as everyone else – more than some. I have six full-time doctoral students. My research is included in the Research Assessment Exercise and I'm the examinations' officer for my department. That's a big administrative job . . .'

'But surely your head of department knows all this.' I was bewildered.

'She does. But she refused to do the scoring. Almost all the departmental heads did. It's a matter of solidarity. They don't want to be responsible for getting their colleagues dismissed.'

'Good for them!' I said. 'But who did do the dreaded deed then?'

'Jenny Sloth, of course . . . who do you think?'

I felt that I was descending into the world of Alice in Wonderland. 'But she doesn't have any idea about your work. How does she know if you have an international reputation or not?'

'She doesn't . . . But somebody had to do it. And so, as chairman of the redundancy committee, she did. And she was determined to mark me down.'

'Are you certain about this?' I asked.

'Oh yes . . . I went to see her. She admitted it. She said that she had definite proof of my disloyalty towards the Acting Vice-Chancellor. Those were her very words . . .'

I was uncomprehending. 'What on earth did she mean?'

'I told you, Harry. Sloth's read all my e-mails. I know it's against my human rights and anyway no gentleman reads someone's private correspondence, but, as I've told you, he tapped into my computer. That's how he knows what I think of him . . . and that's why that cow gave me the score she did.'

'That's disgraceful,' I said. 'You must appeal . . .'

'There's no proper appeal mechanism. It's all happening so fast. I'm going to be out before anything can be done about it. And anyway, I'm not the only one.'

I was alarmed. 'What do you mean?'

'The Sloths hate me because of my e-mails and, as a result, I got almost the lowest score . . . but of the ten people being made redundant, eight either are or have been members of the union committee. Sloth sees this as his chance to destroy the opposition once and for all. He wants to abolish all union activity in the university.'

I had to admit this sounded all too probable. 'Just as a matter of academic interest, who were the other two?' I asked.

Penelope gave the ghost of a smile. 'One was someone in English. His head of department was prepared to participate in the exercise and, in this case, it's fair. The person selected has a serious drink problem. He hardly ever turns up to his classes; he's published no research for more than ten years and he refuses even to think about administration. In any case, it won't be much of a saving for the university; he's due to retire at the end of next year anyway.'

'And the other?' I persisted.

'Olive O'Shea,' answered Penelope. 'She actually scored a little higher than me though I honestly don't see how. She's hardly been into the place since she was appointed and she's certainly never published. She did turn up for a couple of days when she demanded a new room because the one she was allocated was too small. And she did agree to serve on the redundancy committee. Then she disappeared again. I believe she's with her husband in the United States at the moment.'

'Look Penelope,' I said. 'this conversation must be confidential. I'm going to see Sloth in a couple of days. He tried to pretend to me on the telephone that these redundancies were a groundless rumour, but now I know the facts, I'm going to confront him.'

'But what can you do?' Penelope was despairing.

'Well,' I insisted. 'There are two lines of attack. In the first place I am going to insist that the scores are revisited. It's clear that Mrs Sloth is not the person to do them. I'll request that Felix Glass goes through everyone's curriculum vitae and at least then it'll be done fairly. He's a nice man and he won't let his personal prejudices get in the way . . .'

Penelope agreed cautiously. 'That's true . . . but it doesn't solve the problem. If my score is raised, then someone else is going to be at the bottom. And then they'll be sacked. The whole thing's just as ghastly . . .'

'I said there was a second line of attack. Now you must keep this to yourself. He obviously hasn't told you, but I saw Morris for tea the other day. The national office of the union is taking this whole business very seriously. They've got a legal opinion from an expensive barrister who says that Sloth's not followed the correct redundancy procedures. As a result the whole exercise is invalid.'

'No need to go to a posh lawyer . . . I could have told you that for nothing.' Penelope blew her nose again.

'And if necessary the union is prepared to take out a legal injunction in the High Court to stop the university continuing with this course of action.'

'Wow!' Penelope was impressed.

'I know . . .,' I continued. 'Apparently an injunction costs about forty thousand pounds. But hopefully the union won't have to pay. The university is in the wrong and so costs will be awarded against it.'

Penelope found it difficult to get her mind round all this. 'You mean the union is prepared to risk forty thousand pounds to save our jobs?'

'That's what you pay your subscription for,' I pointed out.

'Wow!' said Penelope again.

'Anyway,' I continued. 'I'm going to tell Sloth about what's happening. I'll try to persuade him to delay any action until we know the Funding Council's plans for St Sebastian's. It's stupid to think of getting rid of staff until we know what subjects are going to be taught in the future.'

'So you're going to be the union ambassador?'

'Well . . . I'm going to try to persuade the Acting Vice-Chancellor to see sense, to save money and to try for once to act as a rational human being. That's the sort of thing a university Visitor is supposed to do.'

'From what I know of Sloth,' observed Penelope gloomily, 'he'll be completely bull-headed. St Sebastian's will end up having to pay for an injunction and Sloth will find the money by making even more staff redundant . . .'

As arranged, on Wednesday I set off for Sloth's office. I had to battle my way through a group of noisy French adolescents who were milling around the West Front of the cathedral. They were all eating ice cream and most of them had dropped their wrappers on the steps. I could detect no sign of a supervising adult. No doubt the teachers had gone to enjoy the shops and had left their charges to entertain each other. I watched as the young people shoved and jostled through the entrance of the great church. Perhaps, I thought to myself, there was something to be said for Blenkensop's insistence on admission charges.

When I arrived at the university, I had to wait outside Sloth's door. He was in the middle of a long telephone conversation. When it finally came to an end, he was flustered. 'That was my revered predecessor,' he said.

I was amused. 'Lord Flanagan of Fandonegal? What did he want?'

'Oh he's heard about our staffing rearrangements. He's not happy about one particular aspect. It's nothing important. I'll get Jenny to change it . . .'

I was curious. What could Flanagan be concerned about? He had made it fairly clear that he wanted nothing further to do with

St Sebastian's. Knowing his egoism, it must be something which concerned him personally . . . Then I got it.

'He's upset that Olive O'Shea is to be made redundant!'

Sloth blenched. 'Nothing's definitely been decided yet. And of course Lord Flanagan is quite right. I don't know how Jenny made such a mistake. Olive is immensely valuable to the university. We couldn't possibly let her go . . .'

I realised that I was going to have to tackle the matter head on. 'I'm sorry Robert, but you really must tell me the truth. Whatever you say, these redundancies have been formally decided and the letters of dismissal have already been sent out.'

Sloth could not deny it. I followed up my advantage. 'As Visitor I'm not happy with the way the exercise has been conducted. I know there's been a problem with the heads of departments. But with the best will in the world, Jenny can't be expected to know the full details of every lecturer's career . . . And I have to say that I have detected some very serious anomalies in her judgement.'

'Jenny has done an excellent job . . .,' began Sloth.

I cut across him. 'But you yourself admit she's made a mistake in the case of Lady Barridon. I think we do need to discuss the whole matter from first principles before everything blows up in our faces. After all, as you know, you can't be too careful when it comes to personnel matters.'

I thought Sloth would be furious, but to my surprise he looked rather relieved. 'Shall we have some coffee?' he asked.

I thought this an excellent idea so Sloth rose from behind his desk to ask his secretary to make it. When he came back, he sat down in an armchair and he gestured that I should sit on the sofa.

Then he took a deep breath. 'I'm glad you've come. I need to talk to somebody,' he said. 'It does seem to be more difficult than I thought. I've just received a letter from some expensive lawyer in London. The union is threatening to serve an injunction on the university. They say they're going to take us to the High Court to stop the redundancies.'

'Have you heard from the High Court itself?' I asked.

'No, not yet, but it's only a matter of time. They say we went wrong in some obscure element of the procedure and, as a result, they have the right to stop the whole thing.'

'That's the way employment law works,' I pointed out. 'You've got to get every last detail right. Otherwise the whole thing fails.'

Sloth tried to take a determined line. 'Well we're not going to put up with this. We're not going to give in to a few bolshie union agitators who have no idea about the real world . . .'

'If they're going to the High Court, it sounds to me as if they understand the real world all too well,' I remarked.

Sloth looked more agitated than I could ever remember. He strode over to his desk and rummaged through a large stack of papers. 'Where is it? I know it's here somewhere . . .'

'What are you looking for?' I asked.

'I got the accountant to estimate how much money we'd lose if the Funding Council shuts down the partnerships. It's well over three million . . . Where did I put it? I had it an hour ago.'

'Don't worry . . .' I tried to be reassuring.

'So you see we've got to make cuts. We've no alternative and it's the managers who have to decide where the cuts will fall. Not the unions. After all, managers have to manage . . .'

'So what will you do about the injunction?' I asked.

Sloth tried to sound resolute. 'What can I do?' he asked. 'I'm not going to take any notice of it!'

I shook my head. 'Robert, you've got to be realistic. You can't just ignore it. You'll be in contempt of court. Look, I should tell you about a conversation I had with Morris O'Murphy . . .'

'That Irish troublemaker! He's the one who's responsible for all this mess.' Sloth clenched his teeth. 'If it's the last thing I do, Harry, I'm going to drum out all his wretched union cronies from the campus once and for all . . . What did he say?'

'He approached me as the Visitor.'

'And he wants you to act on the union's behalf? I knew it. He'd resort to anything to get his own way.'

'No, actually,' I said. 'He didn't ask me to do anything. But when I heard what the union is planning, I thought someone ought to talk to you about it.'

Sloth suddenly looked tired. 'What do you want to say, Harry?'

'We both know that it won't do any good for the university to be served with an injunction. The publicity will be frightful and the cost will be enormous . . .'

He was startled. 'Cost? What do you mean cost?'

'Well, if there really is a hearing in the High Court, and it turns out that your procedure was less than perfect, you'll have to pay for their lawyers as well as your own. The final bill could run into hundred of thousands of pounds.'

'No! . . .'

'I'm afraid so. . .'

'Bastards!' he exclaimed.

I continued to try to be soothing. 'Really, Robert, it would be best to avoid it if at all possible. You admit you've definitely made one mistake with regard to Lady Barridon. You don't want to go through all this and end up being humiliated in public . . .'

'But what can I do?' he turned to me like a child.

'Why don't you just hold up the whole process? Of course there'll have to be cuts and of course you must manage them. No one denies that. But there's no need to do it now. Why don't you wait at least until the Funding Council's final report? Then you'll be able to see the way forward.'

'But what about the budget?' he wailed. 'It's supposed to be all sorted out by the end of this month.'

I felt I was gaining my point. 'These are very exceptional times. You've inherited a difficult situation. Why don't you just postpone everything? After all, the new Vice-Chancellor, when he or she is appointed, will want to have some say in the decision. Everything is in a state of flux. Just play for time. In my experience, nothing is very often the best thing to do.'

Suddenly Sloth relaxed in his seat. He looked as if he could go to sleep at any moment. 'That sounds a very sensible solution,' he said. 'Thank you for being so sympathetic, Harry. It always helps to talk things through . . .'

The next day, just after we finished breakfast, the telephone rang. It was Sir William. Victoria looked grave and was clearly upset. She kept saying, 'Oh dear!' and 'I'm so sorry to hear that!' and 'Are all the rest of you all right?' When she hung up, she came to talk to me in the study. 'Mrs Germaney died in her sleep last night,' she said.

I found the news hard to accept. 'But we only saw her the day before yesterday. She came to your class. She seemed fine.'

'Apparently,' Victoria said, 'She wasn't feeling her usual self yesterday. Daddy organised a Scrabble tournament after dinner, but she didn't want to play long and she went to bed early. Well, this morning one of the carers went in to wake her for breakfast, but she couldn't stir her. They called the doctor and he said she had died.'

'That is sad,' I said. 'She was a nice old lady.'

'Daddy's comment was "What a way to go!" and he's quite right. She was eighty-nine you know. Still Matron has asked if you could ring and make an appointment to go over to the Priory. They want you to do the funeral. I said that would be all right.'

'Of course,' I agreed. 'What are the arrangements?'

'Daddy wasn't sure. He rather thought it would be a cremation.'

'That's fine,' I said, and I took the telephone and rang up Matron.

The next day the two of us walked over to the Priory. Matron had arranged that the local undertaker would be present too. There was no family to consult and, beyond a cremation, which Mrs Germaney had paid for in advance, there were no special requests. Victoria went to have a little chat with the residents while we held our conference. I asked Matron what had happened.

'It wasn't entirely unexpected,' she said. 'She's had heart trouble for years.'

'And is there no family at all?' I persisted.

Matron shook her head. 'None that I know of. She told me once that neither she nor her husband had brothers or sisters and they had no children of their own. She certainly never had any visitors. According to our forms, a firm of solicitors is listed as her next of kin. They always paid all the bills for her board and lodging here.'

'Oh dear,' I said. 'It does sound sad.'

'I don't think so,' said Matron. 'She was a cheerful person. When she first lived here, her husband was still alive. They came in together. He died about five years ago.'

'Were they from St Sebastian's originally? Why are there no friends?'

'No. They lived in Manchester and they left their old life behind when they came here. He made a lot of money, I believe. He invented some new form of linoleum and it was very successful.'

'So why did they settle here?' I asked.

'Ah,' said Matron. 'Mrs Germaney told me all about it once. Her husband grew up in a village near St Sebastian's and, when he was a boy, he went to the Cathedral Choir School. After he grew up, of course, he was swept into the Second World War. He was that generation. He fought in the Far East and spent much of the war in a Japanese prisoner-of-war camp.'

'Oh no!' I said.

'Yes. Apparently it was every bit as bad as everyone says. When he came out he weighed about five stone. Anyway, what kept him alive through all the horrors was his memories of the St Sebastian's buildings. He went over and over them in his imagination while he was living the nightmare of building the Burmese railway. So when he retired and there was nothing to keep them in Manchester, he was determined to end his days here. After his experiences, he wasn't religious, but he spent a lot of time in the cathedral. I was always ordering a taxi for him.'

'And were they happy?' I asked.

Matron nodded. 'I hope so. He wasn't an easy man, but they were very fond of each other. I think it was a good time for both of them. Edith Germaney was a very sensible woman.'

The funeral arrangements turned out to be quite straightforward. The St Sebastian's Crematorium was just outside the city, beyond Arrowsmith College and the Law Courts. In the event, the only people present were two representatives from the Manchester factory, a dark-suited lawyer from London, Victoria, myself and a good-sized party from the Priory. It was enough. I think Mrs Germaney herself would have been happy about it.

By the end of April things had settled down. There was no more talk of redundancies at the university and the residents of the Priory were back to their usual routine. Even the cathedral seemed to be running smoothly. Then, on the last Sunday of the month, at Sung Eucharist, Canon Sinclair asked if he could see me after the service.

It was a beautiful spring day and the garden was just beginning to come into flower. We walked across the Green Court together towards the Provost's House, I moderating my steps to his. Standing on the doorstep, he admired the flower beds. 'I shall try to do some gardening in my retirement,' he said as we stepped into the hall.

We went into the study and I poured out sherry for both of us. Canon Sinclair took the glass with a shaky hand. 'Provost,' he said, 'I think the time has come for me to leave St Sebastian's. There's no doubt this Parkinsons thing is getting worse. I don't feel I'm as much use as I should be. The cathedral needs someone more able-bodied.'

I hated to hear him speak in this way. I knew he was devoted to his job and he was much loved by the congregation. 'But, Graham,' I said, 'you're a crucial figure in the Chapter. We can't do without you.'

The old man smiled sadly. 'It's kind of you to say that. I don't deny I shall miss it all very much, but I'm due to retire at the end of the year in any case. I'm not as well as I was and I think I ought to step down by the end of the month.'

I nodded. 'Well if you're really sure . . . We'd be more than happy to have you until December.'

'No, Harry. The time has come. I've talked it over with Jean. We must go.' He looked up at me. 'Do you know, I've been here on and off for more than sixty years?'

'No!' I said.

'Yes . . . I was a choirboy in the cathedral and I was educated in the city. I went away to Oxford of course, but I did my first curacy nearby. Then I was vicar of the parish church for many years before I became a residential canon.'

'And where will you live now?' I asked.

'Not too far away . . . When we inherited a little money, Jean and I bought a small cottage in the country, just outside the city. Over the years we've rented it out. The lease is just coming to an end and the tenants want to leave. So everything's come together. It will be just fine. Yes, just fine!'

'At the very least, I hope you'll continue to worship here,' I said.

Again Canon Sinclair smiled. 'We will indeed! But be assured,

Provost, I intend to take a back seat. No more sermons. And no more duties.' He looked out of the window and sighed. 'It's a pretty place. Full of memories. But there's a time for everything. And the time has come for me to go.'

I had no sooner said goodbye to Graham Sinclair when young Derek Trend appeared on the doorstep. He was someone I always felt vaguely uneasy about. He was polite, helpful, amenable and eager. Yet I had no sense of him as a person. I had no idea of his real views or feelings. I felt I did not know him at all. On this occasion he looked excited and asked if I could spare a minute to talk with him.

'I know you're about to have lunch, Provost,' he said. 'And I don't want to trespass on your time. It'll only take a moment. But I felt I had to see you.'

I led him into the study and asked if he would like a glass of sherry. 'No, really, I don't want to detain you,' he said. 'You see, I've just had a phone call from the Bishop of Morton. He has formally invited me to be his Archdeacon. I've known for a little time that it was a possibility. I come from that part of the world, you know, but I never thought I'd actually be chosen. Anyway, I said that of course I'd have to speak to you about it first.'

I smiled. He was so young and so nakedly ambitious. 'I see,' I said. 'And you want to go . . .'

He took a deep breath. 'Yes, Provost, I do rather. I'll miss St Sebastian's, of course. But there'll be more responsibility. A new challenge. I feel I'm being called to something important.'

'Then you must certainly accept the offer.' I said. 'When do they want you?'

'The Bishop didn't give an actual date, but I have the feeling it's as soon as possible. At any rate by the end of this month. The present Archdeacon has been ill for some time and I'm afraid the prognosis is not good.'

'Oh dear,' I said. 'Well, then it's decided. I'm very pleased for you, Derek. It's a marvellous opportunity and I know you'll do very well.'

Trend looked relieved as he left. With a jaunty step he crossed the Green Court. I stood looking after him. I wondered how far it was possible to reconcile being an ambitious cleric with being an honourable caring Christian. Victoria came out to join me. She had overheard the conversations.

'"So thick and fast they came at last,"' she quoted. 'You're getting rid of them very successfully, Harry. At the university, the Vice-Chancellor's left and Dean Pilkington's on long-term sick leave. And now you're going to be two canons down in the cathedral Chapter . . . Why don't you concentrate on gunning down Sloth and Blenkensop to complete the massacre?'

Victoria and I were due to have dinner with Magnus that evening. Dorothy Upton was staying for the weekend and he was anxious that we should get to know her. He insisted that he was cooking and we were both somewhat apprehensive about what he might serve.

At seven we arrived at his flat. Magnus greeted us at the door wearing his maroon smoking jacket and velvet hat. Dorothy was seated in a battered armchair in front of a low table piled with books and old newspapers. Pushkin was sprawled on her lap and I noticed she was wearing the brooch that Magnus had given her. We greeted each other as old friends while Magnus poured out retsina from a musty looking bottle. There was a peculiar smell of singeing coming from the kitchen and Magnus hurried back to his task.

Victoria immediately focussed on Dorothy's brooch. 'How lovely!' she said. 'It's Victorian . . . What does it spell out? Is it "DEAREST" or "REGARD"?'

Dorothy smiled smugly. 'It's neither. It's "DOROTHY"!' she said.

Victoria leaned forward. 'Let me see . . . oh yes . . . a diamond, an opal, a ruby, another opal, a topaz, a hessionite and a yellow sapphire. Isn't that fantastic? Where did you get it?'

Dorothy looked even smugger. 'Magnus gave it to me!' she said.

Victoria glanced in my direction. 'That's just the kind of thing I'd like, Harry. Is there a precious stone that begins with a "V"?'

Dorothy did not even pause for thought. 'Yes . . . a Vulcanite. Then it'd be Iolite, Chrysoberyl, Topaz, Opal, Ruby, Iolite and Amethyst.'

'Good heavens!' I said.

Dorothy looked apologetic. 'I do crosswords. You pick up all sorts of useless information there.' I noticed that there were two copies of *The Times* on the coffee table. Both were open at the crossword and both grids were completely filled in, but in different hands. I wondered who had done it faster.

'I see you like cats,' I observed.

Dorothy tickled Pushkin under his tabby chin. He stretched himself ostentatiously. 'This one's very handsome,' she said, 'but he's not quite as good-looking as my Hezekiah at home. He's a blue Persian.'

'How lovely!' said Victoria. 'We have two Siamese. Has Hezekiah ever met Pushkin?'

Dorothy shook her head. 'I don't think we should try the experiment. On one occasion I had to have my sister's cat for the weekend. I'm afraid Hezekiah was not very welcoming. It took the visitor several months to recover from the trauma of the experience.' Victoria and I both laughed.

'Dinner's ready,' Magnus called from the kitchen. The three of us sat at a small round table and Magnus served out the food. First there were stuffed dolmades which came from the local delicatessen. This was followed by rather a good lamb stew. 'I got the recipe last time I was in Turkey,' he said. There was also a large mixed salad to go with it. The third course was Greek goats' cheese. Then we had Turkish coffee. This was accompanied by almond biscuits drenched in icing sugar. They were delicious and had been a present from Dorothy.

'There's a good Greek shop in Brambletye,' she informed us. 'I remembered that Magnus liked sweet things.'

Dorothy was delightful. The dimples were much in evidence as she told us how she had first met Magnus. 'You see, in those days, there was no one in my college who was a specialist in Aramaic,' she explained. 'So they farmed me out to Magnus. He was finishing his PhD and he was meant to give me tutorials. He had to check all my exercises, but the problem was he kept making mistakes.'

'You do exaggerate . . .,' said Magnus.

'No I don't!' insisted Dorothy. 'Absolute accuracy is essential in Aramaic . . .'

'I'm afraid she's right . . .,' agreed Magnus.

'And in those days, you have to admit you were a bit sloppy.'

'But I was younger then,' Magnus smiled, 'I didn't know any better.'

Dorothy looked at him fondly. 'I will concede that there has been considerable improvement,' she said crisply.

CHAPTER TEN

All Air and No Substance

As Victoria had observed, the cathedral would soon be very short-staffed. Both Derek Trend and Graham Sinclair would have left us by the end of the month. I too was only supposed to be a stop-gap appointment. I let the remaining members of the Chapter know that I would be willing to take my share of weekly duties until at least one new Canon was appointed and I wrote a desperate letter to the Archbishop. We needed more help.

One Friday morning in early May, I was sitting in my study writing my sermon for Sunday Matins. It was the weekend that Reg was to be away at his Oxford reunion and I saw the Blenkensop car leave the precincts. I am ashamed to say that I felt a certain lightness of heart. For at least three days I would not have to cope with his sullen unfriendliness. Cleo and Brutus were waiting at the front door for the letters to arrive. For some reason the process fascinated them. Then I heard various items drop through the post box and a few minutes later I went to retrieve them.

Victoria had got there first. She was sitting in the kitchen with the cats, giggling at a missive in Sir William's handwriting.

'Why's your father sending you letters all of a sudden?' I asked.

'It's a secret,' said my wife.

'A secret?' I was immediately curious. 'What kind of secret? It's not my birthday yet . . .'

'Daddy said it should only be revealed on a "need to know" basis.'

'Well I'm sure I need to know. You certainly seem to find it funny . . .'

Victoria chuckled. 'Oh all right,' she said. 'You'll find out soon enough, but you're not to stop us . . . You must promise . . .' and she handed over the piece of paper.

The letter was neatly written:

'CONFIDENTIAL: FRIDAY'S CAMPAIGN
attn. VICTORIA GILBERT
Equipment to be assembled:
  i Car in good working order, filled with petrol and ready for a quick getaway.
  ii Large heavy object suitable for blocking cat-flap.
  iii Cat basket with strong fastenings in scullery.
  iv First Aid kit.

14.00: Mrs B. arrives at Provost's House. She is at present caretaking her son's house in the precincts. She should be shown into the study.

14:10: Taxi containing W.D., Bess, Steve and Kev draws up at Provost's House.

14.12: Kev and Steve positioned in scullery with door closed. Unlock cat-flap and stand holding heavy object.

14.15: W.D., from vantage of front door, locates Target and releases Bess.

14.20: Target rounded up by Bess and driven through cat-flap into scullery.

14.25. Kev and Steve place heavy object in front of cat-flap to prevent Target's escape.

14.27: Target captured and imprisoned by Kev and Steve in cat basket. Basket to be securely fastened.

14.30: Kev Steve, and Bess return by foot to the Priory. Mrs
    B., W.D., and Target driven to vet by V.G.
14:45: Appointment at vet (already booked).
16.00: V.G. drives Target and Mrs B. to Blenkensops' house
    and W.D. back to the Priory.
    N.B. Taxi has already been ordered. Kev and Steve will
bring their own heavy gardening gloves.'

I read this missive with a degree of suspicion. 'What's all this
about? Presumably W.D. is your father and V.G. is you. I
suppose Mrs B. is old Mrs Blenkensop. Who's the target? What
are you all planning?'

'It's nothing to do with you, Harry. Don't worry about it!'

Then, of course, I saw it. 'You're going to castrate
Marmaduke!' I said.

Victoria giggled. 'I'm certainly not! You can be sure of that.
No, the vet is . . .'

'But you can't just kidnap him and take him off without a by-
your-leave. He's not your cat!' I was horrified.

'No. But the Blenkensops are away for the weekend and old
Mrs Blenkensop is his official guardian in their absence. Come
on, Harry. That cat is a menace . . . The greatest good for the
greatest number, remember . . .'

'But Reg will have a fit . . .' I was staggered by the boldness of
the enterprise. 'He'll never speak to me again.'

'Well he doesn't say very much now,' pointed out Victoria.
'And anyway it's nothing to do with you. This is old Mrs
Blenkensop's decision. She's a game old bird. She knows what
has to be done and she's enlisted Daddy's help. It's rather a good
plan, don't you think?'

'I don't think this is right,' I said.

'Really, Harry,' argued my wife, 'I don't understand your
ethical position. I thought you believed in the greatest good for
the greatest number. Marmaduke will turn out to be a civilised
creature. All the wildlife in the precincts will be happier.
That includes the Precentor's Otto and our Cleo and Brutus, as
well as countless mice, birds and squirrels. The wailing and
caterwauling which disturbs everyone at night will stop and even
the RSPCA say it's the kindest thing to do. So it's for everyone's

benefit. Now what have you got to set against all that happiness? The possible wrath of Reg Blenkensop. It's obvious that, according to your utilitarian criteria, we're doing the right thing.'

Despite many years' work on the subject, there were times when my faith in my own ethical position was shaken. 'You can't just capture strange cats and haul them off to the vet whenever you feel like it . . .' I said feebly.

'In the first place,' insisted Victoria, 'He's not a strange cat. We all know him and he's a shocker. Secondly, old Mrs Blenkensop is *in loco parentis* and will sign the proper consent form. No vet would do the operation without that.'

I realised I was defeated. 'What are you going to use for the heavy object to block the scullery cat-flap?' I asked.

Victoria laughed. 'I always knew Magnus's fertility goddess would come in useful,' she said.

At two o'clock precisely, old Mrs Blenkensop knocked at our front door. I took her into the study and sat her in an armchair in front of the window. She had an excellent view of the Green Court and had the air of a woman who intended to enjoy herself.

Ten minutes later a taxi drew up. My father-in-law, Steve, Kev and Bess emerged from the depths. I noticed that both boys were wearing thick leather gardening gloves. From my own dealings with Marmaduke, I felt this was a sensible precaution. Victoria ran out to greet them all. She kissed her father, patted Bess and led the two young gardeners through the hall into the scullery. I followed behind.

The two lads were astonished by Magnus's idol. They had never seen anything like it before. They were not sure whether they should be embarrassed or admiring. In any event it was exactly the right size for the purpose. Victoria unlocked the cat-flap and gave Kev the statue to hold.

'You'll see a ginger cat run up the path and into the house from here,' she pointed to the window over the sink. Then she made sure that there were no avenues of escape. She showed them the cat basket and demonstrated how it fastened and finally she presented Steve with the First Aid kit. 'In the event of emergencies!' she said. I wished them both good luck. Then we left them to their vigil, carefully closing the door behind us.

By the time we joined Mrs Blenkensop in the study, the action was well under way. Marmaduke was scratching himself in the middle of the Green Court. Then he started stalking a sparrow who was pecking at a worm about thirty feet away. Sir William, standing by the front door, blew a sharp blast on a silver whistle. Bess, who had dropped down by his feet, was off.

She shot out in the direction of the cat. Marmaduke, who looked up as Bess charged, realised that this was perhaps not the best day for hunting. He ran as I had never seen him run before, but it was not for nothing that Bess had spent her working life rounding up errant sheep. There was no escape. Directed by Sir William's whistle, they did a lap round the Green Court. Then the pair of them shot into our front garden. Somehow Bess had got him at exactly the right angle for the scullery door. He caught sight of the cat-flap and saw it as his salvation. There was a huge clatter as he hurled himself through into the scullery. Sir William immediately called Bess to heel, put her on her lead and the two of them went to join Mrs Blenkensop in the study.

From outside the scullery door, we could hear some terrific spitting and the sound of chairs crashing over. Then there was a long heart-broken wail and the click of a cat-basket being closed. Victoria and I gave the boys a couple of minutes to fasten it before we knocked.

'Is the prisoner secured?' asked Victoria.

'Yeah!' came Kev's voice. 'E's quite a fighter, ain't 'e?' We both went in to see what was going on. There were no casualties. The boys were looking admiringly at their handiwork. Marmaduke was shut in the basket and was bellowing that his feline rights were being infringed. I had some sympathy with his position. Victoria congratulated the two young lieutenants and I went to fetch their commanding officer.

Sir William was immensely pleased with his troops. 'Good work, lads! Well done!' he said and he led the procession out to the car. With many commendations, the young gardeners and Bess were sent back to the Priory. Old Mrs Blenkensop was levered into the front of the volvo. Sir William took possession of the back and Marmaduke was consigned to the boot.

'I told that judge fella that Kev is a useful young man! Damned good show!' were Sir William's last words as the car turned into the Green Court. As they left, I looked at my watch. It was half-past two precisely.

When Victoria arrived home, she was full of triumph. 'Didn't it go well!' she said. 'Everything was like clockwork. The cat's fine. Mrs Blenkensop signed the consent form on behalf of her son. There was no trouble. The operation went without a hitch. Apparently Marmaduke's got to be on a light diet for the next few days. That'll be a shock to his system. When it was all over, I delivered him and Mrs Blenkensop back to the Blenkensops' house and I had to take Daddy back to the Priory. He's cock-a-hoop! Really, he's very good at strategy. I always said he should have been a General!'

'I can't imagine what Reg will say!' I responded.

Blenkensop was to return from Oxford late on Sunday afternoon. I was fearful that he would immediately storm round to the house and berate us for our part in the emasculation. Indeed, I rather expected that he would threaten legal action. However, the precincts remained quiet throughout the evening. There was not even a telephone call. I rose early next morning. I thought there might be a poisonous letter on the door-mat. There was nothing. Monday morning proceeded as usual and my first glimpse of the Canon was at Evensong.

He was a little late and as soon as he had robed, it was time to process into the cathedral. Afterwards, he was delayed by one of the vergers. I deliberately lingered in the vestry. I thought it better to give him the chance to vent his fury. I did not feel it was healthy for him to bottle it up. Yet, in the event, nothing happened. He mumbled something about his stay in Oxford, divested himself of his surplice and disappeared.

When I arrived home, Victoria was in high spirits. She had just bumped into Reg's wife near the Monks' Gate. Henrietta had been very reassuring and had expressed the opinion that Marmaduke should have been neutered years ago. She was thankful it had been done. Victoria had been bold enough to describe her father's campaign. Mrs Blenkensop had laughed immoderately and had said that she wished that she had seen it. They had parted with expressions of mutual esteem. 'So you see utilitarianism is right, after all!' concluded Victoria.

The next day I received a surprising e-mail from the Chief Executive of the University Funding Council. It was marked Urgent and Confidential and was addressed to me as 'The Very Reverend Professor Harry Gilbert, Visitor of St Sebastian's University.' It read as follows:

Dear Professor Gilbert,

I am writing to you as the Visitor of St Sebastian's University. As you will be aware, the Funding Council has recently commissoned its consultants to investigate the university's practices and procedures. The university has already been issued with a draft report which gives a general outline of the findings. However, it did not include the recommendations for future development.

We have now received the final version. It would be very helpful indeed if we could have a private discussion about the situation. I know you must be busy, but I would be very grateful if you could arrange a mutually convenient appointment. Our Chief Accountant will also be present.

Yours sincerely,

Roy Greengrass
(Sir Roy Greengrass, Chief Executive Officer,
UK Funding Council for Higher Education)

Since I was due to go to London for a meeting of the Church of England Consultancy Committee on Medical Ethics on Friday, I asked my secretary to arrange the meeting for that afternoon. It was a sunny summer day when I took the train from St Sebastian's and arrived in London within the hour.

The committee meeting took place in Church House in Westminster. Afterwards, I crossed the river to go to the Funding Council's headquarters on the South Bank. The offices were on the twelfth and thirteenth floors of a tall plate-glass building overlooking the Thames. I took the glass lift and much enjoyed the view.

Seated in the reception area and managing the switchboard was an efficient Indian lady in a sari. She asked me to take a seat. I leafed through brochures about the work of the Funding

189

Council while I waited to be summoned. Several minutes later, Sir Roy emerged. Over six feet tall and stout with it, he was wearing a grey pin-striped suit and had a military moustache. 'Thank you for coming, Provost,' he said. 'It's very good of you to give us your time.'

I was then led into a large office with another superb waterside vista. Already seated at a round table was a diminutive woman wearing a red tight-fitting dress. She was introduced as Mrs Morganstern. Although she looked about eighteen, she turned out to be the Chief Accountant. Coffee was available and she poured it out for all three of us. I noticed that her fingernails exactly matched the colour of her dress.

Sir Roy then handed me the consultants' final report. It was over sixty pages long. 'Now, Provost,' he began, 'this is a copy for you to read at your leisure. As you can see it is extensive. After the report of the Quality Control Agency, we felt that St Sebastian's needed a full review.'

'I see,' I said. The report looked dauntingly dense.

'I regret to say,' continued Sir Roy, 'the consultants found much to deplore. Their conclusions can only be described as damning. Consequently, we at the Funding Council are very concerned about the future of the university. This is why I asked for this meeting.'

I remembered my conversations with Felix and Magnus. This was exactly what they had predicted. I had the unworthy thought that if only John Pilkington had chosen more commonplace names for his imaginary examiners, the university would not be in this predicament. Reluctantly, I turned back to the matter in hand.

'But I'm just the Visitor,' I said. 'I have no real power in the institution. I'm not even on Council.'

Sir Roy surveyed me coolly. 'Yes indeed. We're aware of that. But this is precisely why we wished to consult you. As Visitor, you're now in a relatively independent position – although as an emeritus professor, you are more familiar with St Sebastian's foibles than most.'

I felt this was not the moment to mention that I had left my Chair under a cloud and had never been honoured with an emeritus title. Sir Roy was still speaking. 'We're also aware that you never served under Lord Flanagan of Fandonegal. We do accept that many of the present difficulties stem from that particular regime. Nonetheless, the combination of your familiarity with the university, your independence as Visitor and your position as Provost make you the ideal person to act as mediator.'

Mrs Morgenstern fidgetted during Sir Roy's speech. She seemed to have little patience with his convoluted turn of phrase. He was not to be silenced. 'Now, Provost, you will know that the Funding Council is not in a position simply to take charge. This must be the responsiblity of St Sebastian's own Council. Otherwise the independence of Britain's universities would be meaningless. However, we do have the power to withhold funding altogether. I have to tell you that we cannot see our way clear to financing the university in its present state with its existing managers. There must be a major transformation if the institution is to continue at all.'

'I see,' I said again.

Sir Roy had not finished. I was increasingly feeling that I had not been invited to the meeting to give my opinion. I was there to act as an audience. 'In our draft report,' he explained, 'our consultants indicated that the partnerships established by your previous Vice-Chancellor will need to be curtailed. There's no justification for British taxpayers' money being used to finance students at foreign academies and seminaries.'

I nodded. 'I didn't understand how Flanagan got away with it,' I said.

For the first time in our acquaintance, Sir Roy's composure was disturbed. 'Unfortunately, he was appointed during an interregnum at the Funding Council. I only came on board at the end of last year and I'm afraid my two predecessors were, although admirable in many ways, less than thorough in some of their systems . . . It took me a little time to establish a more vigilant approach.'

'Of course,' I reassured him.

'Anyway,' Sir Roy resumed his old tone, 'the same applies to many of the university degree programmes. We really cannot continue to finance such subjects as Brewing Technology, Professional Golf and Celebrity Studies. However, if they are to be wound down – and in our opinion, they must be wound down

– this will bring about a serious loss of revenue. Of course, we will fulfil our obligation to all current students. But no more can be admitted so the funding will only last for three more years.'

I tried to conceal my impatience. I wondered if my host would ever reach the point. I had already finished my coffee and I thought longingly of the train back to the Provost's House. Then at last the purpose of the meeting became clear. Mrs Morganstern handed me a document entitled: *St Sebastian's University/Arrowsmith College: Proposals for Reconfiguration.*

Sir Roy barely paused for breath. 'This,' he said, 'is the blueprint for the reconfiguration of St Sebastian's University which the Chief Accountant has formulated.' He looked admiringly at his colleague. She was indeed something to look at. 'It is, we believe, the only way forward. As you will see, it's a proposal for the merger of the university with Arrowsmith Teacher Training College. I expect you're familiar with the college . . .'

I nodded. I had certainly driven past it often enough.

Sir Roy was still speaking. 'As I am sure you know, Arrowsmith is exceptionally well managed. Its current Principal, Dr Merlin Meddles, is a man of considerable ability. The college itself achieved the Full Confidence of the Quality Control Agency at its inspection eighteen months ago . . . Unlike the university . . .' The words hung unspoken in the air between us and Sir Roy smiled faintly. '. . . its programmes are well-regarded and its recruitment is healthy. The college is very anxious to achieve university status and an amalgamation would enable it to do so.'

'I see,' I said for the third time.

Mrs Morganstern passed around a plate of custard creams. Behind Sir Roy's back, she winked at me and raised her eyes to heaven. Meanwhile my host took three biscuits. I thought about my waistline and with admirable self-control shook my head. Sir Roy continued regardless. 'The reason we've asked you to join us is because we're going to need your help. We anticipate considerable resistance to these plans from the university employees. People are over-concerned about matters of status, don't you agree?'

'"The last shall be first and the first last,"' I quoted.

He cut across my response. 'As an independent party,' he pronounced, 'we're looking to you to smooth the transition . . . iron out any difficulties so to speak.'

At long last Mrs Morgenstern intervened. 'You should know, Provost, that there's considerable funding for reconfiguration. This is an obvious merger. There will be no need for compulsory redundancies. Over the next three years, there'll be some natural wastage. In addition, we'll put in place generous voluntary severance and early retirement packages. It will work out very well . . .'

Sir Roy was not to be silenced. 'Now there's also the question of the senior management. As I've already indicated, Dr Meddles is an excellent Principal while the university is at present without a Vice-Chancellor. Arrowsmith also has a first-rate Registrar and Dean. In contrast, the university's present Dean is on long-term sick leave and the Registrar is of an age that he could retire with dignity. In both cases, the Funding Council is prepared to offer a suitable severance package. But your help in this matter would be invaluable . . .'

I concealed a smile. 'I'll do what I can,' I said.

'Very good,' said Sir Roy as he helped himself to another biscuit. 'I knew we could rely on you. It really is the only possible solution to the problem. Once you read the report, I'm confident you'll agree.'

He stood up and shook my hand. 'It's been so good to hear your views,' he declared as he guided me towards the lift. I smiled at Mrs Morganstern over my shoulder and I left without another word.

I heard nothing more from Sir Roy and the Funding Council. The final report was not due to reach the university until the beginning of June and I felt no need to enlighten anyone. I had read my copy on the train. When I arrived home, I had locked it in our bedroom safe, together with the cameo necklace Victoria had inherited from her grandmother. In the meantime there was a respite. Sloth had drawn back from the plans for compulsory redundancy. The budget was in abeyance. The university students were busy with their assessment essays and everything was in a state of suspended animation.

I had also had not spoken with Reg Blenkensop. We saw each other at services, but he was very quiet. Somehow, there never seemed to be the opportunity for a proper talk. There was no sign of Marmaduke either. The squirrels were becoming quite bold on the Green Court and I noticed a considerable increase in bird-life. The weather was beautiful and, for the first time, Cleo and Brutus wanted to go out. We unlocked the cat-flap and they put their noses through it and sniffed the air. To our delight, they both hopped out and had a little stroll around the front garden.

Then one tea-time as I was returning home on foot, I came across the ginger menace. He was sunning himself on a low wall near the Monks' Gate. He looked so relaxed and pleasant that I was tempted to put out my hand for him to sniff. 'Good afternoon,' I said.

Marmaduke stretched himself luxuriously and rubbed his head against my hand. I was astonished. I sat on the wall beside him and stroked his head. He purred his appreciation and showed signs of wanting to come and climb onto my lap. I was already late and could not stop for an extended session. I tickled him behind the ears, paid him several compliments and took my leave. He elongated himself out again in the sunlight and went back to sleep.

When I arrived home, Mrs Thomas was dusting the hall. Since she also 'did' for the Blenkensops, I felt I could ask her a question. 'Is Marmaduke more friendly than he used to be, Mrs Thomas?'

'Oh yes, Provost,' she said. 'A different cat he is since he came back from the vet. Mrs Blenkensop told me what your father-in-law did. A good chat we had together while Marmaduke was sitting on her knee! I told Evan about it when I went home. He laughed fit to bust . . .'

Clearly things had changed in the Blenkensop household.

The regular Chapter meeting was scheduled for the next morning. I dreaded it. The admission charge issue could no longer be put off. A decision would have to be made. At eleven o'clock we all assembled in the library of the Chapter House. It was the last meeting for both Graham Sinclair and Derek Trend, so I had brought along a bottle of champagne. I had also prepared a little speech of farewell. In addition, there was to be a visitor. Earlier in the week, the Provincial Registrar had telephoned to ask if he could be present since there was a particular matter he wished to communicate to the Chapter.

We took our usual places around the mahogany table as the long case clock struck the hour. I briefly welcomed the Registrar. He was a jovial rotund figure dressed in a dark grey suit with a crimson and gold tie. He was responsible for all the cathedral's legal work and I had always found him helpful and professional.

'Gentlemen,' he began, 'I have some important news for you all.' He produced a file from his briefcase and placed it on the table. 'This past week,' he said, 'I received a letter from the London firm of James, Lee and James. Mr Griffith-James, the senior partner, who is a great-grandson of one of the founders of the firm, has for many years acted for the late Mr and Mrs Gerald Germaney, sometime residents of this city.'

'Was that the Mrs Germaney who lived at the Priory and who died recently? I asked.

'It was indeed!' The Registrar turned to me. 'I understand you officiated at her funeral. Mr Griffith-James was also present at the crematorium on that occasion.' He cleared his throat. 'There were no relatives and, according to her and her husband's will, the entire estate has been left to the cathedral. I have to say we are talking about a very considerable sum. A very substantial legacy indeed.'

I felt I had to say something. 'That was a most generous gesture. The Matron of the Priory mentioned that she was well-off, but I had no idea that she intended to leave any of it to St Sebastian's Cathedral.'

The Registrar had not finished. 'Before you become too excited, it is my duty to point out that there are some restrictions on the bequest. The money cannot just be deposited in general funds. The principle, and the interest which derives from it, may be spent only on the fabric of the existing buildings. Mr Germaney was apparently anxious that they should be maintained and restored to the very highest standard.'

We looked at each other. We were all thinking about the damp problem in the crypt. I felt I had to grasp the nettle. 'How much are we actually talking about?' I asked.

Putting on a pair of gold-rimmed spectacles, the Registrar

rummaged through the file and took out a thick document with a series of graphs. 'As you will understand, gentlemen, the valuation of the estate varies from day to day so I can only give you a very general figure. Last Friday the grand total stood at eighteen million, seven hundred and sixty three thousand, four hundred and twenty-two pounds and eighteen pence.'

Reg Blenkensop opened his mouth and closed it. Derek Trend quickly made calculations on the back of an envelope. 'Golly!' I said.

'Golly, indeed,' said the Registrar. 'As I said, it is a considerable legacy, but I am sure, with this historic and beautiful building, there is plenty you will find to spend it on.'

He had produced his sensation and it was time for him to go. He packed up his file again in his document case. Assuring us of his best attention at all times, he left us to ourselves.

Canon Sinclair was the first to understand the implications. 'As you all know,' he said, 'I shall be leaving very soon. But my heart will always be in the cathedral. That is the best news I could hear. There is now no reason to levy an entrance fee from those who wish to visit our glorious church. It can remain freely open to all.'

I looked at Blenkensop out of the corner of my eye. He had been very determined to impose charges. I wondered if he was going to be obstinate. To my surprise, there was no bluster. Gravely, he nodded his agreement. 'In the past, I've made no secret of my conviction that entrance fees were necessary if these splendid buildings were to be maintained,' he said. 'Recently in this beautiful sunny weather, when I've seen the tourists enjoying our glorious precincts, I've been beginning to have doubts. In this commercial world, some things should always be free. But until this afternoon, I could not see how it was to be afforded. There is such a pressing need for expensive repairs. But now the way has become clear. With this generous legacy, we're free to continue in the old way . . .'

He was indeed an altered Blenkensop . . . .

'I've done some calculations,' volunteered Derek Trend. 'Such a sizeable sum would give ample scope for a bold investment programme. I'm leaving too, but I think I may be able to offer some advice in this area. My first degree was in business studies and I had two years experience in a city bank . . .'

'Thank you, Derek,' I said, 'Of course we must give serious thought as to how the money should best be invested. But in the first instance, perhaps we should rely on the guidance of the Registrar and Mr Griffith-James of James, Lee and James.'

Then I took control of the meeting. "I think you may wish to know," I said, 'that Mrs Germaney lived to a good old age and she died peacefully in her sleep. For personal reasons, her husband was devoted to the precincts. He had been a pupil in the Choir School and had suffered greatly as a Japanese prisoner-of-war. Their passing is, of course, a sadness, but their legacy will ensure the continued beauty of St Sebastian's Cathedral. We are much in Gerald and Edith Germaney's debt.'

The Canons all nodded their agreement and we passed on to the remaining business of the day.

That evening, Victoria and I had arranged to go with Magnus to the opera. It was the same company that had performed *La Bohème*, but this time it was to be *Don Giovanni*. Magnus had invited Dorothy to join us and she had arrived in the afternoon by train. Since it was a gala performance, we were all expected to dress up. Dorothy looked very striking in a mauve silk dress with her brooch and a string of baroque pearls. Victoria was in dark green and wore her cameo necklace.

We met for a preliminary drink in the White Hart Hotel. Magnus was in a hilarious mood. 'Dorothy has a new MA student,' he announced. 'You may have come across her.'

'Who is it?' I asked. 'Someone famous?'

'A Miss Julia Patterson,' he said slyly. 'Does it ring a bell?'

'I don't think so,' I said. 'Should it?'

Dorothy smiled. 'When she applied, her name seemed familiar. I thought perhaps she had been in the newspapers recently. So I did a little private search of my own . . .'

'And she found out that Julia Patterson is one and the same as the notorious Miss Strict!' announced Magnus. 'The one who got your predecessor into such hot water. You owe her your job . . . you wouldn't be here without her!'

I was bewildered. 'But what in the world is a girl like that doing in a Master's course in Information Retrieval?' I asked.

'She appears to be a very agreeable young person,' said

Dorothy. 'At her interview she said she was interested in learning how to compile and manage a large database. It will be the foundation of the small business she is starting . . .'

'We think,' interrupted Magnus, 'that she's planning to organise an extensive blackmailing scheme which will encompass all the major public figures in England. I should think it'll be a nice little earner. Do you think you could persuade her to sell us shares in the enterprise, Dorothy?'

'I've been very pleased with her work,' insisted Miss Upton. 'She's diligent, eager to learn and substantially more accurate than other people I could mention.'

Magnus chortled. 'Strictly accurate, I hope,' he said, as he summoned the waiter for more peanuts.

Once the Funding Council's proposals were released to the university, I did not have an easy time. Initially, the St Sebastian's Council was appalled by the idea of a merger. The majority of members were local businessmen and county dignitaries. They loved their connection with the university. They were affronted by the possibility that the services of some of them might no longer be required. However, once it was clear that there would be no money for the current institution, attitudes changed. Gradually, realism crept in. I soothed feelings and calmed tempers. Things became easier once it was agreed that the vast majority would be drafted onto the new amalgamated governing body.

The academics were even more difficult. I knew from my own working life that university teachers were prima donnas. They could not stomach the idea that they might in future be working with a teachers' training college. 'What about our research culture?' they wailed. Again I flattered, comforted and pacified. I pointed out again and again that they would be doing exactly the same job in exactly the same place. The only difference would be that their employment would now be secure. There were times when I felt I was trying to persuade a group of film stars to sing a Gilbert and Sullivan chorus in a primary school pantomime. But again, bit by bit, everyone became used to the idea. What had seemed totally intolerable, slowly became regrettably inevitable.

I met Dr Meddles several times. He was highly efficient. He returned telephone calls; he was punctual for appointments and he invariably had the right papers with him. Apparently his doctorate was in Cybernetics and he had written a well-received book on effective time management. Although I could not detect a glimmer of humour in him and I knew that we could never be friends, I had no doubt that he was the ideal man for the job.

Sloth agreed to go quietly. Overall he seemed rather relieved. He and his wife were looking forward to their retirement in Northamptonshire. They certainly received a generous financial package. The situation with Pilkington was more complicated. There was a rumour that he intended to return to St Sebastian's. He said he felt it his duty to contribute to the new institution. In the event, after a private session with Sir Roy Greengrass, he accepted his destiny. He applied for admission to a Methodist theological college in Bristol. Again his final severance payment was not inconsiderable.

By the middle of July everything was sorted out. As a final fling, the Archbishop of Cannonbury agreed to give the address at the university graduation ceremony. It had long been the custom for this to take place in the nave of the cathedral. Subsequently, a lunch was offered to the graduates and their families in a huge marquee pitched on the Green Court. Then, when all the students had left, the Provost, as Visitor, held a tea party in the Provost's Garden for the graduation speaker and invited guests. The wonderful Emma Glass volunteered to organise the food and it was to be served by the Catering department.

On the day, hundreds of students dressed in black gowns, green hoods and mortarboards milled around the precincts. University staff, also in full academic pontificals, assembled just before eleven and processed through the Trinity Gate into the cathedral. It was my role to hand out the diplomas, and I sat in the front on the daïs.

First of all, Sloth, as Acting Vice-Chancellor, welcomed the visitors. Then I went through my routine. I tried to say something individual to each of the new graduates. Things picked up when the Archbishop made his speech. He was at his best, amusing and serious, whimsical and direct, by turn. Then, to conclude proceedings, Sloth addressed the company. He outlined the amalgamation plans. These were exciting times, he said. The Council had agreed that a merger should take place between Arrowsmith Teacher Training College and St Sebastian's University. From now on, the combined institution would be referred to as Arrowsmith-St Sebastian's. He emphasised that this was a time of great opportunity and a tremendous declaration of faith in the future. Finally, he introduced Dr Merlin Meddles, the current Principal of Arrowsmith College, who would be taking over as Vice-Chancellor.

There was a second graduation ceremony after lunch which followed the same course as the first. Everything was finished by half-past three and we had a short break before our guests were due to arrive an hour later.

The Archbishop and his chaplain came first with Robert and Jenny Sloth. They were taken by Victoria into the garden at the back of the house. Glasses of champagne were handed out and Emma Glass supervised the distribution of exquisite tiny scones, and cakes. Next came senior adminstrators, members of the council and representatives of the academic staff. Merlin Meddles and his wife were included and I introduced them to the Archbishop. The Blenkensops, the Sinclairs, the Archdeacon, the Precentor and Canon Robinson, Derek Trend's replacement, were also present. Victoria had invited a little group from the Priory. Matron drove them over in the minibus and Reg Blenkensop found chairs for them all. Magnus was very much in evidence, resplendant in his Oxford DPhil gown, with Dorothy Upton smiling by his side. Felix was on active duty refilling glasses and Victoria and Emma made sure that everyone had enough to eat.

The guests wandered about the garden and admired the flowers. It was a beautiful hot afternoon and Brutus and Cleo sauntered over the lawn and settled themselves on top of the garden wall. They basked in the sun and surveyed the scene. When I next looked up, to my amazement, there were three cats present, not two. Marmaduke had positioned himself a few yards from Brutus. The large ginger and the two siamese sat in perfect harmony, enjoying the warmth together.

While I was speaking with the Sinclairs, the Archbishop's chaplain struck his glass with a spoon and called us to attention. The Archbishop, magnificent in his purple cassock, stepped forward. 'Friends,' he said, 'I want to thank Harry and Victoria for their generous hospitality.' He then looked in the direction of Emma. 'I understand Mrs Glass is responsible for all these delicious scones and cakes. I've eaten far too many already and I intend to eat plenty more!' There was a ripple of laughter and a burst of clapping which Emma acknowledged.

Then the Archbishop continued. 'Now, some of you may know that this past autumn I invited Harry to delay his retirement and take on the role of Provost for a short period of time. To my enormous relief, he accepted the burden and I'm sure you'll all agree that he and Victoria have been a wonderful addition to the cathedral family. Now I have good news. Earlier this week, I asked him if he might consider staying just a little while longer. It is a critical time for the university, and he is much needed in the cathedral. I'm relieved to tell you that he has accepted the challenge. This is indeed good news for all of us. St Sebastian's really needs him.' There was a gratifying burst of applause as the Archbishop finished speaking.

Once everyone was chatting again, Felix took me on one side. 'Congratulations, Harry,' he said. 'Good to have you around for a bit longer!' He grinned. 'You've had a busy year, you know . . . Lots has happened . . . I almost feel as if there might be another novel coming along . . .'

Magnus came up to join us. His plate was piled high with cakes. 'Emma's a genius! Splendid party, Harry!' he said as he accidentally spilled some of his drink. It fizzed spectacularly on his crimson gown. I handed him my handkerchief to mop it up. 'You know what the acronym for our new institution will be?' he chuckled.

'I haven't thought about it,' I said. 'Arrowsmith-St. Sebastians . . .'

'Exactly!' declared Magnus, 'ASS . . . highly appropriate, particulary in view of our new Vice-Chancellor . . .'

'Magnus!' I remonstrated. 'Merlin Meddles is a very competent administrator and is highly regarded by the Chairman of the Funding Council . . .'

'Precisely,' Magnus agreed. 'You could hardly have damned him more completely. He's exactly the kind of person who should be head of ASS. I shall suggest that the new coat-of-arms has a donkey on it with a suitable motto. Something like *Melius Resistere Quam Intellegere* (Better to Resist than to Understand).'

'It's a pity Pilkington's not here,' remarked Felix.

'He's at his interview for the theological college,' I said. 'He wrote Victoria a nice note.'

'All this is due to him, you know,' continued Felix. 'If he hadn't made up those absurd names, we probably would have got through the Quality Control inspection and the Funding Council would never have been alerted to Flanagan's misdemeanours. At the end of the day, the amalgamation is all due to him.'

'Do you know,' I said. 'I haven't spoken to him once since I returned to St Sebastian's. Victoria bumped into Maureen Pilkington in Marks and Spencer, but I've not come across him. Isn't that strange?'

'He's the invisible man . . .,' said Magnus

'The ghost at the feast . . .,' echoed Felix,'

'The ultimate whistleblower,' I concluded, 'an agent of change. He was all air and no substance, rather like your novels, Felix. And now we won't see him again. He's leaving St Sebastian's to preach to the Methodists.'

'It's funny how life turns out,' said Magnus and he went off to find Dorothy in the crowd.